home of our hearts

by ROBIN JONES GUNN

Christy & Todd

THE MARRIED YEARS

BOOK 2

ISBN 978-0-9828772-4-1

Scripture quoted from THE NEW KING JAMES VERSION. © 1982 by Thomas Nelson,
Inc. Used by permission. All rights reserved. NEW AMERICAN STANDARD BIBLE®, ©
The Lockman Foundation 1960, 1962, 1963, 1968, 1971, 1972, 1973, 1975, 1977, 1995. Used
by permission. Scriptures from THE HOLY BIBLE, NEW INTERNATIONAL VERSION®,
NIV® Copyright © 1973, 1978, 1984, 2011 by Biblica, Inc.® Used by permission. All rights
reserved worldwide. *Holy Bible*, New Living Translation. © 1996, 2004, 2007 by Tyndale
House Foundation. Used by permission of Tyndale House Publishers, Inc., Carol Stream,
Illinois 60188. All rights reserved.

This novel is a work of fiction. Names, characters, places, and incidents are either products
of the author's imagination or are used fictitiously. All characters are fictional and any sim-
ilarity to people living or dead is purely coincidental.

Published by Robin's Nest Productions, Inc.
P.O. Box 2092, Kahului, HI 96733

Edited by Lisz Mast and Julee Schwarzburg
Cover Images by Jenna Michelle Photography
Cover and interior design by Taylor Smith, Ringger Design,
Nicolas Ace Wiinikka, and Ken Raney

Printed in the United States of America by Believers Press
Bloomington, Minnesota 55438

"Christ will make his home in your hearts
as you trust in him.
Your roots will grow down into God's love and keep you strong."

~ Ephesians 3:17, NLT

one

*C*hristy was happy. Happier than she remembered being in quite some time.

She sat across from Tracy at their new favorite Newport Beach café and scrolled through the photos on her phone. With a shy smile, Christy turned the screen around. "So, apparently, it's a girl."

"Really?" Tracy leaned closer and tilted her head to get a good look at the image. She didn't seem convinced. "Is Todd still set on the name?"

"Yes. He's definitely set on the name."

Petite Tracy scrunched up her nose. "Gussie isn't exactly the best name, if you ask me. But then, this is your baby, not mine."

"I know. Trust me. Gussie wouldn't have been my choice either." Christy took one more look at the image on her phone before putting it back in her purse and picking up her oversized mug to enjoy a sip of her English breakfast tea latte.

"It does make sense, though. I mean, to Todd's way of thinking, I can see where he came up with that name."

"He's so excited. I hate to douse his enthusiasm." Christy leaned back. Her long, nutmeg-brown hair was folded into a loose braid that fell over her left shoulder.

"Lots of changes are ahead for you guys."

Christy nodded. "I know. Lots of good changes. Amazing changes. So much has been happening so fast."

"Doug and I feel that way, too. Tell me again . . . when do you guys leave for Africa?"

"A week from tomorrow."

The waitress at Julie Ann's Café finished refilling their glasses of water and lingered a moment, giving Christy what seemed like a tender, motherly smile.

Christy smiled back. She loved the cozy and friendly atmosphere at Julie Ann's Café. Returning her attention to Tracy, she said, "Todd said you guys are all set to house-sit while we're gone."

"Yes and we are so grateful." Tracy pinched a nibble from the carrot-and-zucchini muffin they were sharing. "We still can't believe Todd's dad is letting us stay there rent free. The timing is perfect."

"I know. Todd and I felt the same way two months ago when we moved in."

"Has your father-in-law told you yet if he's going to start renting his house again after you get back?"

"No."

"Do you think there's a chance you guys would be able to afford it if he offered it to you?"

"I don't think so. Not until both of us have steady jobs. But Todd said it would be better if we had that conversation in person with his dad next week."

Over the past few months, both Christy and Todd had seen a steady flow of income from various odd jobs. Todd repaired surfboards in the garage and Christy used her sewing skills to create custom tablecloths and place mats. Most of the special orders were prompted by Christy's gregarious aunt Marti, who had convinced many of her wealthy friends to bring their custom projects to Christy.

It had been a dreamy couple of months, especially after both of them had lost their jobs in the fall. But Christy knew the Camelot season wouldn't go on forever. While they were in the midst of it, though, she wanted to enjoy every minute.

Tracy wrapped her hands around her soup bowl-sized tea mug. "It still seems pretty exotic to me—you guys taking off for a month and going to the other side of the world. I don't know anyone who's ever gone to the Canary Islands. And how crazy is it that Katie is getting married in Kenya? Does it seem surreal to you at all?"

"Yes. Very surreal."

"But you seem so calm whenever you talk about it." Tracy flipped her thin blond hair behind her right ear.

"You didn't see me a few weeks ago," Christy said. "When we found out the trip was moved up to the first week of March instead of the original dates in April, panic crept in. I thought it would be impossible to change the flights and all the other arrangements. However, once again, my aunt made it happen."

Tracy leaned in again. "Would it be terrible if I told you that sometimes I'm jealous of you?"

"Of me?"

"Yes, you. I've often wished I had an Aunt Marti who took me shopping and bought me plane tickets."

Christy wanted to mention the many tangled strings that seemed to be attached to Aunt Marti's gifts over the years, but Tracy knew those stories already. "I'm grateful."

"I know you are." Tracy scooted the plate closer to Christy, gesturing that she should have the rest of the muffin. "And I'm happy for you guys. I really am. It's so good that you're able to take this big trip now because everything really does change once you have a baby."

The waitress reached in front of them and removed the emptied muffin plate. She asked if they wanted anything else, and Tracy answered that they were ready for the check.

Christy was lost in her thoughts about how much life had changed for Doug and Tracy ever since their little guy, Daniel, made his grand entrance into the world over two years ago. It got her wondering about all the changes ahead for her and Todd. She really didn't want to think about that right now. After swishing around the last of her tea latte, she sipped it slowly.

As the waitress stepped away, Tracy continued her earlier thoughts. "Although the way our lives are right now, even if I did have an aunt offering me free plane tickets, we wouldn't be able to take off and go anywhere."

"Transition is rough. But once you guys get into a place of your own and Doug gets more comfortable with his new job, you'll start to feel at home here."

"I know. And it will be the same for you guys when you get back from Africa. God will provide a place for you to live. But like you said, transition is rough."

They sat for a moment in comfortable shared silence. Christy was glad they had each other during this time and could be anchored together in the safe harbor of a steady friendship and an abiding hope in God's faithfulness.

"I don't think you finished telling me about Gussie," Tracy said. "When are you going to get her?"

"Todd said we should be able to pick her up on Saturday."

"That soon? Wow, that's great," Tracy said.

"I know. I haven't seen her yet."

"You haven't?"

"No. I've only seen the photos. Todd signed the papers yesterday and took her in to get a new muffler right away."

The waitress placed the check on their table and laughed out loud. Christy and Tracy looked up and she quickly covered her mouth.

"I'm sorry. I wasn't trying to eavesdrop. It's just that I heard you say something earlier about 'Gussie.'"

Christy nodded.

"And then you said she was getting a new muffler." The

waitress laughed again.

Christy and Tracy exchanged glances, not understanding the joke.

"I thought you were talking about a baby. You know. A baby, baby." The waitress cast a bemused glance at Christy and patted her stomach. "I thought you were having a baby girl and naming her Gussie."

Tracy started laughing. "No, we were talking about a car. Her husband is getting a new VW van. Well, it's an old van, but new to them. He had one like it in high school. Show her the picture, Christy."

She reached for her phone and pulled up the photo. "This is Gussie. Gussie the Bussie, in all her vintage cuteness."

"I like the flower-power decal on her nose," the waitress said.

"I know." Christy glanced at the photo again with growing admiration. "That's why my husband decided she must be a girl."

"Makes complete sense now." The waitress chuckled again as if she was really enjoying this little joke. "Well, congratulations on the new addition to your family. I'm sure Gussie will be very happy in her new home." She was still grinning as she walked away.

Christy turned to Tracy and lowered her voice. She felt embarrassed that their conversation had been overheard. "Did you hear me say that Gussie was a baby?"

"No, I think I was the one who called her your 'new baby.'" Tracy giggled again. "It's funny she thought we were talking about a baby and not a car."

"Who would name their child 'Gussie'?"

"You never know. Gussie could be in the next top-ten most popular baby girl names."

Christy reached for the check. "I truly doubt that."

"Hey, it's my turn to pay. Remember?"

"Let's split it."

"No. You paid last time. Hand it over." Tracy gave Christy

a firm look as if trying to fortify her words. The problem was that Tracy's heart-shaped face could never appear threatening. Ever.

"How about if I leave the tip?"

Tracy didn't protest that suggestion. She reached into her large bag and fished around for her wallet. "I almost forgot to ask. How's Todd doing with his dad getting married?"

"Great. He's happy for them. So am I."

"But what about the whole thing about his childhood?"

"What whole thing about his childhood?"

"For all those years it was just Todd and his dad. You know how close they are. Doug told me he thought Todd was having a hard time now that his dad is getting married and won't be his home base anymore."

"His home base?"

"You know, the person he goes to." Tracy looked at the total on the bill.

Christy frowned. *Why is Todd telling Doug and Tracy how he's feeling about his dad's marriage? He hasn't said anything to me about having a hard time with it.* "I know it's going to be an adjustment," Christy said. "But we're still hoping that Bryan and Carolyn will move back here. Mostly we're just really happy for them."

Tracy paid the bill, Christy left the tip, and the two of them stepped out into the brightness of the Southern California morning. "You know, when I told my mom that Todd's dad was getting married in the Canary Islands and planning to live there, she had to look up where they're located. When she saw that the Canaries are off the coast of West Africa, she said he wouldn't last there more than a year. What do you and Todd think? Will his dad stay there indefinitely?"

"I don't know. His fiancée, Carolyn, has a lot of family there. But it feels pretty far away. I'm sure that's what Todd is feeling."

"It is far away. And so is Kenya."

"I know." Christy glanced up at the tall palm trees that

lined the backside of the parking lot. She thought about her spunky and spontaneous, redheaded best friend. Long ago Christy had promised Katie she would be there for her on her wedding day. She just never imagined that in order to keep that promise, she'd have to go to Africa.

They arrived at Tracy's white Mazda, and Christy opened the passenger door. A stuffed animal and a package of baby wipes greeted her on the front seat.

"Just toss those in the back," Tracy said. "This car is such a mess. Sorry."

"Don't worry. I appreciate you offering to drive today."

"Well, I admire you walking here this morning."

"It's not that far," Christy said. "I've been trying to get more exercise because I've been sitting so much while I've been sewing the past few weeks."

"So, where do you want to go first?"

"Gina's Bridal to pick up Katie's wedding dress."

"What will you do if it needs alterations after Katie finally tries it on in Kenya?"

"My aunt bought a small sewing kit for me to take along, and I've got lots of safety pins." Christy's phone chimed. She pulled it from her purse and saw a text from Aunt Marti. "Speaking of my aunt Marti, she wants to know if you'd like to go over to their house next week and clean out their refrigerator."

Tracy shot Christy a puzzled look. "Why? Did her housekeeper quit?"

"No, I think she's asking if you guys want whatever food she has in the fridge so it doesn't go bad while they're gone."

"Sure. That's nice of her to ask. You know my husband would never turn down free food."

Christy quickly texted Aunt Marti, and Tracy returned to their earlier conversation in the café.

"So, are Katie and Eli still planning on an African safari for their wedding?"

"Yep."

"What about your aunt and uncle? Are they still planning to go to both weddings?"

"Yep."

Tracy glanced at Christy again. "You haven't said much about how you feel about that."

"Which part? The safari or my aunt and uncle?"

"Both."

"I was skeptical about the safari at first, but Katie has sent so much info about it that I'm pretty excited now. So is Todd."

"I imagine he would be. But what about your aunt? Really? Do you think she'll be okay with riding around in a Jeep and staying in a tent?"

"She says she is. She researched the whole trip down to the last detail and convinced Katie to stay at a hotel before the wedding rather than in tents. She says we'll be sleeping in luxurious beds and served award-winning meals. According to her, it's world-class accommodations in the Serengeti."

Tracy changed lanes and turned off the blinker. With hesitancy in her voice she said, "Even with the luxury status and everything, I know it's mean to say this, but I hope your aunt won't be . . . "

Christy waited for Tracy to find the right phrase to end her sentence.

"I hope she won't make things aggravating for everyone."

Tracy's delicate description of her aunt's temperament was accurate. Marti did have a way of getting on the nerves of anyone who was around her for very long. But in a deeply rooted, blood-relative sort of way, Christy often felt closer to her aunt than she did to her own mother. She had a level of empathy for Aunt Marti that went a long way in situations that drove other people crazy.

"I love my aunt." Christy spoke the words evenly.

"I know you do. And it's probably a horrible thing for me to bring up, but Doug and I were talking about it and we hope you and Todd don't get bulldozed by her on this trip. The whole point is to be there to give your full attention to

Bryan and Carolyn and Eli and Katie. That's why you're going."

"And that's why my aunt and uncle are going."

Tracy gave Christy a skeptical glance.

"It's all going to work out," Christy said with more optimism than she honestly felt. She knew how difficult it could be to travel with Marti because she'd gone to Switzerland with her a number of years ago. She also knew that everything was locked in place for their extended trip, and the best thing she could do was choose to love her aunt through it all and not take anything personally.

"I hope it does all work out." Tracy paused for a moment. "May I say one more thing?"

"Sure."

"I probably shouldn't say this, but Christy, ever since you guys moved here, I've watched your aunt insert herself into your lives more than ever. It seems like she still thinks you're the naïve fourteen-year-old farm girl from Wisconsin who came to stay with her for the summer. But you've changed since then. We all have."

"I know."

Tracy kept her focus on the road. "I think your aunt treats you like the daughter she never had."

Christy had thought all these same things many times before.

"Again, I'm probably saying too much, but it's too bad that Marti never had a daughter of her own. She could have poured all her socialite training into her, and the bonus would be that you would have had a cousin." Tracy pulled into a parking spot in front of Gina's Bridal and turned off the engine.

Instead of opening her door to get out, Christy drew in a deep breath. "My aunt did have a daughter."

Tracy turned to Christy. Her eyes widened.

Christy's throat tightened as she said, "Her name was Johanna."

two

*C*hristy didn't expect the tears that rushed to the rim of her eyelids the moment she spoke the name, "Johanna" and told Tracy, "My aunt and uncle had a baby girl. They named her after my great-grandmother."

In a small and humbled voice Tracy said, "Christy . . . I didn't know."

"I've never talked about her. The only reason I found out was because my mom told me when I was in high school. Johanna was born premature. She may have been born with a defect. I don't know for sure because I've never asked my mom the details. All I know is that Johanna died when she was only a few days old."

"How sad."

"I know." Christy swallowed before telling Tracy the next piece of painful information. "And then I was born just a few days later."

Neither of them spoke for a moment.

Tracy shook her head. "I can't imagine what I would have done if Daniel had died a few days after he was born. How do you ever recover from something like that?"

"I don't know if you ever do recover completely."

"Especially if your only sister has a baby girl a few days later. And then you spend the years watching that healthy child grow up and remember that . . . " Tracy let her sentence float between them unfinished.

Christy's throat tightened again. "Now that Todd and I are talking about starting a family, I've thought a lot about Marti's loss. I have more empathy for her now, and I think I understand why she is the way she is with me."

"Yes, of course." Tracy fixed her gaze out the front windshield as they sat in the parking lot. "You're the daughter she never got to raise."

"Exactly."

"You know what else?" Tracy turned to look at Christy. "It makes sense to me now. I mean, think about it. Your mom and dad agreed to let you spend the whole summer here with your aunt and uncle. My parents wouldn't have done that when I was fourteen. Your mother's loyalty and love for her sister must have influenced that decision. Did you ever ask your mom about that?"

"No. My mom tends to keep her thoughts and feelings to herself."

"Well, I'm glad she didn't keep you to herself. I'm glad she was bold and shared you with her sister. I mean, what if your parents hadn't let you come? Your life isn't the only one that would have been completely different."

Christy let Tracy's words sink in until her heart raced with thoughts of what her life would have been like if she'd never met Todd, Doug, Tracy, Katie, and the all rest of her Forever Friends. She tried to imagine an alternate life clustered around the hemmed-in childhood she'd experienced in Wisconsin. She was who she was because of what happened to her in Newport Beach. All her most important relationships, including her relationship with Christ, had grown out of the weeks she spent at her aunt and uncle's beach house.

The thought of never having come here sent a shiver up the back of her neck.

Tracy ran her palm across the top of the steering wheel. "Isn't it crazy how one decision can affect a whole series of events and change a life forever? Change a bunch of lives, actually."

Something deep inside Christy grew very still as she thought about everything she knew about the sovereignty of God. He had plans for His children and He accomplished those plans. Her parents had said no to so many things when she was growing up. But to this life-altering decision, they had said yes, even though they had every logical reason to say no.

"I feel like crying at the wonder of it," Christy said.

"God's mysterious ways and His perfect timing." Tracy smiled. "Isn't that the line from the new song Todd and Doug have been working on? God definitely has had His hand on your life."

Christy nodded slowly. "You know what? I think I need to thank my parents for being brave."

"Good idea. When you do, thank them for me, too." Tracy reached over and squeezed Christy's arm. "Thanks for telling me about your aunt. It explains so much. You really are the daughter Marti never had."

Tracy's comment and their poignant conversation in the car continued to roll through Christy's thoughts as they spent the rest of the morning together going through their list of errands.

On their way back home, Christy asked if Tracy would drop her off at Bob and Marti's. "I thought I'd show Marti the wedding dress. She hasn't seen it yet."

"Do you want me to come in or wait for you?"

"No. I'll have Todd come get me later." With the garment bag over her arm and three full shopping bags in her other hand, Christy called out her good-bye to Tracy and trotted up to the recently replaced front door of Bob and Marti's luxurious beachfront home. She rang the doorbell and waited.

Marti opened the door with a startled expression on her perfectly made-up face. "Whatever are you doing ringing the doorbell like that, Christy?"

"I thought it would be the polite thing to do." She stepped inside the entryway and drew in the scent of her aunt's favorite air freshener, a blend of lime and freesia. Lovely and at the same time startling, just like her aunt.

"Why would you say such a thing? This is your second home. It always has been and always will be." Marti narrowed her dark eyes. "Have you been shopping?" She said it as if she could hardly believe that Christy would embark on a shopping trip without her since shopping was Marti's all-time favorite sport.

"Yes. Tracy and I were out and about this morning. I asked her to drop me off so I could show you Katie's wedding dress."

Marti's expression perked up. "Is this it?" She took the garment bag from Christy. "Let's have a look." Marti carried it into the living room and glanced around for a place to hang it. "Come on. Let's take it upstairs to my bedroom. The light will be best up there."

Christy left her other shopping bags at the foot of the stairs and followed her aunt up to her sanctuary. It was, in Christy's opinion, the most beautiful room in the house. It was also the room she had visited the least because of her aunt's preference for privacy.

The midday sunlight filled the bedroom with a trademark golden Southern California glow. The French doors to the balcony were open, and the ocean breeze ruffled the sheer, flowing drapes that had been pulled to the side. The room reminded Christy of an Italian villa with the dark wood floors and expensive wrought-iron furniture on the balcony. The plush cushions were accented by the new, colorful yellow and green pillows Christy had made for her aunt.

Marti hung Katie's dress on an elaborate brass clothing

hook beside her walk-in closet. With an efficient zip, she un-veiled the gown and peeled back the garment bag. She tilted her head and looked at it from the right and then the left. Af-ter removing the garment bag, Marti turned the dress around to inspect the back.

Christy bit her lower lip and waited. Just last week Todd had told her that she bit her lower lip whenever she was ner-vous or anxious. She hadn't realized she did it, but Todd said she started doing it more last fall when their lives were in an upheaval. Now that they were trying to get everything in place for their big trip, he pointed out that she was doing it again.

She moistened her lips and pulled her mouth up in a hopeful smile.

Aunt Marti gave the hem of the simple white wedding dress a wrinkle-reducing tug and fluff. To Christy's immense surprise, she turned to Christy and said, "It's perfect."

"It is?"

"Of course it is. Don't you think so? For Katie, I mean. For a wedding in the wilds? For an exchange of vows beside a hippo pool and under the beastly African sun? It's quite elemental and unglamorous."

"So, you're saying you don't like it," Christy surmised.

"What's not to like? It's a simple dress with a bit of swish in the skirt. What you see is what you get, just like with Katie. Besides, I'm not the one who will be wearing it." Marti looked at Christy more closely. "This is what Katie wanted, isn't it?"

Choosing to draw up all the confident satisfaction she felt when she first tried on the dress, Christy said, "Yes, it's exact-ly what she wanted. I think it's perfect for Katie."

"Isn't that what I just said?"

Christy didn't reply. She lowered herself into the comfy boudoir chair in the corner.

Oh, Aunt Marti. Why can't you just say something nice and uncomplicated at a moment like this? I give up on trying to decipher your hidden meanings. I like the dress. Katie's going to love it. That's all that matters.

Marti fluffed up the flowing gown some more. "Did you buy all the right lingerie to go with this? She'll want a smooth appearance for her backside under this fabric. And no lacy bra on her wedding day. She'll want the bodice to be smooth as well."

"I'm pretty sure I got everything she'll need." With a coy girlfriend-to-girlfriend grin, Christy added, "I also got her a little something lacy for her honeymoon."

"You did?"

Christy nodded, feeling as confident now as she had when she and Tracy found the low-cut, silky negligee with a matching sheer cover-up that tied with a long silk ribbon under the bustline. Both Christy and Tracy thought it was the perfectly poetic look for Katie to don when Eli unwrapped his bride on their wedding night.

"Would you like to see it?" Christy got up from the cozy chair. "It's in one of the bags I left downstairs."

"No, that's okay. If you think it's something Katie would actually wear in a tent on her safari honeymoon, then I'm sure it's fine."

Once again Christy was having difficulty ascertaining whether her aunt was being sincere or sarcastic. It was nicer to believe that Marti was supporting her decisions and entering into the fun of Katie's wedding plans in her own way. It wasn't the girlfriend bonding way Christy had imagined when she asked Tracy to drop her off. But then, Christy had arrived at her aunt's house still running on the tenderhearted feelings that surfaced when she'd told Tracy about Johanna.

Marti gave Katie's wedding dress one final fluffing and said, more to herself than to Christy, "I'm not sure exactly what sort of trousseau one should buy for a missionary in Africa."

Christy stepped closer to her aunt and tried to get her to look at her. "Eli and Katie are just like any other young couple who are getting married and want to celebrate and enjoy each other on their honeymoon."

"Not exactly." Marti turned to Christy and raised an eyebrow. "They're virgins, aren't they?"

Christy nodded.

"Then what you said isn't true. They're not like most other young couples in this generation."

Christy agreed with her aunt and tried to explain that even though Katie and Eli were on staff at an international mission organization that facilitated bringing clean water to African villages, they were still normal twenty-somethings in love and about to get married. The fact that they had chosen to save themselves sexually for each other didn't mean they were repressed or restricted from expressing themselves fully on their honeymoon. That was, after all, the point of waiting. Coming together was a true celebration because they would give themselves as a gift that had never been opened before.

Christy concluded with, "Why wouldn't Katie want to have something elegant and flattering that will make her feel like a beautiful gift to her husband on their wedding night?"

Marti blinked several times and then turned away. Again, under her breath, she said, "It's not like that for every young woman, is it?"

Christy wanted to reach out and touch her aunt's shoulder and ask what she meant by that. Was she giving a hint about her own honeymoon? Or was it more than that? Had Marti been with another man before Bob?

Christy's thoughts were spinning with all the possible secrets that had remained locked away in her aunt's very private heart. In typical conflict-avoiding fashion, Marti abruptly changed the subject.

"We'll pack Katie's wedding dress in my suitcase since I'm taking the largest one I have. I'll roll it. Even with the bulky garment bag, that should still keep it from getting too wrinkled or crushed. Then as soon as we get to Nairobi, we can unroll it and use my travel steamer to get out all the wrinkles."

"That sounds like it will work. I also bought an adaptor so

Todd and I will have a way to plug in all our electrical gadgets and not have to borrow your adaptor."

"Good. Now what about your ears?"

"What about my ears?" Christy's right hand automatically went to her ear as if something was wrong with it.

"You haven't gotten your ears pierced yet."

Christy was caught off guard by her aunt's comment. "Why would I get my ears pierced?"

"You told me weeks ago that Todd had given you a special pair of pearl earrings for Christmas and you wanted to wear them to Bryan's wedding."

Christy nodded, vaguely remembering the conversation.

"You also told me that it was a problem because the earrings were for pierced ears and you'd never gotten your ears pierced."

"Yes, but . . . "

"We should go." Marti glanced at her watch. "Right now."

"Go where?"

Marti gave Christy a withering look. "To get your ears pierced."

Christy's stomach did a queasy little flip-flop. It was childish but there was still something in her that felt squeamish whenever she thought about having a needle stuck through her earlobe. Christy remembered feeling the same way when she was eleven and lived on a farm in Wisconsin. Her best friend, Paula, had gotten her ears pierced and did her best to convince Christy to get hers pierced, too. When Christy asked her no-nonsense dad, he had told her, "If God had wanted you to have two more holes in your head, he would have made you with holes in your earlobes already."

That was the end of the discussion on pierced ears while Christy lived under her parents' roof. Since pierced ears and earrings in general weren't that big of a deal to Christy, she was fine with leaving her ears "the way they came from the factory," which was another of her dad's sayings.

The problem now was that the pearl earrings Todd had

given her at Christmas were special. Marti did remember that correctly. Christy had promised Todd she'd wear them to his dad's wedding. She just didn't feel like getting her ears pierced right now.

"I can go do it later this week, Aunt Marti."

"Why wait? Do you have anything else pressing on your schedule today?"

Christy reluctantly admitted that she did not.

"Well, it's up to you." Marti zipped up the garment bag on Katie's wedding dress.

In her mind's eye, Christy could see the pleased expression of her surfer-boy husband when he noticed she was wearing the earrings. Todd didn't always notice little details like when she added decorative touches to the house or took the time to put on makeup. But he always noticed and commented when she wore her hair down and flowing. He would notice the earrings. She was sure of that.

"Well?" Marti's tone made it clear she was at the end of her patience and required a final answer this very moment.

The queasy feeling escalated from Christy's stomach to her throat. In a pinched voice that made her feel like she was fourteen again and Marti was daring her to grow up, Christy said, "Okay. Let's go. Quickly. Before I change my mind."

With an arched eyebrow Marti said, "Change your mind? Since when did you ever have a difficult time making decisions?"

She was not a hormonal teenager anymore who couldn't decide what to order at the fancy restaurant her aunt had taken her to. Over the last decade Christy had made plenty of excellent decisions. The very reason she had stopped by Marti's with the wedding dress was an act born of a heart full of compassion. She didn't deserve to be demeaned this way.

Before Christy could rally her flared-up emotions to give a succinct response, she caught a glimpse of the mischievous grin on her aunt's face.

Clearly, a return trip to South Coast Plaza wasn't about

Christy's big step to "put two more holes" in her head. It had nothing to do with her floundering when it came to making quick decisions. This was Marti's glib idea of what girlfriend bonding time meant to her.

Once again, Christy was willing to play by her aunt's rules. It was the best way, perhaps the only way, she knew how to do as her own mother had done and provide Aunt Marti with a smidgeon of the love she longed for. No one could bring Johanna back. But they could help fill in a few of the thousands of holes left in Marti's heart when her only daughter had stopped breathing.

three

*C*hristy intentionally did not set her alarm on Saturday morning. She planned to sleep in, knowing that the next few weeks would be filled with jet lag and irregular sleeping times.

The night before, their home had been filled with laughter and meaningful conversations until well after midnight. Doug and Tracy and a dozen other friends had come together for what was becoming a regular Friday night gathering. The group decided they'd continue to meet while Christy and Todd were gone, and Doug agreed to have his guitar on hand to lead a time of worship.

Christy had left most of the cleanup from last night until after she got going this morning. She assumed Todd would go surfing first thing as he usually did on Saturdays. When he got back she'd have the kitchen cleared and be ready to make waffles, Todd's newest Saturday morning favorite.

However, when she felt her husband's slightly scruffy chin on her bare arm and his nose burrowing into her hair as it fell across the curve of her neck, she thought she must have really slept in if Todd was back from surfing. With her eyes still closed she murmured, "I'm still sleeping."

In a husky whisper Todd said, "Are you dreaming of your manly husband?"

"Always." Christy rolled into his arms and received his morning kisses on her cheek and on her smiling lips.

Todd kissed her cheek again and then drew her hair back from her ear. "Hey."

Christy opened her eyes. She gazed into his screaming silver-blue eyes and her heart did a little flutter. "Hey, yourself," she said playfully.

"No, I mean, hey, what's this? In your ear?"

Christy's hand went to the small silver post earring in her earlobe and gave it a gentle twist the way the woman at the jewelry store had instructed her. "I got my ears pierced."

"When?"

"A couple days ago."

"Why did you do that?"

"So I could wear the pearl earrings you gave me for Christmas. Remember? I promised I'd wear them to your dad's wedding."

"Hmmm."

Christy propped herself up on her elbow. "What do you mean, hmmm? Did you forget you asked me to wear them?"

"No." He continued to focus on the earring as if he'd never noticed her earlobes before. "I remembered."

"Why are you staring at them?"

"This one is kind of red. Is it supposed to be?"

Christy's fingers went to her left lobe. It felt tender to her touch. "I have some solution I'm supposed to use while they heal up. I just forgot to use it last night." She looked over at the clock on the nightstand. Almost eight thirty.

"Did you go surfing already?"

"No." Todd rolled onto his back and put out his arms for Christy to come cuddle up with him. He kissed her on top of her head. "I had something more important to do this morning."

Christy tilted her head up from her side snuggle position and planted a row of kisses along his jawline. She was waiting for him to romantically say that the most important thing on his schedule that morning was to love his wife, and then she would say something equally romantic and the kissing would pick up at a steamy pace.

"Yeah, today's the day," Todd said.

Christy paused her chin kissing and tried to figure out what he was talking about.

"Do you want to go with me to pick her up?"

That's when it was Christy's turn to remember. Todd had another girl in his life now. How could she forget?

"Sure," Christy said. "I'll go with you to pick up Gussie. When do you want to go?"

Todd wrapped his brawny arms around her. "After."

"After what?" Christy asked playfully.

"After this." Todd kissed her with the passion of a man who had waited many hundreds of empty Saturday mornings so he might fully and unashamedly experience what he and Christy shared now.

The sweetness of their morning communion lingered over them as they drove to the car repair shop in Huntington Beach. Christy rubbed the back of Todd's neck.

"Both hands on the wheel, mister." Christy smiled.

"Oh, so you can touch me but I can't touch you? Is that how it is?"

"Yep. That's how it is when you're driving."

"What about when you're driving?"

Christy laughed. "You and I both know that when I'm driving, the last thing you're thinking about is giving me a little squeeze."

A cute, dimple-inducing grin spread across Todd's face. "Listen, *Kilikina*. If you haven't yet figured it out, you need to know that I am always thinking about giving you a little squeeze. Day and night. Night and day."

Christy smiled the way she always did when he called her

by her Hawaiian name. She thought about how naïve she had been about men in general when she and Todd first got married. Todd had been a patient teacher and an understanding husband. Most of all, she was glad the two of them had been able to figure out everything together. It allowed them to share the sacredness of love as a couple. They had the freedom to take their time to explore and learn the best ways to express their affection for each other.

To Christy, it seemed that the luxury of having decades to figure out how to get closer and closer as a couple was a huge benefit of marriage that no one ever talked about. She felt safe and settled when she was with Todd.

"I love you," Christy said spontaneously as they sat at a busy intersection waiting for the light to change.

Todd glanced at her with a warm, affectionate gaze that turned into a mischievous grin. He jammed the car into Park and opened his door. "Come on!"

"Todd! What are you doing?"

He was in front of the car, motioning wildly for Christy to join him. As she looked out the windshield at her crazy husband, she noticed the stoplight. This was their intersection. This was where Todd kissed her for the first time when she was fifteen.

She leaped out and dashed to the front of the car. Her lips found their way to his waiting lips easily, and both of them burst into laughter. The person in the car behind them honked his horn and Christy glanced up to see that the light had turned green.

She squealed as they both scurried to get back in the car. Todd released the parking brake and slammed the car into Drive. He sailed through the intersection just as the light was turning yellow.

Christy couldn't stop laughing. She felt young and breathless as if they had just done something truly daring.

"I think that should be our thing," Todd said.

"Our thing?"

"Yeah. We go through this intersection all the time now that we live here, and it seems like any other intersection. But it's not. It's *our* intersection."

"Yes, it is. It's the intersection of carnations and kisses."

Todd grinned. "I didn't have any carnations for you this time."

"But you always have kisses. I'll take those anytime."

"You never know when you might receive one of those kisses at this intersection again." He was looking straight ahead, but he comically flexed his eyebrows up and down. "You'll just have to be prepared at all times."

"I can do that." Christy looked out the window, content-edly smiling as they drove past many familiar Newport Beach landmarks. She remembered the conversation she and Tracy had earlier that week and repeated it for Todd.

"Did you tell your parents yet how glad you are that they sent you here?"

"No."

"Why don't you call them now?"

Christy pulled her phone from her purse and saw that she'd missed a text from Tracy.

"Tracy said we should go by her parents' place after you get Gussie. They want to see her."

"Sounds good. Better yet, how about if we all go down to San Clemente this afternoon and take Gussie out on her maiden voyage? We can pick up some sandwiches on the way."

"That would be fun. I'll tell Tracy." Christy sent a long text back with the beach-day suggestion and then placed a call to her parents.

"Hi, Dad. How are you guys doing?"

"I'm fine but your mother is under the weather."

"She is? What's wrong?"

"She's right here. I'll let her talk to you."

"Hi, honey." Mom sounded tired and her voice was a bit wobbly.

"Hi, Mom. Dad said you're not feeling well."

"It's just the stomach flu, I think. It's put me in bed, though."

"I'm so sorry to hear that. Is there anything we can do for you? Do you want us to come down there?"

"No, don't come. I don't want to run the risk of you getting this bug right before your big trip. I'll be all right. I just need to get some rest. Once this fever breaks I'm sure I'll be fine. How are you two?"

"We're doing great, Mom. We have some fun news. Todd found a VW van and we're on our way to pick it up right now." Christy spent the next few minutes updating her mom on Gussie as well as a few more details about the trip and how Katie's dress turned out.

As Todd pulled into the parking area in front of the car repair shop, Christy said, "I need to go, Mom. I'll call you tomorrow, okay? Take care of yourself and get some rest."

"I will. Thank you, honey."

Christy hung up and rubbed her earlobe. She'd forgotten to use the cleansing solution before they left. "Remind me to put the stuff on my ears when we get home."

"I'll probably forget. Why don't you send yourself a reminder on your phone?"

"Good idea."

"Also remind yourself to thank your parents."

"For what?"

"Isn't that why you were calling your mom? To thank them for sending you here so you could meet me?" Todd grinned and opened his door.

Christy was busy typing in her notes to self when her car door opened. Todd stood there, looking all gentlemanly and little-boy anxious at the same time. Dropping her phone into her purse, Christy got out and thanked her polite prince. They walked into the car repair bay holding hands.

When her eyes adjusted to the darkness inside KarMart, Christy could see that Gussie was on a lift and two mechanics were examining her underbelly. She looked a lot more dusty and rusty from the backside than she'd looked in the photos. But she was still a cutie and Christy was glad Todd had gotten her.

"She was leaking oil like crazy," one of the guys said to Todd. "And the catalytic converter won't pass California inspection. Did you know that already?"

"Yeah, I knew I'd have to work on getting that fixed. What about the carburetor?"

The mechanic shook his head, indicating it wasn't good news.

Christy found her way to the frayed sofa next to the Coke machine while Todd continued discussing Gussie's special needs and examining her front, back, and center. She read a new text from Tracy:

CAN'T GO THIS AFTERNOON. DOUG SAID HE'D TALK TO TODD LATER AND FIGURE OUT ANOTHER TIME WE CAN ALL GO.

By the time Todd finished and shook hands with both the mechanics, it was clear that Gussie wasn't going anywhere that morning or by Sunday afternoon.

"We won't get her until after we get back from Africa," Todd said as they returned to the parking area.

"Did they give you an idea of how much the repairs will cost?"

"No."

Christy bit her lower lip. Todd looked at her. "Don't worry. We're swapping, like I told you earlier."

"How much more are you going to need to swap? I'm guessing it will be more than the original agreement of two refinished surfboards." Christy really hoped he didn't say he wanted to swap one of their other two cars. Their reliable Volvo was the car her aunt and uncle had helped them buy after Todd was in a bad accident in his original VW van, Gus the Bus. Their other car was practically brand new. Katie had given it to them last May when she left for Kenya. Even though Katie had said they could do whatever they wanted with the car, including sell it, Christy felt they needed to keep it in case Katie and Eli ever moved back to the States.

"I'm adding some painting to the deal."

"Painting?"

"Yeah, I'm going to paint the outside of Darren's mom's house this week before we leave on our trip. Do you want to walk across the street and get something to eat?"

Christy sized up the taco stand and thought it looked promising. Todd was a die-hard taco consumer. Ever since they'd moved out of their apartment near Rancho Corona University at Christmastime, Todd had been on the hunt for tacos that were as good as the ones he used to consume weekly at Joe's Taco Stand. So far his search had been unfulfilling.

Todd held her hand as they crossed the street and Christy asked, "Do you think you'll be able to get the painting done by Wednesday?"

"Shouldn't be a problem. The house is in Costa Mesa. Nice and close. Two days max is my guess."

Todd's estimate of "two days" turned into three ten-hour days. It seemed that all they could do was grab a few hours of sleep each night and go back at it the next morning. He finished just before sunset on Wednesday and came home dirty, sunburnt, and fried out of his brain. But he'd finished the work, and that was a huge relief.

Christy thought all along that he had underestimated the time for the project, but she kept her opinion to herself and managed to do most of the packing for both of them. She'd gone over all the details of the house with Tracy so they'd be ready to turn the keys over to them the next morning before the airport shuttle picked them up.

Christy had also spent a lot of time over at Bob and Marti's the past two days as her aunt evaluated everything she was packing. If Christy had time to think about anything other than the trip, she probably would have gotten frustrated with Todd for cutting the timing so close.

On Wednesday night after Todd, the weary house-paint-
er, had showered, he came downstairs and pulled the remainder of a sub sandwich out of the fridge. He sat beside
Christy on the kitchen counter stools and looked over at her
checklist. "So, tell me what I need to know."

Christy jumped right in. "The shuttle will pick us up at
Bob and Marti's at one fifteen tomorrow afternoon so we
need to drive over there at one o'clock, and we'll leave our car
in their driveway. That way Doug and Tracy can park their
car here."

"Got it." Todd chomped into his sandwich.

"We need to eat before we leave because the flight doesn't
go out until five and we don't know how much time we'll
have at the airport."

Todd nodded.

Her phone rang but she let it go unanswered. She guessed
it was Marti with more last-minute details. It would be easier
to call her back with answers after she'd gone through her
own list with Todd.

"We fly to Chicago, have a two-hour layover, and then we
fly to Madrid and from Madrid to Las Palmas. I didn't pack
your carry-on because I'm not sure what you want to have on
the plane with you. I'm guessing you'll want your sweatshirt.
It's in the dryer right now."

"Thanks for thinking of that."

Christy nodded. Before she could go on to the next detail,
Todd's phone vibrated on top of the counter like a jumping
bean. She wanted to tell him not to answer it, but he'd already
picked it up and read the name on the screen.

"It's your mom," Todd answered. "Hey, Margaret. How
are you?"

"It's Norm. I'm on Margaret's phone. Is Christy there?"

"She's right here. I've got you on speaker."

"Hi, Dad!"

"Your mother is in the hospital."

"What?" Christy felt the room close in.

"What happened?" Todd asked.

"She couldn't shake the flu. When I got home she didn't look good, so I called the doctor. He said to bring her into his office, but she passed out on the way there so I took her to the emergency room. We're waiting for the doctor now."

Christy's heart raced. "Dad, which hospital are you at? Are you at Palomar?"

"Don't come down here. There's no call for that. I just wanted you kids to know."

"We can come, Dad. We can leave right now."

There wasn't a reply.

"Dad?"

Muffled voices came through the phone before Christy's dad came back on and reverted to his usual clipped sentences. "They just said I can't use a phone in here. I'll call you back. Tell your aunt and uncle."

"Of course, Dad. Call us."

"I said I would."

"Okay. Bye, Dad. I love you."

He replied in a low, gravelly voice, "Pray for your mother."

four

*T*odd wrapped his arms around Christy and drew her close. Her mother had always been so sturdy and robust. The news that she was in the hospital rocked Christy to the core.

"We need to call my aunt and uncle." Christy uncurled from Todd's comforting hug and reached for her phone.

"Let's drive over instead." He took the lead and drove them the few blocks over to Bob and Marti's with the car windows down. The chilly coastal air assaulted her senses.

As soon as Todd delivered the news, Marti went for her phone.

"Are you calling Norm?" Uncle Bob asked.

"No. I'm calling Palomar Hospital. I want to talk to Margaret's doctor right now."

Bob convinced her to hang up and wait until after the doctor had a chance to offer a diagnosis. "Norm said he'd let us know."

Christy could tell by the look on her aunt's face that Marti's plan-making skills were running at high speed. "Well, then he can let us know while we're in the car driving down to Escondido. I'm certainly not waiting here for an update."

"I don't know if we should go just yet. My dad said he wanted us to wait for him to call back."

"Of course he did." With the sound of wild frustration, Marti said, "But he's not thinking clearly." She sprang to her feet. "I'm going to Escondido. Are the rest of you coming with me? Or do I have to drive myself to the hospital?"

Ten minutes later all four of them were in Bob's Lexus as he sped down the 5 freeway headed for Escondido. Christy had to agree with her aunt on this one. It helped to at least be in motion and on their way to the hospital instead of just waiting for the phone to ring.

The traffic was fairly light, which helped them to make good time most of the way. As they passed the signs for the turnoff into San Clemente, Christy thought of the plans Todd had dreamed up last Saturday. That trek to San Clemente was going to be in Gussie with surfboards on her roof and lots of laughter among the passengers in her belly.

This was quite a different journey.

They were rolling past Camp Pendleton when Todd's phone buzzed. He picked up the call from Christy's dad on the first ring and put it on speaker.

"They've just taken her into emergency surgery."

Marti gasped.

"Looks like it's her appendix."

"Did it burst?" Marti asked.

"They weren't sure. The doctor said they needed to open her up to find out." His voice cracked as he added, "She's in a lot of pain."

"Is David with you?" Bob asked.

"He's on his way. I called him at work. He's coming."

"We're on our way, too, Norm. We'll be there soon." Bob turned to Marti as soon as Todd ended the call. "I'm glad you got us out the door, hon. Good call."

"I knew it was serious. I just knew it. Family has to be there for each other at times like this. Can't you drive any faster, Robert?"

Christy tapped out a text to her younger brother, David. He replied a few minutes later: AT THE HOSPITAL. DAD'S WORRIED. Christy texted back: TELL DAD WE'LL BE THERE SOON.

Even though a burst appendix seemed fairly common, it could be serious. There could also be complications, depending on what they found once the exploratory surgery began. Marti speculated on dozens of those complications and railed against the dangers of general anesthesia as Bob drove through Oceanside and turned inland toward Escondido.

"I'm going to let Doug and Tracy know." Todd sent out a text asking them to pray for Christy's mom. Within minutes lots of their friends from the Friday night gathering started sending encouraging messages to both Todd's and Christy's phones, letting them know they were praying.

When they arrived at the hospital, they found Christy's dad and her brother in the waiting area. Everyone spoke in low, nervous voices and got teary eyed as they hugged each other. More than Christy remembered her family ever hugging each other.

Dad seemed out of place in the setting. He was a large man with bushy eyebrows and reddish-brown hair that had thinned over the years. His hair was shorter than she'd ever seen it, and his bald spot had now taken over his crown. For the first time in her life, he looked old to her.

"Does anyone want something to drink?" Todd asked.

Marti replied with an odd name and Christy guessed it was her favorite cocktail drink.

"Something I can get in the hospital cafeteria," Todd added. "Like coffee?"

"I'll take some coffee." Bob reached for his wallet.

"I've got this. Anyone else?" Todd pointed to each of them and took their order.

When he got to David, the seventeen-year-old version of Christy's dad confidently said, "I'll go with you." Last year

David had exchanged his thick glasses for contact lenses, and Christy was convinced the switch had made a noticeable difference in his appearance as well as his personality.

The next hour and a half of waiting was torture. Marti spent the time interrogating every nurse who passed through the waiting room. Christy took a corner seat next to her brother and asked him every question she could think of about school, work, church, and girls. David said he wasn't interested in anyone particular at the moment. Christy wasn't entirely sure if she believed him or not. Knowing David, he would probably keep such things to himself until he was certain that the girl he was interested in was actually interested in him, as well.

The eight-year difference between Christy and her brother had meant that she grew up feeling like his babysitter and always viewed him as a pest. She didn't feel that way now. Whenever she had a little slice of time to talk with him like this, she always wanted to spend more time with him.

On a whim she said, "Why don't you come and hang out with us during spring break? Will you have to work the whole week or could you come? At least for a couple of days."

David's somber expression lightened. "I could work it out. Thanks." He tilted his head and looked at her more closely, as if trying to discern if she was genuine in her invitation.

"I'm serious," Christy said. "Todd and I would love to have you stay with us."

"Are you still going to be living in his dad's house then? I thought Mom said you would be moving again when you got back from Africa. She's been cleaning out your old bedroom because she wants to be ready in case you guys are homeless again."

David's words fell like a stone that had been dropped to the bottom of her stomach. She'd forgotten how uncertain their future was, and she hated the thought of her mother trying to prepare a room for them. For the past few years, Christy's old bedroom held the overflow of everything that didn't fit anywhere else in her parents' small home. It was a combination craft room, pantry, and storage room. Todd said once that the room would qualify to be on a reality TV show if they ever started a series called *Junk Rooms Gone Bad*. Christy defended her mom and tried to explain to Todd what their farmhouse had been like in Wisconsin the whole time she was growing up.

Todd seemed to understand when Christy had told him, "People who have a barn and a basement and an attic naturally save things, even if they're broken because when your finances are limited, you learn to make do with what you have. If you can fix something rather than buy a new replacement, you feel like you're being a good steward, not a hoarder."

Marti, however, had the opposite philosophy. She wanted nothing to do with her Midwest upbringing and always insisted on the newest, best, and most expensive.

As Christy was trying to cheerfully assure her little brother that she and Todd wouldn't move back in with their parents, Marti was negotiating with one of the nurses, trying to insure that once she came out of surgery, her sister would be given a private room with a view.

The nurse patiently said she would look into it and walked away as quickly as she could. Another nurse entered the waiting area just then. "Mr. Miller?"

Christy's dad rose to his feet. He stood eye to eye with the large male nurse.

"The doctor will be out in a few minutes to give you a full update. I just wanted to let you know that your wife came through the surgery without any complications. She's in the recovery room right now and is still sedated."

Marti stepped forward. She looked like a child next to the two large men. "I'm Margaret's sister. I'd like to be with her in the recovery room. Will you take me there now?"

The nurse looked like he was caught off guard by Marti's boldness. "I'm not able to allow you into the recovery room. As soon as the anesthesia has worn off, we'll get her in a room upstairs. You'll be able to see her then."

"That's ridiculous. Why can't I be with her now?"

"Hospital policy. We put our patient's privacy and safety first. I'll let you know as soon as you can see her." The nurse turned before Marti could pepper him with more questions. He walked away quickly, his thick-soled shoes making a soft squeaking sound on the tile floors.

"Hospital policy," Marti muttered. "If I were the one in the recovery room right now, I'd want my family beside me. I wouldn't want to wait until I was wheeled up to some room on another floor to know if anyone cared enough to come be with me. All I can say is, she better get a private room. And with a view. I requested a room with a view."

"A view of what?" David said under his breath. "The parking lot? It's the middle of the night."

Christy wasn't sure if Marti had heard David's comment. She was most likely choosing to ignore him, as usual.

"We'll be able to see Margaret soon enough," Bob said calmly. "You've done all you can. Do you want to walk around a little or get some fresh air?"

"I'm staying right here. He said the doctor would be out soon. We need to hear the full report." Marti picked up a magazine and flipped through the pages. "It's not going to be good. There's something wrong. I just know it."

Twenty minutes later the surgeon entered the waiting room. He made eye contact with Dad. "Mr. Miller? May I speak with you in private?"

Marti popped to her feet, but Bob reached for her hand to urge her to sit by him. She reluctantly conceded and said in a low voice, "It's more than her appendix. They probably found fibroids."

Christy wasn't sure what her aunt was talking about, but the sound of fear in her voice prompted Christy's heart to pound fiercely. Todd put his arm around her and drew her close as they waited for her dad to finish his conversation with the doctor.

Dad came lumbering back into the waiting area and sat down with a blank expression. The five of them gathered in a circle around him so he wouldn't have to broadcast the news to the other people seated in the small area.

He looked down at his large hands. "She's going to be all right. Her appendix didn't burst. It was about to. She had an infection and . . . " He looked up at David. "Could you get me a cup of coffee, Son?"

David looked confused. "We got coffee for you already. You didn't drink it."

Todd glanced at Christy and she knew he'd picked up the same clue she'd just read.

"I could use some coffee, too. I'll go with you." Todd stood and motioned for David to join him.

"But you don't drink coffee, Todd." David looked at Dad. "I'm not a kid. I want to know how Mom is, too."

Worry shadowed her dad's eyes as he firmly said, "David, just go get me a cup of coffee."

"Come on." Todd herded David out of the waiting area. Christy realized she had been holding her breath, waiting for what her dad was going to say next. All the worst-case scenarios blitzed through her brain. *Is it something terminal? Did they find cancer when they opened her up?* Tears began to fill her eyes.

"Well, Norman? Tell us. What did the doctor say to you?" Marti leaned in closer. "Was it her fallopian tubes? She had fibroids, didn't she?"

He looked at Marti with unmasked surprise at her diagnosis. He nodded and seemed relieved that she had spoken the words for the female body parts out loud so he didn't have to.

Marti drew in a deep breath. "I knew it. Just like all the women in our family. Did they perform a hysterectomy?"

Norman nodded again. "Partial. The doctor said it was partial."

"That means they must have removed the uterus and fallopian tubes because of the cysts, but left her ovaries. Is that right?"

"Yes."

Christy thought it was irritating and at the same time oddly endearing that her dad looked like he was blushing when Marti said, "ovaries" and "uterus." But she wasn't sure what this diagnosis meant.

"Did the doctor say there was anything else?" Christy didn't want to say the word *cancer* out loud, but she wanted to know the whole diagnosis now.

"They have to wait for lab reports. She'll be here in the hospital for at least three days."

"Of course she will." Marti rubbed her eyebrow. "I was in the hospital four days. Our mother was there for a week. It's no small thing to go through a surgery like this."

The four of them looked at each other, none of them sure what to say next. It seemed that her aunt slowly softened around the edges and took on a calmer and settled demeanor. "Your mother was there for me when I needed her," she murmured.

Christy didn't remember her aunt ever having major surgery. Nor did she remember her mom going to care for her. That didn't matter at the moment because she was focused on her mother's diagnosis and what would happen next. Pulling Aunt Marti to the side, Christy pelted her with questions about the medical history of the women on her mom's side of the family.

Marti's answers were direct and eye-opening. After explaining how they were genetically polyp prone, Marti added, "But there's no history of breast cancer on our side of the family, which is rather peculiar when it's so prevalent."

"I appreciate you telling me all this," Christy said.

With an unusual tenderness in her expression and her gestures, Marti placed her cool hand on Christy's forearm. "This might be the best reason for you and Todd to start a family sooner rather than later. Or at least try to start a family. There's no guarantees you'll be able to get pregnant or that the baby will live."

The pain in Marti's eyes was as clear as time-washed pebbles at the bottom of a Wisconsin lake.

Christy leaned in and in a low voice she revealed to her aunt that she knew about Johanna. "Mom told me when I was in high school. I always wanted to say something to you about her but didn't know what to say."

Marti's eyes misted over. It was as if Christy had disturbed the tranquil waters of deep sorrow and the pebbles of pain expanded into elongated proportions. Marti whispered, "I think of her nearly every day of my life."

Christy never expected such a vulnerable confession from her aunt. Her throat tightened, choking back any words she might say. That was probably a good thing because Christy had no idea what to say after that.

"This is not the time or the place to talk about my daughter." Marti drew in a deep breath and sat up straight. "It's my sister we're here for." In a voice loud enough for Christy's dad and Uncle Bob to be invited back into their private conversation, Marti said, "What matters now is that we all have positive thoughts for Margaret and decide what must be done. It's clear that you'll have to go on this extensive trip without me. I need to stay here and care for her the way she took care of me."

"You're right, sweetheart," Bob said. "We'll stay."

"No, you need to go," Marti said firmly. "There's nothing you can do here. And with the world the way it is these days, don't you think it's safer for you to go along with Christy and Todd in case something goes wrong?"

Christy wanted to remind her aunt that both she and Todd had been on extensive trips to Europe over the past few years, and they had managed just fine without a chaperone.

Todd and David returned with coffee for Dad. He said, "Thanks," and put it next to the other cup of coffee that was now cold.

Christy gave Todd a simple summary of what he and David had missed. "My aunt was saying that my mom's recovery will take a while."

"Several weeks," Marti added.

"So, we're trying to figure out who should stay back from our trip and help out."

Todd gave Christy a questioning look followed by a nod. She slowly turned her head and looked at her dad. "I can stay. I think I should be the one to help out."

"No, Christy. You need to go. You can't miss Bryan and Carolyn's wedding."

"Marti's right," Bob said.

"And as for Katie's wedding," Marti continued, "I certainly don't need to fly halfway around the world just to see some elephants and attend a safari wedding. Katie is the closest thing you've ever had to a sister. You'd never forgive yourself if you missed her wedding."

Christy felt torn. "It seems like I should be with my mom at a time like this. I'm her daughter."

"Well, I'm her sister and I know what she's going to need."

"But Aunt Marti . . . "

"Great-day-in-the-morning!" Christy dad slapped his palms on his thighs. "You can both go on your trip around the world. Margaret is my wife and I'll take care of her like I always have. That's the end of it."

Christy and Marti exchanged glances that felt weighted with the sort of unspoken understanding that could only be shared between two women. Especially after the heart-to-heart conversation they just shared. Christy knew all too well what it would be like if her mom was left entirely in the care of her no-fuss husband and never-home teenage son.

"Actually, Norman, that's not the end of it." Marti stood and faced her brother-in-law with her hands on her hips. "No offense, but there are times in a woman's life when she needs more attention than what any well-meaning husband can give her. This is one of those times."

Marti continued giving orders to the rest of the crew. "Christy, you must go with your husband to your father-in-law's wedding. And on to Katie's wedding, of course. These are important life moments you'll never be able to experience again."

She pointed at her husband. "Robert, you need to go with them. And Norm, you need to go back to work in the morning. I'll take care of Margaret. That settles it."

Silence reigned within their small circle as they all exchanged glances. David broke in and asked, "What about me?"

Marti looked him up and down. "You need to get a haircut."

Marti's trite comment made them all chuckle. Christy was a little in awe of this vulnerable, sweet side of her aunt. Her demeanor continued as they waited to see Christy's mom. The peaceful resolve that floated around them helped Christy to feel like going on the trip was the right thing to do.

Her emotions waffled, though, when they were finally able to visit Mom. The attending nurse allowed in two at a time. When it was Christy and Todd's turn, she held her mom's limp hand and spoke to her in a soothing voice. Her mom didn't respond, which was disturbing yet understandable. She was too sedated and on too much pain medication to open her eyelids more than a flutter.

Todd kissed his mother-in-law on the brow and prayed for her before he and Christy slipped out of the room and Bob and Marti went in for a second time.

It churned Christy up inside to see her mom so completely incapacitated. She wished they weren't flying out the next day. If she could at least look her mom in the eyes and tell her they were going, it would help her feel better about going on the trip. She wanted her mom's blessing. Not a memory of her with tubes in her arms and hooked up to machines and an IV drip.

Her dad looked even more concerned than she felt. She

could tell because his eyebrows resembled two caterpillars in a head-on collision. Christy went over to him and offered a comforting look.

"She'll be okay," Christy said with as much courage as she could find in the moment.

"The incision was six inches long." Her dad didn't look at Christy when he said it. He seemed to still be processing the information the doctor had told him in private. "Cut her clear open."

Christy put her arms around her teddy bear of a dad and gave him a big hug. He stretched out his arms around her and Christy rested her head against his chest.

In a low rumbling voice, her dad said, "They told me she won't be able to have any more children."

Christy looked up, surprised at the muted emotion she could feel coming from him. In an effort to add a lighthearted touch, she said, "Don't you think you and Mom are a little old to start adding to your family?"

He looked confused by her comment.

Christy grinned. "I thought David and I were the only two kids you ever wanted. Didn't you used to say that after us they broke the mold?"

His somber expression remained.

Christy gave up on the quips and rested her head back against her dad's chest. She kept hugging him even though she knew he was probably uncomfortable with her excessive affection. "It's going to be okay, Dad. Mom will get better. You'll see."

Christy could hear a sigh rumbling deep in his chest but refusing to come out. She wanted to believe that everything with her mom would be fine, and she wanted her dad to believe it, too.

"The doctor said the surgery went well," Christy reminded him. "No complications. That's what he said. The hospital staff will take good care of her for the next few days, and then Aunt Marti will be there to help with her recovery time. She'll bounce back quickly. You'll see."

A long sigh released at last from the caverns of her dad's spirit.

Christy pulled back and looked up at him with a slight smile. "You know what, Dad? When it comes to the next round of babies, why don't you let Todd and I take it from here?"

He looked at her with hope in his eyes. "Are you saying . . . ?"

"No. I'm just saying that sometime . . . eventually . . . hopefully . . . " Christy left her thoughts dangling the way her father had left so many of his sentences unfinished over the years. She couldn't determine when she'd get pregnant. Or as Marti reminded her, what might happen. But she and Todd had talked about it so much lately that it felt natural to bring it up as the next significant event in their lives. They just didn't know if or when their wished-for blessing might come to be.

Christy's dad touched the side of her face with his large hand. "Don't rush to have a child. Make sure your husband has a job first. A steady job."

Christy nodded. "I know. We're praying about that."

He still looked concerned. With what seemed like a great amount of effort, he said, "Go on this trip, have a good time. But when you get back, both of you need to buckle down and get your lives in order."

"We will, Dad."

Christy was quiet on the long drive back to Newport Beach in the dead of the night. She wished she felt like she was doing the right thing by leaving while her mom was still in the hospital. She thought about how Marti had told her to hurry up and have babies and then her dad told her to take their time. She wished her dad had more confidence in Todd and her and how their future would fall into place. The answer was to trust God because that was all any of them could do.

Why is it so easy to say "trust God" and yet at moments like this so hard to do?

five

Small waves of regret washed over Christy as she and Todd sat with Uncle Bob in the Red Carpet room at Chicago's O'Hare Airport. Aunt Marti, who had arranged for the first-class treatment on their long journey, wasn't with them to enjoy the fruit of all her planning.

The comfortable chairs, complimentary beverages and snacks seemed tasteless as Christy thought about her mom and the phone call she had just made to her dad. He said her mom wasn't herself yet. The nurse had told him that was to be expected. It would still be another day or two before they'd be able to cut back on the pain medication so she'd be more alert and able to talk with him. But he wasn't happy with that diagnosis, and the worry came through in his voice.

Christy could also tell that Aunt Marti was already driving her dad a little crazy with her impatience and overorganization of everything in the hospital room and beyond. The waves of regret kept rolling in and receding.

Todd gave her a grin. "You doing okay?"

She nodded and returned her gaze to the gardening magazine in her lap, even though she wasn't paying attention to the images as she slowly turned the pages. Even if she had stayed in Escondido and was sitting in the hospital room, there was nothing she could do for her mom right now, and she didn't want to start another discussion about it with Todd. All her dad and Aunt Marti could do was wait.

And that was all she, Todd, and Bob could do now at the airport, as well. Waiting in a cheerless hospital room was just about the same as waiting in a first-class airport lounge. The luxury setting did nothing to alleviate the sense of helplessness.

Their flight to Madrid was scheduled to leave in less than an hour, and it would be at least nine hours before they landed and could place another call to Christy's dad for an update. Until then, all Christy could do was pray for her mom.

Todd put down the motorcycle magazine he'd been reading. "Do you want some more tea?"

"No, thanks."

Christy knew this probably wasn't the best time to bring up another delicate subject, but with the flurry of all that had been happening over the past week, she hadn't had a chance to ask Todd how he felt about his dad's marriage.

Reaching over and resting her hand on his forearm, Christy said, "I heard something from Tracy that sort of surprised me. She said you'd told Doug you were uneasy about your dad getting married."

Todd gave her a surprised look. "I wouldn't say I'm uneasy about it."

"How do you feel? Really? I mean, I know you're happy for them. I am, too. But do you feel like you're losing your father?"

"No."

"Do you think he won't be as interested or involved in your life once he has a wife?"

Todd's expression clouded over. He pulled away from Christy and put the magazine down on the end table. "It's his

life. His turn, you know? He was there for me when it count-
ed and now I want to do everything I can to support him. He
doesn't owe me anything."

Judging by the agitated tone in Todd's voice, Christy
knew Tracy had been right. This was difficult for him.

Doesn't he see that I'm his home base now?

"My dad has waited a long time for this. He wants to be
with Carolyn."

"I know," Christy said quietly. She also knew that if she
said anything else at this moment she'd be sorry later. Todd
and his dad had to make their own peace over this change in
their relationship.

She'd learned long ago that the way to get Todd to open
up to her was not by shooting him so full of questions that
he finally bled out all the information she desired. It was better to wait. Let him think and process and then come to her
with his summarized thoughts and feelings. That was Todd's
idea of intimate communication. She preferred being more
involved in the process so she could offer her insights on the
topic.

But not this time. This time she would wait, just like she
was waiting for everything else. And she would pray.

Uncle Bob returned to his spot on the lounge sofa with
a plate full of crackers and cheese. "I am looking forward to
getting some shut-eye on this next flight. How about you
two?"

"I could sleep anywhere right now," Todd said.

"This is the flight Marti paid extra to upgrade our seats.
We should be able to stretch out more than on the last flight."

"It's a bummer that Marti did all the planning and now
she's missing the whole trip."

"When we call her from Madrid, let's mention the upgraded seats. She'd appreciate hearing that."

Their upgraded seats were more than just seats, the three
of them discovered. They were among the first to board and
were directed to space age-looking, fully reclining seats in

individual sleeping cubbies, complete with personal TV screens and reading lamps.

Todd kept grinning and Bob gave him an enthusiastic thumbs-up as the two of them settled in across the aisle from each other. Christy had the seat next to Todd by the window and was secretly ecstatic. She'd seen this sort of first-class cabin a few years ago when she was flying home from Switzerland. That time it had only been a glance before turning and shuffling to the back of the plane. She couldn't believe they were actually occupying the luxury seats on this flight.

The well-dressed travelers around them appeared blasé about the spacious accommodations. It seemed this was the way they always traveled. Christy also noticed that their fellow first-class comrades also had no reaction to the steak and sautéed mushroom dinner with asparagus that was served on fine ceramic plates and delivered on trays covered with crisp linen cloths. With the wave of a hand, one of them even turned down the dessert of chocolate ganache cake with raspberries.

Christy, Bob, and Todd didn't turn down any of it. Christy especially liked the warm, lemon-scented washcloths that were handed to them with wooden tongs before the meal was served and then again afterward. She stretched out in her easily prepared capsule bed, smelling of fresh lemons and feeling like a princess.

Todd leaned over from his adjoining space and gave her a lingering kiss. He drew back and smiled at her. "Not bad."

Christy tilted her head. "What's not bad? My kiss, or flying first class like this?"

Todd slipped his hand around the curve of her neck. "I think I need another kiss before I can decide which I like more."

Christy eagerly provided him with a stellar kiss, still laced with chocolate and raspberries. Todd pulled back and with a playful grin said, "Don't go starting something you can't finish, Mrs. Spencer."

Christy grinned at her handsome husband. "You started it."

"Yeah, I guess I did." With one more gentle kiss on her cheek he whispered, "Later."

Christy knew what he meant. She also knew she would have no difficulty falling asleep as the plane streaked its way across the skies and delivered them to Madrid, where they'd catch another plane for the three-hour flight to Las Palmas in the Canary Islands.

Her sleep was sweet and deep. She put aside her gnawing concern for her mother and dreamed of hiking with Katie through the verdant tea fields of Kenya.

Right in the middle of a slumbering image of Katie and Eli exchanging first bites of their wedding cake, Christy was jolted out of dreamland. Her eyes opened all the way. Quickly taking in the darkened first-class cabin, she realized in a moment that the thought in her dream was not something conjured up in her imagination. The thought was true.

She bolted upright and bumped her head on the edge of her capsule. "Todd!" Christy jostled the shoulder of her sleeping lion. "Todd! Wake up!"

He squinted at her as if he had no idea who she was or where they were. Christy knew how difficult it was for Todd to be roused when he was in a deep sleep, but this was an emergency.

"Todd, are you awake?"

"Yeah. Yeah. What is it? What's wrong?" He pushed himself up on his elbow and squinted at her more intently.

"Todd." Tears began to fill Christy's eyes before she could get the words out. "I messed up. I messed up so bad."

"No you didn't. Your mom will be all right. Marti is with her. You did the right thing by coming."

"No, it's not my mom. It's Katie." Christy covered her face with her hands.

Todd drew her hands away and turned on the reading light. "You're not making any sense. Did you have a bad dream?"

"No. It wasn't a dream." Christy wiped away the tears rolling down her cheeks. "Todd, I forgot Katie's wedding dress."

"What?"

"I forgot to bring Katie's wedding dress with me!"

"I thought you said you rolled it a certain way and put it in the suitcase."

"I did! Aunt Marti and I took extra care to pack it just right. But we put it in her suitcase, not mine. It's still there. At Bob and Marti's house, rolled up in Marti's big suitcase."

Todd was quiet for a moment. "Well, there's nothing you can do about it now."

Christy didn't like his easy answer. Of course she couldn't do anything right that moment, but what could she do? How could she get the dress in time? She needed to come up with a solution. She needed to fix this awful mistake.

Todd turned off the reading light. "When we call Marti from Madrid, you can ask her to mail it to you."

Christy snapped the light back on. "How can she mail it to me? She's in Escondido and the wedding dress is in Newport Beach." Her emotions swelled like a puffer fish.

"Then ask Tracy to send it to you."

Christy contemplated that possibility for a moment as Todd lay down and got comfortable again.

With one eye opened, he gave her an earnest look. "Don't worry about it. It'll work out."

"How?"

"I don't know." Both his eyes were closed and he was making it clear he wasn't willing to lose any more sleep over her horrifying dilemma. "You'll just have to trust God."

Once again, Christy felt as if those words sounded awfully flippant in the midst of a deep, dark moment.

"Come on. Have a little faith, Kilikina. God will work this out somehow. We'll just have to live inside the mystery of *how* He's going to do it while we get some sleep."

Christy wanted to throw something at him. "Live inside

the mystery" had sounded beautifully poetic when he and Doug used it in a song they were writing. However, at this moment and in this instance, it was the worst thing he could possibly say to her.

How can he be so at ease about this? He has no idea how long it took me to find that dress for Katie and how hard it was to get the alterations done in time. Even if Tracy is able to get into Bob and Marti's house and ship the dress to Nairobi, how do we know if it will get there in time?

Christy started biting her lower lip. There was no way she would be able to doze off again the way Todd had.

She had one thing to do as Katie's matron of honor. One thing. Get her a dress and bring it to the wedding. *I can't believe I forgot it. If Katie had done this at my wedding, I'd be so upset.*

Christy thought about her wedding and all the little things that went wrong or almost went wrong. Katie had sprinted to their getaway car at the very last possible moment in order to give Christy an important item she'd packed for her honeymoon. It was the little bundle of letters she'd written to her future husband and tied up with a ribbon. Doug and Rick had tried to slip a "honeymoon survival kit" into Christy's luggage and removed the letters in order to make room for the gift Tracy had put together for them.

When Katie found out about the removal of the letters, she went to heroic efforts to make sure nothing was amiss on Christy's big day.

Now it was Christy's turn. She wanted to be there for Katie 100 percent. And she'd failed.

I can't believe I forgot Katie's dress.

Todd was right about not being able to do anything about it right now. She had to wait. Just like she had to wait to hear an update on her mom. The feeling of being suspended was terrible. She even felt clammy about being suspended in nothing but invisible air as they jetted across the Atlantic Ocean.

Todd's admonition to "have a little faith" returned to her, and she turned off the reading light. She had a little faith right now. But that was it. Just a little.

"I'm sorry," she whispered as she curled up in her flight bed. The apology was as much for Katie as it was to the Lord. She was sorry she had so quickly given up any faith she had in Him and in His mysterious ways. Instead of faith, she had opened the door to fear. Whenever she did that, whenever she let fear jump into the driver's seat, she was destined for a careening, soul-draining ride. She did not want fear to take over.

Christy whispered the words of Second Timothy 1:7 that Todd had often repeated to her whenever he saw fear grabbing the keys and trying to take her for a wild ride. "God has not given us a spirit of fear but of power and of love and of a sound mind."

Her heart and mind immediately calmed. She let out a long, deep breath and then another. If Todd were awake right now, he'd be reminding her that nothing comes as a surprise to the Lord. God knew all about Katie's dress. He wasn't stressed about it. He was working out His bigger plan behind the scenes.

But what kind of bigger plan could God possibly have in all this?

Christy tried to imagine what sort of good might come of this. None of her scenarios seemed plausible. The only thing that gave her some bit of cheer was knowing that this was Katie, her Forever Friend and favorite Peculiar Treasure. Katie didn't care about fancy dresses and event details as much as Christy did. Katie would probably be just as happy if she married Eli in a pair of jeans and one of her old T-shirts from Bargain Barn.

But this is her wedding. It needs to be special and beautiful. No one has ever honored Katie and celebrated her the way she should be. I wanted to be the one who did that on her wedding day. Aunt Marti and Christy talked about this for hours. They were going to go all out and make sure Katie felt pampered and beautiful and loved.

Christy pulled the thin airplane blanket up to her chin and released the last few straggling tears she'd held back when she was kicking fear out of the driver's seat of her thoughts. In this final release of her amplified emotions, all she could think was that she wished her aunt had come on this trip. Marti would know what to do.

The wish surprised her. *I miss my aunt. Hmm. Interesting. I don't think that's ever happened before.*

Finally giving in to the emotional exhaustion of the last twenty-four hours, Christy closed her eyes and slept fearlessly for the remainder of the flight. When the cabin lights came on, the first-class passengers were roused with the offering of another lemon-scented warm towel. The fragrance of coffee brewing helped convince her it was a new day, even though her body was telling her it was still the middle of the night and she needed to get more sleep.

"You feelin' all right?" Todd asked.

She nodded. "How about you?"

"I'm doing good."

The flight attendant served them glasses of orange juice and offered a basket of warm croissants before the breakfast of omelets and fruit were served. Todd helped himself to two croissants. "This is the way to travel, isn't it?"

Once the three of them were off the plane and had found their departing gate for the flight to Las Palmas, Uncle Bob tried to give Marti a call. He had added extra services to his phone in order to make it easy to place international calls. Something wasn't working right with the system, and Bob was unsuccessful in placing a call before it was time to board their next flight.

Christy sat in the middle and immediately felt claustrophobic. After their last luxurious flight, this smaller plane felt like a school bus with a narrow aisle down the middle. The welcome and flight safety instructions were repeated in

Spanish, English, and French. The people around them were speaking other languages, which made the fact that they were in Europe start to feel real. Before the plane took off, Todd was already asleep with his head against the window. Christy leaned her head back. She wished she had a travel pillow or at least an extra sweater she could roll up and use for support.

Christy turned to Bob who was flipping through movie selections on his iPad. "I think that last flight ruined me for life. It's terrible knowing how much nicer things are at the front of the plane."

Bob smiled. "As they say, 'ignorance is bliss.'"

"I still feel sad that Marti wasn't able to come. She would have liked that last flight."

"Listen." Bob looked at Christy over the top of his reading glasses. "I'll tell you something, but don't tell your aunt I said this. She was relieved about not coming with us."

"Relieved? Why?"

"The more she researched all the details, the more her anxiety grew. She doubled up on the 'serenity' pills she gets from her naturopath doctor. They take the edge off when she feels a panic attack coming on. She started taking them a week ago. They've actually been helping with her migraines, too."

"I didn't realize any of this. She seemed so eager to do all the planning."

"She was. The anxious feelings started the day we went to get our shots for Africa. When she brought the malaria pills home, she stared at them as if they were going to rob her of her youth."

"She was afraid to go to Africa?"

"I think she was actually more nervous about the Canary Islands. I don't know why. My only guess is that it had to do with the lack of five-star resorts where we're staying. She likes things to be comfortable when she travels. Predictable and safe. Between what she considered the subpar accommodations in Las Palmas and the possibility of getting bitten by a mosquito in Africa, she was pretty nervous. Not to mention the fear of a plane crash and potential political unrest in Kenya."

Christy's eyes narrowed. Faith and fear were doing a teeter-totter routine once again in her heart.

"Don't you start thinking about those problems now." Uncle Bob reached over and gave her hand a squeeze.

Christy told fear to go away and thought about how eager her aunt had been to volunteer to stay with her mom. She wanted to believe that Marti's motivation came from her love and concern for her sister. Was it possible that as Bob was saying, Marti was looking for an easy way to excuse herself from this trip?

Sometimes Christy didn't understand her aunt at all.

The other thing she didn't understand was the gathering of Carolyn's family who met them at the airport. They were all speaking Spanish and hugging and kissing Christy, Todd, and Bob as if they were long-lost relatives who had been shipwrecked at sea and now returned to the home of their childhood. Their effusive welcome was unlike anything Christy had ever experienced before.

They drove the winding roads of the arid island in a swirl of conversation and ended up at a seaside restaurant just before sunset. Another dozen or more enthusiastic relatives were on hand for another round of hugs and kisses and questions about Christy's mom and Aunt Marti in heavily accented English.

Christy had never felt so encompassed and welcomed anywhere in her life. She could see why Todd's dad liked it here so much and why he loved being a part of Carolyn's family.

The best part of the affectionate reunion had been what happened between Todd and his dad. When they first saw each other at the airport, they had hugged and smiled and laughed. It was a joyful reunion and lots of full circles being completed when Bryan introduced Todd and Christy to Carolyn. She was as lovely as her photos. Her shoulder-length, coffee-colored hair bounced as she linked her arm in Bryan's and the two of them led the way to their compact car in the airport parking lot.

The flurry of hellos had been wonderfully sweet and lighthearted.

But when they were at the restaurant, Bryan motioned for Todd and Christy to get up from the seats they'd taken at the far end of the table. He insisted they come to where he and Carolyn were seated at the head of the table and that Todd sit at his right hand. That's when the poignancy of this moment set in.

Before Todd could take his chair, a look of wild realization came over Bryan's face. It was as if it had suddenly hit him that he had his only son with him, beside him, only inches away.

Bryan's expression tightened and his pale-blue eyes widened with a willful intent not to blink. It was the same look Christy had seen a number of times on Todd's face when he was trying to be strong and brave and not give way to tears.

After rising from his seat of honor, Bryan went to Todd and placed his worn hands on Todd's shoulders. The two of them looked so alike in that moment. Todd's expression mirrored his father's. Bryan gazed into his son's eyes and gave a nod of deep satisfaction as if this was a moment for which he had waited a long time.

The two men embraced with a father and son fervor that had to be sinking deep into Todd's soul.

Christy's vision began to blur with happy tears. This was exactly what Todd needed, she was sure of it. If they hadn't come, he would have missed this embrace that encompassed a lifetime of unspoken feelings.

Time doesn't heal all wounds. But a single moment in time, like this one, certainly can.

six

The next morning Christy was the first to wake in the narrow bed where her back was pressed against the cool concrete wall. Todd was still asleep on the air mattress on the tile floor. A smile pressed her lips upward as she remembered where they were and all that had happened last night.

She felt a soft contentment still settled on her as she remembered the celebration dinner last night and all the love that had been poured out on them since they arrived in the Canary Islands.

She and Todd had fallen asleep in each other's arms in the narrow bed, but sometime in the night Todd found his way to the air mattress on the floor where he was now spread out on his stomach. He had his right arm up and bent and his left leg bent at the knee. He looked like a 3-D chalk drawing on a sidewalk in a murder mystery, snoring softly in a deep way that made it clear he was indeed dead—dead to the world.

Christy rolled onto her back and pulled the crisp white sheet and puffy down comforter up to her chin. The small room was cool and quiet. It was great room for sleeping once the shades were down to block out the brightness of the new day.

Christy gazed at the ceiling and thought about how concerned Carolyn's mother had been last night at dinner when they told her Christy's mother was in the hospital. "Abuela Teresa," as all of the relatives called Carolyn's mom, had asked to get on the phone when Bob got ahold of Marti.

"You are a good sister," Abuela Teresa had said. "You are missed here very much, but what you are doing is the work of angels. May God bless you doubly for the way you are blessing your sister."

Christy wondered how Aunt Marti had taken the blessing over the phone. It certainly was delivered with sincerity from the matriarch of Carolyn's family. Abuela Teresa was a striking woman with white hair worn up in an attractive twist. She had a lot of sisters. And cousins. And second cousins. And nieces and nephews and uncles. Christy lost track of who was who, but she had no trouble telling which of the women were related to Carolyn because they all seemed to resemble Abuela Teresa in some way. Not all of them were as demure and elegant. Carolyn came the closest in face and form. All of them were lovely in their own way and exuded a confidence Christy found compelling. It wasn't arrogance. It was a steady sort of calm that didn't come from a "serenity" pill.

Christy thought about what happened last night at the restaurant when Abuela Teresa learned that the three of them had plans to stay at a hotel. She rose to her feet and made a declaration, first in English and then in Spanish—they were family and should not stay at a hotel. End of discussion. It was similar to Aunt Marti's declaration at the hospital and that made Christy smile. Abuela Teresa somehow managed to deliver her decrees without the sharp edges of Marti's announcements. Her words rolled out with soft corners and honeyed tones.

Roberto, as everyone was now calling Uncle Bob, was

to stay with Bryan at his new house. Add Christy and Todd would stay with Abuela Teresa and . . .

Todd stirred on the buoyant air mattress on the guest room floor. He slowly moved both arms to his side. He opened one eye and then the other. His actions reminded Christy of a curious lizard as he held up his neck and stared straight ahead while the rest of his body remained still.

"Good morning," Christy whispered.

Todd propped himself up on his elbow. He smiled and looked at Christy with great contentment.

"You're a happy camper," she said.

"I definitely feel like a camper on this air mattress."

"Did I kick too much last night and hog all he covers?"

"A little." Todd gave her a wink. It was a silly wink because his eyes were puffy. "I thought we'd both get more sleep if we had space to stretch out."

"Thanks for taking the floor."

"I don't mind. This is pretty comfortable, actually. It reminds me of my bed in the apartment I shared with Doug and Rick back in our San Diego State days."

"Except that bed was filled with sand, not air." Christy didn't include the usual comment Katie always added whenever this topic came up. Katie called it his "kitty litter box" and insisted that no one could truly sleep in a bed of sand. Todd assured her that it was just like stretching out on the beach and taking a long nap.

"The bed I had as a kid was filled with air, like this one, only not as comfortable. It was green. One of those ninety-nine cent air mattresses you buy at the grocery store in the summer." Todd shifted his position and stretched his stiff neck. "I don't think I ever slept on a real bed until my dad bought the house in Newport Beach and I went to live with him."

Since Todd rarely talked about his childhood, Christy felt her heartbeat quicken at his unexpected comment. "How old were you when he bought that house?"

"First grade. What age is that? Six? Seven?"

Christy nodded. She loved that he was opening up so effortlessly and didn't want to do anything to hinder the flow of his words.

"Probably would have been sooner, but it took my dad a couple years to get custody of me. He said that was a good thing because it gave him time to save up money to buy the house. He had to look as stable as he could because the courts had deemed my mother fit to raise me."

"Was she?" Christy asked cautiously.

Todd leaned back and stared at the ceiling. He didn't answer.

Christy wasn't sure if she should say anything else. She wanted to go to Todd and curl up next to him and kiss his sad face. But she waited, watching for a clue as to what he wanted.

After a moment, he said, "You know the girl in the movie Bob was watching on one of the flights? The movie with the guy with the box of chocolates at the bus stop?"

Christy nodded. She knew what Todd meant even if he couldn't remember the name of the movie.

"My mom was like the girl in that movie. Only I was born way before she got sobered up and could hold down a respectable job."

Unpleasant images of what Todd's earliest years must have been like ran through her thoughts. While she was raised on a farm, eating fresh corn on the cob and waving sparklers in her grandparents' front lawn on the Fourth of July, Todd was alone in a small apartment sleeping on a green swimming pool raft. His only idea of what a loving extended family looked like came from the shows he watched on TV.

"I'm glad your dad was able to get custody of you," Christy said quietly.

Todd drew in a deep breath and sat up. "Me, too."

"I loved the way he hugged you last night at the restaurant."

"Me, too." The contented half grin on Todd's face showed his dimple, and Christy knew the embrace had, indeed, been infused with all the healing and resolve she had envisioned.

Todd sniffed the air. "Do you smell breakfast?"

Christy didn't smell anything.

He reached for his phone that was connected to the adaptor and plugged into the wall socket. "Whoa! Forget breakfast. That must be lunch I smell. Did you know it was almost eleven thirty?"

"Is it really?" Christy decided that Todd's glimpse over his shoulder at his childhood was over. She tossed back the covers and placed her bare feet on the cold floor. "Weren't we supposed to go over to your dad's house first thing this morning?"

"He told me to call him once we were up." He grinned at Christy again. "I'll tell him the same thing that one aunt kept saying last night. What was her name? She kept asking if we had 'jet drag.'"

"I heard her say that, too. Jet drag. Yeah, that's what it feels like." Christy pulled some clothes from her open suitcase and grabbed her cosmetic bag. She showered and dressed quickly.

A chorus of voices echoed in the small apartment as Christy headed down the short hallway to join the group in the living room. Abuela Teresa had a bird that was twittering wildly in its cage by the large open windows behind the sofa. One of the aunts was reaching for a cloth to cover the cage in order to quiet the bird.

The women were happy to see that Christy was up, and all of them spoke at once. What she picked up from the pieces of English spiced with a few Spanish exclamations and mixed with lots of hand gestures was that the aunts were going to have a party for Carolyn tomorrow and they wanted to make sure Christy understood that she was invited.

Carolyn wasn't among the group of eager celebrators in the living room so she couldn't translate. Christy nodded, agreeing to be at the party. "What time is it tomorrow?"

They all looked at each other.

Christy had discovered at the dinner last night that near-ly all of Carolyn's relatives understood English much better than they let on. They preferred to speak Spanish, of course, but since Christy's Spanish was abysmal, they were willing to be accommodating with all the communication. Christy pointed to her wrist where she would be wearing a watch, if she had one, and asked again, "What time is the party to-morrow?"

"All day," one of the women said. "At the spa."

"Oh!" Christy liked this idea even better. "What time should I be ready to go?"

"Nine." One of the aunts held up nine fingers.

"Okay. I'll be ready. How fun! Thank you for inviting me."

All the women gave Christy an odd look as if she had no need to thank them. Of course she was invited.

Abuela Teresa entered the room wearing a flowing kaf-tan-style dress embroidered in deep-green trim around the neck. She carried a tray of stemmed glassware. Carolyn fol-lowed her mother with another tray of small sausages along with small slices of baguettes and a bowl of brightly colored dipping sauce of some sort.

"Mojo sauce," one of the aunts told Christy. "Try."

The women found places to sit in the small living room and cleared a space on the coffee table for the two trays. They each reached for a glass and held it up as a salute first to Car-olyn and then to Christy. They said something in Spanish and all sipped in unison. Christy tasted the beverage and found it to be a refreshing blend of bubbly mineral water spiked with what appeared to be fresh lemonade, judging by the small bits of lemon pulp floating in the glass like confetti.

Todd stepped into the room and all the eyes went to him.

"*Buenos días*," he said, giving a manly sort of half bow to the women of the court. Christy thought his gesture was cute and silly at the same time since it was so out of character for him to play the role of the gallant gentleman. The influence of the ancient Spanish culture that prevailed in this corner of the world must be having an effect on him.

The sisters began chittering all at once, and the bird in the covered cage directly behind Christy joined in. It was a glorious sound in her ears. If she was Abuela Teresa and had shared her life with sisters and daughters like the ones in this room, this was exactly the sort of sounds Christy would want to fill her home in her lingering years.

The woman next to Christy reached over and squeezed her arm. "He is so handsome, like his father. *Muy guapo.*"

Christy smiled and nodded her agreement. Blond-haired, blue-eyed men must be a rarity here. It was quite a change from the steady flow of bleached-out beach boys she saw every day in Newport Beach.

"And your uncle?" the woman asked in a lowered voice. "He is still married?"

"Yes. My aunt had to stay home and take care of my mother."

"Ah, *sí.*" The woman pursed her lips. "He would make a good husband for my friend."

"He already is a good husband to my aunt." Christy delivered the words with a soft smile and lifted her glass in a toast to her faithful uncle.

With evident delight that Christy had initiated the toasting gesture, the sister gave a lighthearted laugh and clinked her glass with Christy's.

Todd joined the group, piecing together his conversation with bits of Spanish. He didn't need to try so hard to connect with his new relatives. They'd still be crazy about him if all he did was sit there and eat all the sausages, which he pretty much did.

Bryan arrived after all the food was gone. He was wearing painting clothes and greeted everyone at a distance, indicating that they risked getting paint on them if they came too close. He turned down Abuela Teresa's offer to make him some more food and asked Todd if he was ready to come back to his house and lend him a hand.

"Sure." Todd turned to Christy. "Would you like to stay here?"

"No, I'll go with you guys. I can help with the painting or whatever it is you're doing."

One of the sisters protested, indicating that Christy should leave the men to do the painting and she should stay with the women. Christy looked to Carolyn for direction.

With a warm smile, Carolyn rose from her chair. "You are now officially a Woman of the Canaries, Christy. That means you are a woman of options. You can do whatever you'd like. No one will think better of you or worse for what you decide."

"I'll go with you." Christy tried to get up from the couch, but first she had to receive and give a little cheek-to-cheek kiss to each of the aunties before she could leave the room. Abuela Teresa gave her a lingering, closed-lip smile and said as she had last night when they first arrived at the apartment, "*Mi casa es su casa.* We are family. You do whatever you wish while you are here."

"Thank you. *Gracias.*"

Abuela Teresa smiled broadly showing teeth that were slightly crooked and slightly yellow. No wonder she kept her lips together when she smiled. The imperfection caused Christy to like her even more. She liked all the aunts and cousins. How would the dynamic be in this group if Aunt Marti had been there? It was hard to know. Marti might have embraced them all with the same gentle kindness she'd shown to Christy in the hospital waiting room. Or she could have run out of her serenity pills and been completely flustered by the way the women did life here.

Carolyn slipped her hand into Bryan's as they walked to the elevator of the large apartment complex and rode down to the underground parking. Christy loved watching the two of them express their affection for each other. They had met here in the Canary Islands as teens and had a bumpy summer romance that ended badly. When they saw each other again for the first time last year, it was, as Bryan told Todd and Christy, as if no time had passed. His attraction to Carolyn was still there. He was elated when he discovered she felt the same way.

Carolyn's husband had died as a result of a violent act over eight years ago, and she needed that time to process her grief. Their love was brimming with hope and new beginnings for both of them. Their wedding in five days was going to be a grand celebration.

"How's your mother doing?" Carolyn asked once they were in the car and threading their way into the heavy traffic on the main road in front of the apartments.

"We haven't had an update since last night, but Uncle Bob said she was responding well."

"I heard Bob talking to Marti this morning," Bryan said. "It looks like your mom will be able to go home today or tomorrow. He said that was sooner than expected."

"That's good to hear," Todd said.

Carolyn turned around in the passenger seat and reached back, offering her hand to Christy. Christy took it and received the firm squeeze Carolyn offered. "It looks like you and I will have to be the ones who keep each other cheerful. I know you must be concerned about your mother and missing your aunt since she couldn't come."

Christy nodded even though her thoughts about Aunt Marti's presence on this trip had waffled over the last few days.

Carolyn said, "I'm so sad Tikki and Matthew aren't coming for the wedding."

"They're not coming? I thought they were arriving on Thursday."

Carolyn let go of Christy's hand and shook her head. "In all the chatter last night I wasn't sure if you had heard. Tikki is pregnant."

Christy's eyes grew wide. She knew how close Carolyn was with her only child, just as Bryan was close to Todd, his only child. The crazy part was that Christy and Todd and Matt and Tikki had all gone to Rancho Corona University. Tikki and Matt had been at Christy and Todd's wedding. It didn't seem right for them to miss Bryan and Carolyn's big day.

"I hadn't heard that she was pregnant," Christy said. "That's wonderful."

"Yes and no. She's had some difficulties. Two days ago the doctor said he wouldn't release her to travel this far. It's too risky for the baby at this stage."

"I'm so sorry to hear that. I was looking forward to seeing them. And I'm sure you must be really disappointed that they can't come."

Bryan looked in the rearview mirror. "I thought I'd told you, Todd."

Todd shook his head. "This is the first I've heard of it."

"We talked about postponing the wedding," Bryan said. "But you guys were already in the air and Tikki insisted that we go ahead."

Carolyn gave Bryan a loving look. "Tikki and Matt promised they'd come out and see us after the baby's born."

"Dad, you're going to be a grandpa," Todd said.

Bryan laughed and glanced at Todd in the rearview mirror. "I know. A groom and a grandpa in the same year. How 'bout that? Five years ago I never would have guessed this would be happening." He shot Carolyn a smile. "I am blessed beyond belief."

Carolyn smiled back. She turned in her seat again and looked at Christy with an open expression of pure honesty. "I have a favor to ask of you, Christy."

"Sure."

"We tried to keep our wedding simple, as you know. As you also know, I asked Tikki to stand with me. We planned to just have Todd and Tikki at the altar with us."

Christy nodded. *Todd and Tikki*, the new stepbrother and sister pairing that would be one of the results of this union.

Even their names went together.

"When I realized that Tikki wouldn't be able to come, I asked my twin sister to stand with me instead."

"Which one is your twin?" Christy asked. "I don't remember meeting her yet."

"She's not here. She lives in Northern California and was supposed to arrive on Wednesday. But she's . . . " Carolyn glanced at Bryan as she seemed to be trying to find the right words.

"Her sister isn't like any of the other women you've met here," Bryan said. "She's self-absorbed."

Carolyn tried to soften his evaluation. "She's in a difficult marriage right now and her two daughters are both in some complicated situations. Marilyn e-mailed me last night and said she didn't think she should come."

"That's awful," Christy said. "Both Tikki and your sister not being able to be there on your special day. I'm sorry to hear that, Carolyn."

Carolyn drew in a quick breath and tilted her head as she fixed her gaze on Christy. "I know this is last minute, but is there any way you would be willing to stand with me at the altar at our wedding?"

Christy didn't know what to say. She hadn't expected the invitation. "Are you sure there isn't someone else you'd like to ask? You have so many wonderful aunts and cousins here."

"I know. I do. And that's a problem, you see, because they are all so close. If I single out one of them, I run the risk of offending all the others. But that's not the only reason I'd like you to be my attendant. Bryan and I talked about it, and I'd really like you to be by my side on Saturday just as Todd is going to be next to Bryan. You're our immediate family."

"I'd be honored, Carolyn. I really would. Thank you for asking me."

A look of relief washed over Carolyn's face. "Thank you, Christy. This means more to me than I can say."

In a matter-of-fact voice, Christy's father-in-law said to

his bride-to-be, "I told you she was gold. Pure gold."

Todd reached over and covered Christy's hand with his. She felt so loved and so wanted at that moment. This bond that had just formed between her and Todd's side of the family felt different than what both of them had with her side of the family. This was, as Bryan said, golden.

seven

$\mathscr{I}$t wasn't until they pulled up in front of the house Bryan inherited that Christy let it sink in. They were on an island that was a province of Spain. The Sahara desert was less than seventy miles to the east. The weather was warm without being humid. The tropical foliage reminded Christy of Hawaii and the air was scented with honeysuckle. This wasn't a dream. She was on the other side of the world.

The house, the land, and the mature citrus trees that surrounded it suddenly made her feel as if they had arrived at an old hacienda where something important had happened in history. In a way, it had. This was the house Bryan's stepmother had lived in and had left to him in her will. The important history playing out before their eyes was that Todd's dad now had a home and acreage in the Canary Islands, and he was about to get married and start a whole new season of his life.

The beauty of new beginnings was evident when they got out of the car and Bryan opened the ornate wrought-iron gate that led them down a cement pathway to the front door.

On either side of the path were freshly planted flowers that spread out like a variegated carpet of deep magenta, bright persimmon, and vivid lapis blue. Christy felt like she was walking into a painting.

"This is so beautiful." She paused to admire the birdbath that was lined with stunning yellow, green, and blue tiles.

"You should have seen this house before we started the renovations," Carolyn said. "We have pictures we'll show you."

"Todd showed me some of the photos Bryan sent him."

"It's such a great old house," Carolyn said wistfully. "It was falling apart. Don't you think it feels alive now?"

Christy agreed with Carolyn as they walked past the double wooden doors that opened to a spacious tiled entryway. The main living area was straight ahead, one step down. Large tarps covered the furniture that had all been moved to the center of the room. Uncle Bob stood on a ladder with a paintbrush in his hand. He had earbuds in and seemed focused on whatever he was listening to as well as the detailed work in front of him.

"I brought reinforcements," Bryan said in a loud voice.

Bob turned with a look of surprise at their arrival. He gave the four of them a nod and a grin and returned to carefully dabbing the creamy-colored paint along the top of the wall without getting it on the ancient-looking wood-beam ceiling.

"I suppose I should give you a tour first," Bryan said. "Kitchen is here on the left. We are still waiting for the new refrigerator, but the rest of the appliances and the new sink have all been installed."

"When will the refrigerator get here?" Todd asked.

Bryan shrugged. "It was supposed to be here last week."

"We're hoping it arrives before Friday." Carolyn let out a notable sigh. "My aunts are counting on using it for all the food they're making for the reception."

A missing refrigerator was something Christy would consider a major issue and worthy of a string of panicked phone calls. Her father-in-law seemed unusually relaxed about it.

"If there's one thing I've learned being here," Bryan said, "it's that you can't rush anything. We're definitely on island time here in the Canaries. The refrigerator will show up eventually. If it's not here by Saturday, we'll improvise."

Carolyn didn't look quite as relaxed about the topic. But she seemed to have accepted the situation with a quiet resolve.

"Come see the bedrooms." Carolyn led the way to the other side of the house where they had expanded one of the original rooms into a master bedroom and added a bathroom. The bed was a large four-poster crafted from dark wood. A flowing, white mosquito net covered the top and was pulled to the side by long ties that matched the deep orange-and-lapis blue bedspread. It seemed the mosquito net was more for decoration than necessity. With the bright colors in the bedspread, the dark wood of the furniture and in the dark beams of the ceiling, along with the soft light coming in through the large open window, this room looked like something from a magazine.

"Wow." Christy turned all the way around to take in the entire space.

"Yeah," Todd echoed Christy's impression. "Nicely done, Dad."

"Carolyn had a lot to do with this room." Bryan leaned over and gave his fiancée a kiss on the cheek. He whispered something in her ear. Her face turned rosy and she shyly kissed him back.

Christy had secretly wondered if Bryan and Carolyn were waiting until their wedding night before being intimate with each other. It was none of her business, but she still wondered how it would be for them now that they were both Christians. Bryan had said a few years ago that since he'd given his life to Christ, he was only interested in "doing things God's way." He told Christy he'd spent most of his life doing things his way and that hadn't "yielded much of a harvest."

Seeing the blush on Carolyn's face and the way Bryan had whispered to her, Christy thought they certainly must have waited and saved their most intimate moments as a couple for their wedding night. The signs of integrity and purity were evident regardless of a couple's age. She couldn't help but smile inwardly to think of them having such a romantic space to come to and start their love life together as husband and wife.

Todd slipped his hand into Christy's as they finished the tour of the main bathroom and the other two rooms: a guest room and an office.

What is Todd thinking right now? Even though he keeps saying he's happy for his dad, I know this has to be unsettling for him to see Bryan starting this whole new life so far away.

Christy gave Todd's hand three squeezes. It was their secret message of "I-love-you." He responded by holding her hand more tightly, as if trying to draw some of her strength to process all this newness. They stepped into the guest room and saw that Uncle Bob's suitcase was open on the tile floor and the bed was unmade. Christy smiled inwardly. Her aunt would never stand for such clutter or an unkempt bed. Perhaps Bob was enjoying the freedom of sharing Bryan's bachelor pad for these final days before the wedding.

"What can we do?" Todd asked when the tour circled them back to the large central living room area. "Put us to work."

He let go of Christy's hand and seemed resolved that this was the new reality. His dad was getting married and living in this house. He was here to help. Todd had responded this way in other difficult emotional situations. He dealt with his feelings in the moment by doing something.

"We need to get the cabinets installed in the main bathroom," Bryan said. "They're out on the back patio. Why don't you help me carry those in and we'll tackle that beast. The only other project is to wipe out all the kitchen cupboards and start filling them with the plates and dishes in the boxes stacked up in the dining area."

"I can help with that," Christy said.

"And we need to set up the chairs on the patio," Carolyn said. "My uncle is supposed to bring them over this afternoon."

"Your home is beautiful. All of it."

"Thanks, Christy." Carolyn smiled at her.

Bryan beamed at her comment. "It feels like home. And as long as I can keep working here remotely, we don't see an urgency to move back to the States any time soon."

"That might change once your first grandchild arrives."

Carolyn and Bryan exchanged glances. It seemed as if they hadn't yet gotten ahold of the idea that Tikki and Matt were having a baby. They were too focused on their new love and new life together, as they should be.

"I'm secretly praying there might be a way for Tikki and Matthew to move here," Carolyn said. "I know it's a farfetched dream, but I've seen God do much more than I ever imagined in the last few years so I'll keep wishing and praying and dreaming and see what He does. A daughter needs to be near her mother during certain seasons of life."

Christy nodded. Her heart had definitely tugged her to stay with her mom during this unexpected season of surgery and recovery. She also wanted her mother to be near when the time came for her first child to be born.

"It's been more important than I realized for me to be close to my mother this past year." Carolyn gave Bryan an admiring look. "Bryan has been so supportive of that."

Todd shifted his weight to his back foot, the way Christy had seen him do dozens of times when he was surfing a low, curling wave and wanted to balance himself in order to ride it all the way to shore. "I'm happy for you, Dad. For both of you. This is what you've wanted for a long time."

"Thanks, Son." Bryan cast an affectionate glance at Carolyn. "That means a lot to us."

Todd glanced at Christy as if looking for support. Remembering what she'd read in Todd's expression earlier and sensing it again, Christy awkwardly added, "Although we were kinda hoping you guys were going to say you'd be moving back to California. Your house there is looking pretty good now, too."

Bryan rubbed the back of his neck the same way Todd did when he was processing a decision or trying to solve a problem. Christy wondered if there came a time when parents felt a sense of guilt over pursuing their own lives and dreams instead of sacrificing everything to help their children have every advantage in life.

"You know, I wasn't sure how to tell both of you this, but this might be the time to discuss it." He looked at Carolyn.

She gave him a sympathetic look and then projected the same expression onto Todd and Christy.

"The thing is," Bryan shuffled his feet as if looking for the right words, "we've looked at it from every direction, and the conclusion Carolyn and I keep coming to is that we need to sell the Newport Beach house."

Christy's breath caught in her throat. She glanced at Todd and saw his jaw clench. He didn't blink.

"We wanted to hold on to the house, especially after all the renovations you two did on it. We tried to find a way to make it possible for you two to stay there indefinitely. But we just couldn't make it work."

"We understand." Todd cleared his throat. "It's your house, Dad. You need to do what's best for you and Carolyn."

"You can stay there until the house sells," Carolyn said, giving them a hopeful look.

"Rent free," Bryan added. "At least for the next few months. Then we'd really be up against a wall."

"We can start paying rent now, Dad. We wouldn't be able to pay as much as you'd get if you rented it out, but between now and when it sells we can—"

"No. I don't need you to pay anything. At least not yet.

If the house doesn't sell in the next three months, then we'll talk about it if you're still there."

"Okay." Todd's expression remained steady.

Christy bit her lip so she wouldn't get teary eyed.

"We can talk more about this later," Bryan said. "We just wanted to have a chance to tell both of you before the wedding."

"We appreciate that, Dad. And we appreciate you letting us stay in the house until it sells. It's very generous of you."

"Of course. Like I said, we tried to figure out how to make it work, and the numbers just didn't add up."

The four of them stood in a tight sort of silence for a moment before Bryan said, "Well, let's see if we can haul those cabinets in here."

Christy quietly excused herself to go use the restroom. As soon as the door closed, she clutched the edge of the bathroom counter and tried to breathe steadily through her nose. Todd might be able to hold it together in the face of such news, but she felt like she was about to lose it. The small space felt dry and tight as if the walls were closing in on her.

How can Todd appear so calm and businesslike about this? That's the only real home he's ever known. He put so much into helping renovate the house after the last renters messed it up. These last two months of living there had been perfect. Absolutely perfect. Where are we going to live now?

Christy turned on the cold water and let it pour over her wrists, cooling her down. She knew that if she tried to talk to Todd about any of this now, he would tell her to trust God for their future and live inside the mystery, and all that. She drew in a deep breath and exhaled slowly.

Faith is such a precarious thing. I feel like I have to start trusting God fresh each day, as if the steps forward I took yesterday were for that day alone.

Christy looked at her reflection in the mirror. Her eyes were red from holding back her tears. Her hair had started out that day in a haphazard cluster. She took out the tie and gave her nutmeg-colored mane a vigorous shake. Christy folded her long hair into a loose braid, then smoothed back the sides with her palms and took another deep breath.

You can do this. You came to support your new mother-in-law and your father-in-law. Now's your chance to do that. Don't give in to all the crazy-making emotions. Todd is staying strong. You can, too. God will work this out. He always does.

Christy put away all thought of the Newport Beach house and returned to Carolyn's beautiful new kitchen with a brave face. As the two women worked side by side unloading the boxes of kitchen items, Carolyn gave Christy an overview of the plans for the wedding ceremony. It was to be held in a small chapel in the center of the old part of town, and afterward the guests would come to the house.

"I have a dress for you to try on," Carolyn said. "It's the dress I got for Tikki. It's at my Aunt Isobel's apartment, where I've been staying. But if you don't like it or it doesn't fit, we can go with something else. You're my only attendant so you don't need to match anyone else. If you think the dress you brought with you might work, we can have a look at it later today."

The dress Christy was wearing for Katie's safari wedding was long but simple and flowing. The fabric was a pale blue and it had cape-like sleeves that came down to her elbows. If she lifted her arms out straight, the sleeves looked like butterfly wings, according to Katie. It wasn't the sort of dress Christy would ever select for herself. Katie had found it online and begged Christy to try it on and take a video of it.

Christy had obliged. When she went to the bridal shop, Katie's college friend and RA partner, Nicole, had gone with Christy and took the video of Christy floating around the dressing room. Katie loved it and so Christy willingly bought the dress.

That was also the shopping trip when Nicole and Christy found the perfect wedding dress for Katie.

The dress that is still rolled up in my aunt's suitcase over six thousand miles away.

"I'll be right back, Carolyn. I need to check on something with Uncle Bob." Christy went into the living room just as her uncle was descending the tall ladder.

"What do you think?" he asked, removing the earbuds. "See any spots I missed?"

Christy gave the ceiling a quick scan. "No. It looks great. Hey, I was wondering when you were thinking of calling Marti again. I haven't figured out the time difference yet. I'm eager to hear how my mom is doing and I need to talk to Marti about Katie's dress."

"Ah yes. The forgotten wedding dress. I'd almost forgotten about it again."

"I know. Me, too." Christy began to feel anxious again about how she was going to solve this problem. "There's so much going on right now."

Bob put down the paint and the brush and pulled his phone from his pocket. "We can call right now if you like."

Christy nodded eagerly as Bob placed the call. He held the phone out with the speaker on so they could both hear Marti. She picked up on the second ring and her voice sounded like gravel.

"Robert, you would not believe the living nightmare this has been."

He quickly cut in and said, "Sweetheart, I've got Christy here with me. And I've got you on speaker."

An awkward pause followed.

Christy leaned in closer to Bob's phone. "Hi, Aunt Marti. Is everything okay?"

"Yes, yes. I'm tired. That's all. It's been more difficult than any of us expected."

"How's my mom?"

"She's improving. She'll be able to go home tomorrow. Your father and I have agreed that it's best if we take her to my house for the recovery."

"Isn't that a long way for her to have to ride in the car?"

"I've arranged for a medical transport. She'll be quite comfortable and they'll be able to carry her up to my bedroom suite. She'll have the room all to herself. I'm moving into the guest room. All of us felt that the ocean view and the private balcony should help her recover more quickly. Norman and David can will come up for the weekend and help out. I think it'll work out very well for all of us."

"I appreciate you being there for her, Aunt Marti. I'm sure it's been really difficult. Are you able to put my mom on the phone?"

"She's resting right now."

"I hope you'll get some rest, too," Bob said.

"I will. Why don't you call me back in a couple hours?"

"Sure," Bob said. "We can do that. We'll talk to you soon, then."

"Oh wait! Aunt Marti, are you still there?"

"Yes."

"I can't believe I almost forgot. Well, actually I did forget. I forgot Katie's dress. It's in your suitcase. At your house. I forgot to get it before we left. I need to figure out how to get her wedding dress sent to me in Nairobi."

There was no response.

"Aunt Marti? You still there?"

"You forgot Katie's dress?"

"Yes."

"Christy, how could you forget Katie's dress?"

Uncle Bob drew the phone closer and in a calming voice said, "You know that all of us had a lot on our minds that night before our flight. What matters now is that we figure out how to get the dress shipped to Nairobi. Do you think you can help us with that?"

"Of course." Marti's words came out clipped. "I'll work on it after I get Margaret settled."

"Thank you so much, Aunt Marti. I really appreciate it."

"One thing at a time. I'll take care of it."

"You're the best," Bob said cheerfully.

ROBIN JONES GUNN

Her aunt released an exaggerated sigh right before Bob hung up, and Christy tried not to feel bad all over again for forgetting Katie's wedding dress. She turned to see Carolyn standing a few feet away.

"Is everything all right?"

Christy nodded. She didn't want to add any of her problems from home or from Katie's wedding to the list of yet-to-be resolved problems for this wedding.

"We got a good update on Margaret," Bob said. "She's leaving the hospital tomorrow."

"I'm so glad to hear that." Carolyn looked at Christy more closely. The golden flecks in her soft brown eyes caught the sunlight coming in through the living room window. "I heard what you said about your friend's wedding dress. Is there anything I can do to help? Did you want the dress to be sent here?"

"I think it's best to send it directly to Kenya."

Todd bounded into the living room just then, his face glistening with perspiration. "Hey! Anybody free to help unload chairs? They just arrived."

"At your service," Bob said.

"The chairs for the reception are here? That's encouraging," Carolyn said. She and Christy followed Bob and Todd out the front door to where the delivery truck had parked by the front gate.

"Christy, I'm serious about helping with Katie's dress. If there's anything at all I can do, please ask me, okay?"

Christy felt like wrapping her arms around Carolyn and soaking up all the kindness that came with her words. With all that Carolyn had to sort out for her own wedding, she was still offering to help Christy solve her problem for Katie's wedding. This was the sort of mother-in-law any young woman could only dream of. No judgment, no shame. Just a whole lot of extravagant grace.

Nothing more was said about Katie's dress until the next day when all of Carolyn's women were gathered at the spa for their version of a pampering bridesmaid party.

That's when Christy made two important discoveries about the Women of the Canaries.

eight

"*The* Women of the Canaries," as Carolyn's aunts and cousins referred to themselves, lived and moved as a cohesive flock bound by their love for each other. That was the first discovery Christy made on the way to the spa the next morning: Loyalty reigned among the Women of the Canaries.

The second important fact she learned was: The Women of the Canaries had no secrets from each other.

It was such a different dynamic than the unspoken rules Christy grew up with. Everything was private between the women of her family, and they didn't share their problems with each other unless they were at crisis level.

These two significant discoveries became evident as they were on their way to a spa at a resort in Maspalomas. Carolyn was the intended object of their celebration. But as soon as they packed into the small van with second cousin Rosa at the wheel, all their focus seemed to be on Christy. They wanted to know how Christy's mother was doing, which was very kind. She was happy to report that her mom was leaving the hospital that day and the doctor said she was right on schedule with her recovery.

Next, the Women of the Canaries wanted to discuss which dress Christy had decided to wear when she stood up with Carolyn at the wedding on Saturday.

"I'm going wear the dress Carolyn got for Tikki. It's a little tight but I think it will work. As long as I don't try to sit down."

The women nodded and chattered their approval. What Christy understood from the mix of Spanish and English darting past her was that it was obvious she should wear Tikki's dress. It was Carolyn's choice. The fact that Christy thought the dress was a little tight was not a problem. Not when Christy was so young and so shapely.

The Women of the Canaries diverted into a discussion of the food they were each preparing for the reception. Christy wasn't able to follow all the Spanish so she focused her attention out the window as Rosa navigated the winding roads to the resort on the far side of the island of Gran Canaria.

"The view is so pretty." Christy pointed out the window to the pale-green water of the Atlantic that filled their view just below the steep cliffs.

None of the other women looked out the window to take in what was for them an everyday view of vast horizons and wind-tossed, rolling waves. The whitecaps scattering across the sea looked like a great box of commas had dropped from the sky and were bobbing along, trying to find their missing sentences on the shores of this rocky island.

The conversation slipped into English as Carolyn defended her twin sister and explained why she decided to cancel at the last minute. One of the aunts, Frieda, insisted it wasn't Marilyn's fault. It was her *terrible* husband and her *horrible* daughters that kept her from coming.

Frieda had arrived yesterday and was the only one of Abuela Teresa's sisters who lived in the US. Apparently she lived close to Marilyn and defended the missing twin with passion.

"I will tell you this." Frieda pointed her bright-red finger-nail at Carolyn. "*A donde el corazón se inclina, el pie camina.*"

Christy waited for the translation, which came from Rosa. Catching Christy's eye in the rearview mirror, she said, "It means, 'To where the heart is inclined, the feet will follow.'"

Carolyn added, "My aunt is trying to say that my twin doesn't have the same inclination to return to the Canaries as I did. This island is the home of my heart. It's not hers."

More discussion flitted in and out and around Christy like a charm of hummingbirds all coming in and drinking from Carolyn's statement about the home of her heart. Christy kept her gaze out the window as a precise thought settled on her.

Newport Beach is the home of my heart. It's the home of Todd's heart, too.

She wished she hadn't looked into the face of that small discovery just then. If Newport Beach truly was the home of her heart and of Todd's heart, then they had to find a way to stay in Newport Beach after Bryan's house sold. The thought of having to live anywhere else caused Christy's stomach to tighten up like a sea turtle pulling itself into its shell. She folded her arms across her midriff and exhaled slowly.

Trusting God for the unknown future was turning into a gut-squeezing exercise. She hoped the spa would help her relax.

When they arrived at the resort, Christy stuck close to Carolyn and followed everything she did. It was a large hotel and the facilities were as luxurious as any resort in the Southern California beach area. Marti would have been impressed.

They checked in, received their plush white robes, scuttled to the dressing area, and all proceeded to disrobe. Entirely. Christy had brought her bathing suit and put it on before covering up with her robe. She was glad to see that Carolyn had done the same. The other women teased them, but there was no way Christy would be comfortable going along with the local custom and using the spa facilities wearing only a tiny bikini bottom.

"Are you okay with this?" Carolyn asked quietly as they moved as a group to the first station of the spa treatments.

Christy nodded. The truth was, she was completely out of her comfort zone, but she didn't want any of these women to know that. Especially the way they shared everyone's personal secrets with each other.

They entered a quiet room dug out like a cave with muted red lights. The slightly reclined beds that formed a circle around the room were designed to make the women feel weightless as they listened to the steady, pulsing sound of a heartbeat. Once they felt calmed and centered in this room, they were to move on at their own pace and enjoy all the other amenities.

Christy leaned back on the softly cushioned bed and closed her eyes. She didn't care that she kept her robe on over her bathing suit, and she didn't want to see if the others were dropping their robes. This space was, as intended, extremely relaxing. It seemed weird to her that the sound played over the speakers located next to each cot was of a heartbeat instead of soothing music. But once she closed her eyes and drew in a deep breath, her own heart rate slowed to match the pace of the strategic heartbeat surround sound.

Christy floated off to sleep. All worries about Katie's wedding dress or their future housing problem were left outside of this lulling space. Christy dreamed of walking on the beach and picking up small white shells that she tucked into the pocket of her plush spa robe.

She was ruffled back to the present by Carolyn's soft touch on her arm and a quiet whisper. "I didn't ask if you wanted to go through the stations on your own or go with me."

As much as Christy wanted to stay in this cocoon and spend the entire spa day sleeping off the effects of jet lag and dreaming of walking on the beach, she'd seen pictures of all the other stations in a brochure handed to her when they checked in. She wanted to try the mineral pools, the sauna, the waterfall shower, and the Turkish steam bath. She was especially looking forward to the hot stone massage scheduled for her later in the day.

Christy swung her legs over the side of the bed and gave Carolyn her answer by silently following her out of the hive-shaped room and into the dimly lit hallway that led to the other stations. "I better stick with you, if you don't mind."

"Good. I was hoping you'd say that. My aunts all love coming here. They have their favorite stations and know what they're doing. This is only my second time here and I'd much rather go to each spot with you."

Christy followed Carolyn for the next two hours and they experienced each of the rejuvenating treatments. They saw the other Women of the Canaries in the pools and sauna as they quietly proceeded in tandem. To Christy's surprise, the aunts and cousins had nothing to say. Each of them was silently entrenched in their own private renewal experience. It was unexpected after the endless volley of conversation Christy had witnessed since she arrived. They seemed to treat the spa experience with a sacred sort of isolation.

Christy entered into the same peaceful silence. She used the time in the saltwater pool to effortlessly float and pray. She felt weightless and problem free. It was like nothing she'd ever experienced before.

In the sauna, Carolyn and Christy sat at opposite ends of the wooden benches and neither spoke nor made eye contact. As the sweat poured from Christy and soaked her bathing suit, she understood the reason why the other woman in the sauna had entered with nothing but a towel wrapped around her to absorb the flow of detoxifying perspiration.

The absence of full coverage on the other women in the spa began to grow on Christy. She didn't look at them. She didn't feel like any of them were trying to show off. It felt very European and normal for the women who had come here on vacation as well as the Women of the Canaries who sought this experience as a private refuge.

Christy tried to explain to Todd her interesting and relaxing spa experience once the two of them were alone late that night. She could tell right away that giving him the visual image of a spa full of partially naked women was a bad idea. She'd learned enough as a young married woman to know that any man was going to immediately conjure up a matching image when given any sort of suggestion of any sort of female nudity.

She quickly changed the subject and asked how his day had been with Bob and his dad.

"We got the cabinets to fit in the bathroom. That was a challenge. They look good, though."

"What about the refrigerator?"

"It didn't come yet."

"Is your dad starting to worry a little more?"

"I heard him on the phone lining up ice chests to borrow for Saturday."

"From what I heard, the aunts are starting their cooking and baking marathon tomorrow. They expect over a hundred people at the reception."

"Are you going to help?" They were seated on the sofa in Abuela Teresa's living room. The windows behind them were letting in the cool night air and the bird was silent in her covered cage. Abuela Teresa had gone to bed after the relaxing spa day. From one of the other apartments across the way came the vigorous sounds of staccato guitar music.

Before Christy could answer Todd's question, he turned to look out the open window. "There it is again. Did you hear this guy the other night when we first arrived? He's gotta be playing a flamenco guitar. Did you hear that last riff?"

Christy listened with Todd. He stretched his arm across the back of the sofa and ran his fingers through Christy's hair. "Can you hear how it's crisper than a classic guitar?"

She couldn't tell the difference. Todd had tried to teach her to play guitar more than once, but she wasn't able to get used to the feel of the strings pressing into her fingertips. Todd promised her fingers would toughen up the more she practiced, but she wasn't motivated enough to keep going. It suited her just fine that Todd was the musical one in the family.

"He must have a tap plate on it. Can you hear the way he's stomping his fingers right there? You can't get that sort of sound on a classical guitar. That has to be a flamenco guitar because of the staccato sound. Hear it? There's less sustain."

"What does that mean?"

"The notes don't resonate as long as on a classic guitar."

Christy could hear the differences when Todd pointed them out. "It sounds like music to dance to." She lifted her arm over her head and snapped her fingers. "Flamenco dance."

Todd grinned. "When we were in Spain I almost bought a flamenco guitar. Remember that?"

"I do." Christy reached over and brushed Todd's sandy-blond hair off his forehead. Todd had been letting his hair grow out for several months. It was the longest Christy had ever seen it and had almost reached a straggly looking stage. She did love it though, when he got out of the shower and raked his fingers through his golden mane so his hair went straight back and showed off his screaming silver-blue eyes. Once or twice she'd convinced him to use some of her hair product so his hair would stay back in that just-groomed look all day. Hopefully, she could convince him to wear it that way for his dad's wedding.

"Maybe I'll find one here before we leave," Todd said.

Christy didn't reply. She had lost track of the conversation as she was gazing at her handsome husband, enjoying the way he was playing with the ends of her hair and listening to the romantic flamenco music dancing through the open window.

"What would you think?" Todd asked.

"Hmmm?"

"A flamenco guitar. I could buy one while we're here."

"You should. I still feel awful that you sold your mandolin last Christmas in order to pay the electric bill."

"Hey, that's in the past, Christy. It was the right choice at the time. Thought I'd ask around and see if one of our new uncles can help me find a used flamenco guitar."

"We sure have a whole lot of new aunts and uncles, don't we?"

"Yeah. I like it." Todd leaned back, folded his hands over his stomach, and stretched out his legs. "I like having people. Relatives. It's a good thing. I totally get why my dad loves it here."

Christy tried to imagine how it would feel to grow up without knowing any of your relatives. She gingerly asked the question that had been rolling through her thoughts ever since they'd toured Bryan and Carolyn's new home. "How do you feel about your dad and Carolyn staying here the rest of their lives?"

"It's his choice. Their choice." Todd looked down at his hands and rubbed his thumb over a callus on his palm. "If I had what my dad has here, I'd stay, too."

"You mean the house he inherited?"

"Not just the house. The people. I think that being 'home' is being with the people you want to do life with."

Christy agreed but she still wanted to know how Todd felt about all these changes. The warm embrace he and his dad shared at the restaurant clearly had a powerful healing effect on him. But that was before he knew his dad was staying in Las Palmas permanently.

Christy asked a second time, "How does it make you feel that your dad will be living here, so far away?"

Todd looked at her as if he didn't understand what she was getting at.

"Yesterday, when your dad told us they planned to stay here and sell the house in Newport, it hit you in a deep place. I know it did."

Todd waited for her to make her point.

"So, how do you feel about all this?"

He straightened up and looked uncomfortable. "What do you want me to say? That I feel sad and abandoned and fearful of being without a place to live again? Do you want me to tell you that I feel like a terrible husband because I can't provide for my wife?"

Christy was stunned by his answer. "No," she said in a small voice. "I mean, unless that's how you really feel. Then, yes. I want you to share these things with me. I want to know how you're doing with all the changes."

Todd thought a minute, looking at his hands. "I'm okay."

She gave him a look that made it clear she wasn't convinced.

"The way I see it, all the pieces are shifting in my dad's life and in ours." His expression was somber, fixed. "That doesn't mean it's a bad thing. It's just going to take me some time to adjust. The Lord is our dwelling place. I believe that."

Christy still felt edgy and wasn't sure how to respond. Her husband was hurting. She wanted to say something that would comfort and encourage him, but she didn't know what to say.

Is it a good thing that he's leaning on that Bible verse right now? Or is he hiding behind it so he doesn't have to tell me how he really feels?

The guitar music out the open window came to a quick-strumming crescendo and ended. For a full minute, Christy and Todd sat side by side in the silence. The music continued to reverberate in her thoughts.

Drawing from the influence of her new aunts, Christy decided that a wise woman didn't keep pressing her husband on a topic he's not ready to discuss. She put aside all the probing questions she'd started rehearsing and decided this was one more area where she needed to learn to trust God.

"Let me ask you something," Todd said calmly. "How do you feel about this place?"

"About this island? This town?"

"Yeah. All of it. Do you think you could ever live here?"

Christy felt her heart stutter and then start again. "No."

"No?" Todd looked surprised at her immediate honesty.

"I think it's a nice place and all the new relatives are great, but I can't picture us living here. I just can't. The language barrier alone would be a big issue for a long time. And what would we do for a living? I mean, where would we live? What would be the purpose in coming here? It's your dad's dream and I'm happy for him, but I don't think that necessarily makes it our dream, does it?"

Todd placed his hand on her shoulder to calm her. "I was just asking. Just considering the possibilities."

Summoning the same courage she'd had to draw from every time her husband started talking about moving to Papua New Guinea, Christy formed the question that needed to be asked. "What about you? Would you want to live here?"

She pressed her lips together, waiting for his answer. As long as she'd known Todd, there had been a sprinkling of wanderlust in his eyes. He carried with him romanticized ideas of what life would be like in remote corners of the world, where a bed was a hammock strung between two palm trees and dinner included some sort of unpronounceable fruit.

In some ways, the Canary Islands was a civilized version of the island living he had long dreamed of. Should she have been more enthusiastic about living here? This island was better than Borneo any day.

Todd calmly shook his head. "No. This is my dad's place on the planet. But I don't think it's mine—ours."

Christy released a slow breath. "It's not the home of our hearts."

Todd leaned forward and looked back at Christy over his shoulder. He smiled slightly so his dimple showed as he echoed Christy's line. "Exactly. It's not the home of our hearts. I think the best thing you and I can do right now is just be present in the present. I mean, we came here for my dad and Carolyn. I don't want anything to interfere with us being able to celebrate with them."

Christy nodded her agreement. Todd leaned over and kissed her on the cheek. "Come on. Let's get some sleep. We have some pretty full days ahead of us."

Christy took Todd's hand as he offered to help her up from the couch and led her to the bedroom.

Over the next two days she kept telling herself, "Be present in the present."

Home of Our Hearts

nine

On the day of the wedding, Aunt Frieda with her fire-cracker red fingernails was the first aunt to show up at Bryan and Carolyn's house. She arrived with food, advice, and a roll of duct tape.

"You said your dress was tight. I have the solution." Aunt Frieda held up the duct tape. "We'll put this along the seams of the lower half of your dress and trust me. It will hold you together the entire day."

Christy laughed and received the gift from Aunt Frieda with a warm, "Gracias." She hadn't begun to get dressed yet for the wedding. There were too many other things to do around the house. She had taken her role of matron of honor seriously and was efficiently snuffing out little fires here and there before Carolyn even heard about them.

Carolyn had already moved the rest of her clothes and cosmetics into the master bedroom earlier that morning. At about the same time, Bob had moved his belongings out of the guest room. He and the rest of the guys were gathering at Aunt Isobel's. She had promised them a big wedding day breakfast and insisted that all of them clear out of the house to give Carolyn complete serenity and as much time as possible to get ready for the festivities.

Aunt Frieda hadn't seen the house yet so she took herself on a tour. She ended up where Christy was, in the small space between the kitchen and the covered parking area that had been turned into a laundry room. Christy was loading the sheets from the guest room into the compact dryer.

"I saw the before pictures," Frieda said. "What Bryan has done here is nothing short of miraculous."

"It's beautiful, isn't it?" Christy stepped into the kitchen and with a tip of her head she said, "Did you hear that the refrigerator was delivered yesterday afternoon?"

"Yes. That was cutting it too close. If I were Carolyn, I would have been a wreck. Speaking of the bride, where is she?"

"She was headed for the shower the last I checked."

The two of them ventured to the other side of the house where they found Carolyn in the bedroom with a bath towel wrapped around her wet hair. She put the phone down and smiled. "I was just on a video call with Tikki. She said to tell you she's so glad you're here."

"Oh! I wish she could be here. How is she feeling?" Christy asked.

"Better. The doctor put her on bed rest and she hasn't had any more spotting for two days now. The baby's heartbeat is strong."

"What a relief," Frieda said.

"Yes, it is." Carolyn reached into her cosmetic bag and pulled out a tube of mascara. "Aunt Frieda, could you keep my phone with you during the wedding and reception and send pictures to Tikki? I told her I'd try to keep her connected in real time the best I could. Do you know how to take videos and send them to her on this sort of phone?"

"Of course. I'll be glad to do that for you. What else do you need?"

"Nothing else that I can think of right now."

Just then a rousing chorus of female voices echoed through the house as the front door opened and the Women of the Canaries let themselves in.

"They're here with the food. Perfect!" Frieda's expression lit up. "That's my other job. I'll take care of everything. The two of you should not lift a finger. And Tikki will feel as if she's right here with us." She snapped a photo on the phone of Carolyn and Christy, sent it to Tikki, and hurried away.

Christy couldn't be sure but she thought the aunts had all discovered the new refrigerator at the same moment. The sound of elation reverberated throughout the house. *If they get that excited about a refrigerator, this is bound to be a lively wedding and reception!*

Christy took a shower and got ready in the guest room. She decided to try Aunt Frieda's duct tape suggestion. With one long strip, she fortified the main seam down the back of her dress and smoothed it down before slipping it over her head. As far as she could tell, turning to the side and trying to see in the small mirror over the dresser, all was as it should be.

At Todd's request, she was wearing her hair down. It had gotten so long that it often felt too hot or too tangled to leave it down. Most of the time she wore it pulled back in a loose braid or up in twist on the back of her head. Today, though, she brushed it thoroughly, used some of her expensive Moroccan oil hair balm Aunt Marti had gotten for her months ago, and tucked the sides behind her ears. Christy went heavy on the mascara and played with the eyeliner and eye shadow in her cosmetic kit. She'd gotten used to wearing very little makeup the last few months they'd been in Newport Beach so it made it fun to go all out today.

As soon as she was ready, Christy returned to the master bedroom and tapped on the door with her nice Canon camera in her hand. "Carolyn? Do you mind if I take some pictures? I thought Tikki might enjoy seeing the before images."

"I'd love it. Thank you for thinking of that, Christy."

It had been a long time since Christy had gotten her camera out, and she had to fiddle a bit with the settings before she was able to capture the sunlight on the windowsill just right. That helped her calibrate her settings and focus on the rest of the shots in the bedroom.

Carolyn slipped into her wedding dress and Christy helped zip her up and fasten the hook and eye at the neck. It was an elegant, fitted gown with lace long sleeves similar to the sleeves on the bridesmaid dress Christy was wearing. The bodice had inset lace with a collar that came up higher in the back but dipped modestly in the front.

"Carolyn, this is a beautiful dress. It looks so good on you."

"Thank you. It was my cousin's dress and needed only a few alterations. It's my something borrowed." She faced Christy. "You know the old saying, 'Something old, something new, something borrowed, and something blue.'"

"I've heard that before." Christy reached for her camera. "Stand just like that and look out the window. The lighting is perfect."

Carolyn's shoulder-length, coffee-colored hair was up in a sophisticated twist. She turned to show Christy the gorgeous jeweled hair comb to the side. "This was my grandmother's. It's my something old. The velvet clutch on the dresser is my something blue, and the something new is Bryan and me." Carolyn's grin lit up her face. "We're new. Our love for each other is new."

Christy caught a perfect close-up shot of Carolyn's profile. The crystal teardrops in her eyes glistened as did the jewels in her borrowed hair comb. Christy was so grateful that she had these special few moments with her new mother-in-law-to-be. Abuela Teresa had made it clear to the eager aunties that they were not allowed into Carolyn's inner sanctuary while she got ready. Surprisingly, they honored her wishes.

The one person who was not restricted from the bride's chambers was Abuela Teresa. She tapped on the door and entered looking like royalty. Her hair was up and she was wearing a long, deep-blue satin dress cut in the style of what a vintage Hollywood icon would wear down the red carpet on opening night at Grauman's Chinese Theatre.

Abuela Teresa approached Carolyn with shining eyes and carrying a long white veil crafted of light and airy lace. Christy had heard about this lace veil. It had been in the family for well over a century, and the delicate lace barely showed the signs of age. The pale white lace fell from her hands like a cascading waterfall.

The two women embraced and Christy quietly stepped to the side and kept her camera clicking. Carolyn's mother lifted the veil and placed it on her daughter's head as she whispered to her in Spanish. Carolyn's eyes were closed, as if she were receiving a long-awaited, highly valued blessing. The lacy veil fell over her shoulders and floated all the way to her waist.

It was one of the most beautiful, sacred prewedding moments Christy had ever seen. A deep sense of peace seemed to enter the bedroom, riding on a soft, warm breeze through the open window, encircling them and adding its own sacred whispers to the moment.

Christy kept taking pictures and felt a physical ache that Tikki couldn't have been here to share this moment with her mother and grandmother. Christy was determined to take as many pictures as she could of the Women of the Canaries and send them all to Tikki so she could feel as if she was part of this special day.

Tikki and Matt had gotten married here in Las Palmas last fall in the same chapel where Carolyn and Bryan would exchange their vows this afternoon. She could only imagine that all those memories must be flooding Tikki right now as she remembered her own special day with this extraordinary family. What added even more to the deeply entrenched traditions and history of this family was that the chapel was five hundred years old. According to tradition, Christopher Columbus prayed at this chapel before embarking from the Canary Islands and sailing west on his first voyage to the New World.

It was, as Carolyn had explained to Christy on the drive home from the spa, a sacred place of seeking God's blessing before new beginnings. The chapel was a popular locale for small weddings not only because of the history, but also because of the beauty of the opulent golden altar and the reverent feeling everyone reported to feel when they entered the darkened, holy place.

The tender moment between Carolyn and her mother concluded as sweetly as it had begun. Abuela Teresa led Carolyn to the bedroom door and opened it to usher her daughter out into the gathering of women.

Carolyn was met by an eager cluster of more aunts and nieces and cousins than Christy had seen so far. The praises for the stunning bride rose like a flock of twittering starlings at sunset. They moved as one, examining the front of her dress, the back of her dress, her hair, her makeup, and cooing over the veil, but none of them dared to touch it. Every single one of the Women of the Canaries breathed their approval and blessings with tears and a procession of kisses on the cheek.

Christy stood to the side, capturing the moment with her camera and enjoying being part of all this. The spa day was in lieu of an American-style bachelorette party. Last night there had been no rehearsal or rehearsal dinner. Their special dinner had been the night that Christy, Todd, and Bob arrived. The times of prewedding celebration had been deliberate and respectful. Christy appreciated that none of the women had introduced bawdy games or excessive drinking or a time of opening gifts that were embarrassing to the bride. In every way they elevated the sanctity of marriage and had come alongside with nothing but love, enthusiasm, and honoring support. This was the moment set aside for all the women to gather around and share their best wishes for Carolyn. Christy loved the way this family did weddings in the Canary Islands. It was so much more respectful and celebratory than some of the bridal showers she'd attended over the years in California.

Aunt Frieda sidled up to Christy. "She's beautiful, isn't she?" She snapped a photo and texted it to Tikki.

"Yes. She's glowing."

"There is such a contrast between Carolyn and her twin," Frieda whispered. "Carolyn has the beauty on the inside, first. That is why it shines out at a moment like this. And the dress is perfect."

"Yes. It is."

"What about your friend's wedding dress? Has it arrived in Africa yet?"

"I don't think so. My aunt let me know she's working on it and she assures me the dress will be delivered in time."

Frieda pointed her red fingernail in the air. "Trust your aunt."

In that moment Aunt Frieda resembled Aunt Marti in some ways but with a more brazen and dramatic flair. As if Aunt Frieda had read Christy's thoughts, she reached over and gave Christy's backside a firm pat down. Startled by the gesture, Christy pulled away and nearly dropped her camera.

"I was just checking to see how the duct tape is holding up."

"So far, so good, I guess."

Aunt Frieda patted the back seam of Christy's dress one more time as if Christy's explanation was equal to an invitation. "You used a lot. That's good."

"I haven't tried to sit on a chair yet, so we'll see if it holds up to that supreme test. Or I could just stand all day."

Aunt Frieda raised a thickly penciled-in eyebrow. "You won't just stand, *mi niña*. Before this day is over you will dance like you have never danced before in your life."

"Well," Christy replied with a nervous laugh. "That will be a first because I'm not much of a dancer. Neither is my husband."

Aunt Frieda looked shocked. "What about at your own

wedding?"

"We didn't have dancing."

"A wedding without dancing? Oh, my dear child. That will all change for you today." She stretched her left arm over her stomach and held her right hand in the air with her red fingernails held high. "Flamenco is the dance of life. You will see what I mean at the reception."

For some reason, Aunt Frieda's motions appeared graceful and her passionate words sounded intriguing and not at all comical.

As the other Women of the Canaries giddily escorted Carolyn to the car that would deliver her to the church, Christy dashed back to the bedroom to get the blue velvet clutch Carolyn had forgotten. She hurried out the front door to the street where Rosa had saved the front seat for her in the same car that Abuela Teresa and Carolyn were in. Christy slid in carefully and listened to make sure she didn't hear the sound of the back of her dress ripping.

The duct tape worked! Now if I just don't eat too much at the reception, I might be okay.

The cars all pulled away in a procession with a few honks and swerves. She turned to check on Carolyn and her mother in the backseat. Both wore the same content expression of deep happiness.

Christy pulled out her camera and turned around to subtly take their picture. The midafternoon sunshine had illuminated the two women as they were sitting close with their fingers laced together in an abiding pose of mother/daughter understanding. Abuela Teresa's weathered skin was subtly contrasted by the firmness of Carolyn's smooth hand crowned with her exquisite blue sapphire engagement ring. Christy loved images of people holding hands and she knew this would make a gorgeous picture. She snapped quickly and felt a tight clenching in her stomach.

At that moment, Christy missed her mother and loved her mother more than she ever had in her life.

ten

*T*he parade of cars arrived at the parking lot in the old town section of Las Palmas and Christy felt as if she had stepped back in time. The buildings in that area were painted deep yellow and had ornate carved wooden doors.

The women extracted themselves from the vehicles parked side by side. They adjusted their outfits, smoothed their hair, and moved as one across the uneven cobblestones. They were on their way to the chapel.

Carolyn, Christy, and Abuela Teresa waited with Rosa in her car until all the guests had found their way into the chapel. Rosa pulled their flowers from the trunk and presented them with creative satisfaction. A wrist corsage of red and white rosebuds for Abuela Teresa and a single long-stem red rose for Christy with a long, trailing white ribbon. The simple yet dramatic single rose and ribbon would look stunning against her black dress. Very Old World classic.

Rosa returned to the trunk and came back with the wedding bouquet hidden behind her back. With a little girl expression of hopeful expectation, she held out the gift of her handcrafted creation to Carolyn and blurted out, "I hope you like it."

"Oh, Rosa, I love it. You outdid yourself. It's gorgeous. Thank you so much." Carolyn dipped her nose into the tiny cluster of barely opened white rosebuds that made up the center of the bouquet. The pristine white roses were circled by a bounty of velvety red roses that had fully bloomed and exuded a heady fragrance that filled the car.

Christy didn't know if the bouquet was intended to symbolize the bride's pure heart encompassed by vivid, mature Women of the Canaries, but that's what she saw when she looked at the delicate white buds surrounded by the deep red roses. Carolyn was the classiest-looking bride she had ever seen, with her elegant dress, lace veil, and sumptuous bouquet.

Apparently, several dozen complete strangers thought the same thing.

As soon as Rosa got the call that it was time to head to the chapel, Carolyn, Abuela Teresa, and Christy carefully slid out of the car and demurely made their way across the old town square. Tourists who had come to visit the nearby museum stopped to view the stunning bride. Some took pictures. Christy couldn't blame them. In fact, she wished she could stop and take a few pictures. In her elegant gown and with the long lace veil fluttering behind her, Carolyn embodied all the romance of this ancient square.

They strolled past a lovely tiled fountain that sprayed them with a refreshing mist. Carolyn stopped and smiled. She plucked a petal from her bouquet and tossed it in as if making a wish, lost in a private dream.

"This is where Bryan proposed to her," Abuela Teresa whispered to Christy. "Right after Tikki's wedding."

Christy had heard the story from Todd's dad over the phone months ago. She could hardly believe she was standing here now in this place of world-changing history and life-changing romance. She felt caught up in a swirl of events that overlapped the past and the present and found it easy to believe that she was observing a love and a beauty that belonged to another time.

A man in all black who was holding an expensive-looking camera with a large lens slipped around to the opposite side of the fountain. He exchanged a few words with Rosa. Abuela Teresa stepped away from Carolyn and Christy did the same. She realized that he was the professional photographer and he was on the job now, ready to capture Carolyn and Bryan's special moments.

The women continued their procession to the small, tile-roofed chapel and clustered in a bit of afternoon shade provided by the bell tower. Rosa scooted into the chapel and came back out into the sunlight with a squinting grin. "Okay, Abuela. They're ready for you."

Abuela Teresa gave Carolyn one last kiss on the cheek and with her head held high, she entered the darkened chapel where she would take Bryan's arm and be ushered to her place of honor in the front pew.

Christy noticed a plaque affixed to the side of the chapel that indicated this was the chapel where Columbus had come to pray. She tried to picture him walking through this entryway.

Rosa was carrying Christy's camera as well as Carolyn's "something blue" velvet clutch. Christy asked for the clutch and pulled out the dainty handkerchief, which Carolyn wrapped around the stem of her bouquet so it would be ready if she needed it during the ceremony.

Christy used the lipstick to give Carolyn a last bit of freshening up. She smiled at her almost-mother-in-law and whispered, "You look beautiful."

Carolyn smiled back, exuding a calm that whisked away the slight nervous tremors Christy felt as they were walking toward the chapel. Rosa touched Christy's arm, giving her the cue to enter next. She drew in a deep breath and led with her right foot, calm and steady.

It took her eyes a moment to adjust to the candlelit darkness. She could smell the heavy, lingering scent of all the beeswax candles that had burned in this place for hundreds of years. A violinist stood to the far left, playing a majestic tune that filled Christy's heart with joy.

She blinked and caught her breath when she saw the stunning altar that rose to the high ceiling and filled the front of the chapel. It was the most intricate gold-covered altar piece she'd ever seen. The center statue was lit with the brightest light, and at the very top was a dramatic crucifix. She had no idea that the simple white-stucco chapel with the minimalistic benches would house such a magnificent work of art.

To the right, looking somewhat diminished in comparison to the huge edifice behind him, stood Bryan. He looked so handsome in his dark suit with black velvet lapels and a straight black tie. He was half smiling at Christy but mostly gazing past her, trying to get a glimpse of his bride.

Christy looked to the right of Bryan now that her vision had adjusted. Her heart felt as if it had leapt out of her chest when she fixed her gaze on Todd. He was far more handsome than his dad with his blond hair slicked back and wearing a distinctive European-style suit with a narrow black tie. The imminent glow from the ornate gold-inlaid altar seemed to illuminate Todd and Bryan from behind. Each step down the aisle took her closer to her true love, her Forever Friend, her husband.

This felt like a holy moment to her. It was different than how she felt at their outdoor wedding, where the evening light rolled across the meadow and the shaggy palm trees clapped their praises. This moment felt hidden and sheltered. The chapel hadn't appeared to be much on the outside. But on the inside, the beauty of the golden altar was all consuming.

The expressions of pure love on the faces of the bridegroom and the best man were compelling and life giving.

If Christy had ever wondered in her ten years of knowing Todd whether or not he was truly attracted to her, his fixed gaze on her at that moment would have put all doubt permanently to rest. His expression brimmed with wonder and deep abiding admiration and affection. He was looking at her as if she were the most beautiful woman in the world. At that moment, she felt as if she were.

As Christy turned to take her place on the left side, she felt her long hair swish as she made the turn. She knew that simple movement would endear her to Todd even more and embed this moment on his mind. He loved it when she wore her hair down, but it had been a long time since she'd worn it that way.

Once Christy was in place, the violinist changed tunes. Christy didn't recognize what he was playing, but the sweet strains filled the ancient space and seemed to elevate the spirits of everyone in the pews. Abuela Teresa rose to her feet and turned to the back of the chapel where the afternoon sunlight burst through the open door. All eyes were fixed on the entrance, awaiting the arrival of the bride. Aunt Frieda leaned into the aisle slightly from the second row to start videoing the moment for Tikki.

Carolyn stepped into the light in the doorway and a soft murmur of admiration rose from the guests. She seemed to glow like an angelic being as the light fanned out behind her and pierced through the long lace veil, making an elongated, intricate pattern that stretched out on the aisle before her.

Carolyn came forward to her groom slow and easy. She didn't rush the moment. It was as if she decided that she had waited for this and she was going to luxuriate in every second of it.

Christy glanced at her father-in-law. He was transfixed. This was his bride and she was coming to him, at last.

That image of Bryan, the bridegroom, gazing on his bride with such unmatched adoration and pure love, fixed itself in Christy's heart and mind. She'd never forget the way Todd had looked at her. But she'd also never forget the way Bryan looked at Carolyn as she seemed to float down the aisle.

The ceremony, all in Spanish, seemed fairly easy to follow. The Scripture they had asked to be read was Psalm 23. Christy tried to pick out some of the familiar Spanish words and silently repeated parts of the popular passage as it was read.

"The Lord is my shepherd; I shall not want. He makes me to lie down in green pastures; He leads me beside the still waters. He restores my soul . . . Surely goodness and mercy shall follow me all the days of my life; and I will dwell in the house of the Lord forever."

Christy had a clear view of her father-in-law from where she stood. Tears welled up at the sincerity in his expression during the exchange of vows and again when he placed the ring on her finger. Every time Christy looked at Todd, his jaw was forward and his eyes narrowed. She knew he was trying not to cry. However, a small army of renegade tears burst through the line when Bryan solemnly leaned in and kissed his bride.

Christy cried, too. Partly in response to the joyful sacredness of this moment but also because her heart went out to Tikki. Carolyn's daughter should have been the one standing beside her mother right now. She should have been the one watching her new father-in-law turn into a happy mess of tears and a wild grin as he offered his arm to his beaming bride and the two of them headed down the aisle. Tikki should have felt this surge of joy that Christy felt, knowing that Bryan and Carolyn were leaving this prayer-filled chapel to embark on their own adventure as they discovered the new world of being one as husband and wife.

Thinking about Tikki missing out on this made Christy even more grateful that Aunt Marti had offered to be there for Christy's mom. Marti was right. Christy needed to be here for her new mother-in-law, and she definitely needed to be there for Katie. Some moments in life only happened once.

As Bryan and Carolyn neared the door at the back of the

chapel, Christy took four steps across the front of the altar and met Todd in the center. His face was still moist from the tears. Christy wanted to tenderly reach out and dry them with her finger. Then she wanted to kiss her husband and tell him how deeply she loved him.

But she did none of that. She simply blinked back her own tears and slipped her arm through his waiting arm. Todd drew her close and covered her hand with his left hand, squeezing it three times as they began their walk down the aisle, looking straight ahead in a position of reverence.

Christy squeezed his arm three times, too. As soon as they were outside the chapel in the softened twilight, Christy leaned in and gave her husband a kiss. He kissed her back meaningfully and held her face with both his hands.

"I love you," he whispered.

"I love you, too," Christy whispered back. If at some distant time in the future their feelings for each other should diminish at all, which didn't seem possible at this moment, all the two of them needed to do was go to a wedding. The weight of the vows and the sacredness of the exchange of the rings seemed to infuse both of them with an invigorating reminder of the same covenant relationship they shared.

The wedding party headed for the fountain where Carolyn had requested they get a photo of the four of them. Todd kept his arm around Christy's slim waist and as they walked he leaned over and whispered, "You're so beautiful." He kissed the side of her head. "I love your hair and you look amazing in that dress."

"It's a little tight."

Todd pulled her closer to his side. "Says who?" he murmured.

"You look pretty amazing yourself in that suit."

"You like it?"

"I do. But I like who's wearing it even more."

Todd leaned over and planted another kiss just above Christy's ear. He gently pulled her hair back and kissed her just above the pearl earring he'd given her for Christmas. "You wore them."

"Of course I did." She leaned in and added, "You noticed."

"Of course I did."

Christy couldn't stop smiling. To be loved like this by Todd was what she had dreamed of for so many years. All during their dating years he had been so reserved. He held back on compliments and expressions of affection at times when she wished with all her heart that he would hold her and kiss her and tell her she was beautiful.

Now Christy was grateful beyond words that Todd had saved even these intimate touches and nuances until after they were married. If they had been this openly affectionate and expressive while they were dating, it would have been much more difficult to wait until they were married before they gave themselves to each other.

All those years when I thought he wasn't paying enough romantic attention to me, he was just saving it up. He noticed everything back then. I'm sure of it. And it's so much better now because we can give ourselves to each other with complete freedom.

As they assembled by the fountain and took a family picture, Christy observed the way Bryan and Carolyn were looking at each other and affectionately exchanging whispers and long kisses. From every indication, they had waited as well. The days and nights ahead for them would be especially blessed because of their patience.

For the next few hours Christy and Todd barely left each other's side. They rode together to the house sitting especially close in the backseat of Uncle Jorge's car. They held hands as they walked into the house and went out on the back patio, where several of the aunts were beginning to fill the serving table with dozens of delicious-looking tapas.

Dozens of ornate lanterns were placed around the patio and out in the yard and were giving off an inviting golden glow. The sun had sailed over the edge of the world leaving behind a dozen pink party streamers unfurled against the pale-blue sky. A few puffy, white clouds gathered over the rooftop of Bryan and Carolyn's blessed hacienda and took on a tinge of butter yellow around their fluffy edges. Two little girls in frilly dresses and shiny black shoes chased a little boy wearing a bow tie. Laughter spilled from the kitchen. The setting was enchanting.

Todd led Christy over to one of the small tables under a very old palm tree. The distressed table had once been painted aqua blue, but the paint was now chipped and peeling across the top. She sat across from him and reached over to cover his hand with hers.

"I know this is the right thing for my dad," he said. "I have no doubt."

Christy gave his hand a squeeze and nodded.

"When I start to really miss him in the future, I just want you to remind me of this moment. Remind me that I sat here and said that this is where my dad belongs."

"Okay," Christy said softly. "I will."

They sat at the table, holding hands for a few more minutes while guests continued to pour in. Uncle Bob made the rounds, sharing conversations with a few of the relatives who spoke English. The Women of the Canaries kept a continuous supply of food coming to the serving tables, and everybody found something to drink from the variety of beverages offered. Todd went over to talk to the guitarist who was setting up a stool in the corner. Christy had a pretty good idea Todd would find the flamenco guitar he was after before this evening was over.

Christy got up and went to the beverage table. She reached for a fluted glass and filled it with sparkling lemonade. Seeing an open chair next to one of the younger cousins, she made her way to the other side of the patio and sat down. The music stopped and the conversations lulled. Christy crossed her legs and as she did, she heard the horrifying sound she had so desperately tried to avoid. Aunt Frieda turned to Christy with the phone in her hand, videoing the moment.

No! No, no, no, no.

It wasn't the reinforced back seam that gave way. The reverberating rip in the dress happened on the right side and had opened up four inches at her widest part. Quickly uncrossing her legs, she felt the rip give way even more.

I can't believe this is happening!

Christy got up and, spreading a wide jazz hand over the torn side of the dress, she scurried to the guest bedroom. After quickly closing the door behind her, Christy slipped out of the dress and fumbled through her bag to find the sewing kit. Aunt Marti had predicted that Christy would need the needle and thread for Katie's dress, not for a borrowed bridesmaid dress that couldn't contain her girth.

This is so embarrassing. I wonder who else saw what happened. I wish I'd brought something to change into.

Christy stitched swiftly. The roll of duct tape was still on the dresser, so after she sewed the seam she pulled off several strips and reinforced both sides of the dress at the hipline.

I wish I wasn't so wide. I'm built like my mom in that area and I hate it. I wish I'd gotten the same genes Marti was blessed with from some other skinny branch on our family tree. It would be so much nicer to be petite and narrow like her.

As Christy slipped back into the repaired dress, she thought of how quickly her self-image had gone from feeling loved and adored by her wonderful husband who had made it clear that he thought she was the most beautiful woman in the world, to feeling like she was back in high school comparing herself to all the skinny girls and pondering radical ways to adjust her basic body type and structure.

With her back to the door, Christy smoothed the dress and mumbled to her reflection in the mirror, "You'd think by now I would have made peace with the way I look." Placing her hands on her hips she squeezed, trying to make herself smaller. "Shrink, you blinkin' hips. Come on. Why do you have to be so wide?"

The door squeaked open and Christy turned to see Abuela Teresa. Embarrassed at being caught in her self-deprecating moment, Christy fumbled with an explanation. "Too much good food, I guess." A nervous laugh leaked out. "I'm bursting at the seams. Literally." She laughed again and patted her hip.

Abuela Teresa ushered herself all the way into the room and gave Christy a tender look. "I am surprised. You are angry with your frame."

"I just wish I wasn't so wide. That's all."

Even though Christy had been getting used to the way the Women of the Canaries invited themselves into each other's lives and private thoughts, she wasn't prepared for such direct words.

"This is what matters." Abuela Teresa folded her hands over her midriff and pressed in on her stomach area. "Only this."

Carolyn's mother didn't necessarily have a flat midsection so Christy wasn't sure what she was saying.

Does she think it's better to have a flat stomach than wide hips?

If this was going to be a pep talk about self-image, Christy would have expected Abuela Teresa to touch her heart and say something very American about how beauty begins on the inside.

Instead, Abuela Teresa kept both her hands on her midsection. "Here. Right here. This is where you live. In your gut. This is where your feelings go when you swallow them. This is also where your best laughter comes from."

She lowered her voice as if sharing an ancient secret. "Don't you see, Christina? This is where you love. This is where you, as a woman, are given the privilege to nurture and carry new life. Right here, in your gut, this is where you die a little each day when the one you loved for all your life leaves this earth before you."

Christy felt as if the whole world had gone very still.

With a smile drawing up the corners of her eyes and emphasizing a sunburst of well-earned wrinkles, she added, "And when you dance, *mi niña*, this is where the music comes from."

Christy had come to love the gutsy Women of the Canaries and had seen at the spa how comfortable they were with their bodies. None of them had tried to hide their flaws. As far as Christy could tell, they hadn't spent the time comparing their flabby parts with each other. She'd never been around a group of women at any age who were so comfortable in their own skin.

Abuela Teresa reached out her hand. Her skin was sprinkled with age spots but her motion was graceful. She cupped her palm under Christy's chin. "You are now a Woman of the Canaries, Christina. You are one of us. As your Abuela I say to you, make peace with your curves. Honor your bones. Live from here." She pressed her palm against Christy's midsection. "Live from the stomach up."

Christy nodded. "Thank you," she said in a humbled voice. "Gracias."

"De nada. Now, come with me." Abuela Teresa took Christy by the hand. "They are about to start the dancing. That's why I came to find you. You must dance with us."

Christy was about to protest as she had with Aunt Frieda and insist that she didn't dance. But if she was ever going to learn how to live from the stomach up, this would be the place and tonight would be the night.

eleven

$\mathcal{C}$hristy and Abuela Teresa returned to the backyard patio, and Christy wasn't surprised to see that her husband had taken off his suit coat and rolled up the sleeves of his white shirt. He'd loosened his tie and unbuttoned the top button. What she was surprised to see was that he had pulled up a stool next to the guitar player and had somehow managed to find a guitar that he was now playing alongside the professional musician, picking up the melody as he went.

The song ended with a bold stroke across the strings and the musician turned to Todd with a wide smile and nodded. Apparently Todd had been able to keep up with him and turned the last solo into a duet.

Todd returned the guitar to the stand behind the musician and shook his hand. The musician looked over at Abuela Teresa. She gave a nod and he gave an announcement in Spanish. The guests began to step back, clearing the floor and opening up the center of the patio so there was enough space for an area to dance. Todd came to Christy and put his arm around her shoulder.

"Did you see that? It was awesome. I wish Doug were here. He would have loved jammin' with this guy."

"Where did you get the guitar?"

"He had it in his car. He's going to sell it to me. We'll work out the price later. I'm so stoked."

"I can tell." Christy was happy to see Todd so ecstatic. To share with him her bit of pending excitement, she leaned closer and said, "We're going to dance."

"Who's going to dance?"

"You and me."

Todd's silver-blue eyes narrowed. "I don't know about that."

"Just one dance?" Christy did her best cute-wife-please-oh-please look.

"You've seen me dance, Kilikina. It's not attractive."

"Actually, I'm not sure I have ever seen you dance."

He leaned over and pressed a raindrop of a kiss against the side of her head. "What if we just keep it that way?"

"Todd, seriously. I want to live from the stomach up."

"From the what?"

"I'll tell you later. Just say you'll dance with me. Promise me. Please?"

Before Todd could answer the musician struck a vibrating chord on his guitar and all the conversations ceased. Abuela Teresa stood in the center of the floor. Bryan and Carolyn sat directly in front of her as if they had pulled up their chairs for a family performance. It reminded Christy of the way patient parents might become the audience when their children had come up with a play they're eager to perform.

Only this time it was the children watching the mother.

Abuela Teresa struck a pose with her hands on her hips. The musician played the next chord followed by a string of soul-stirring notes and Abuela Teresa began to dance. The heels of her shoes clicked on the cement and every staccato step echoed across the patio.

Christy was amazed. This unassuming, quiet woman who

was over seventy years old was dancing flamenco in front of everyone. Her movements were convincing and elegant. Her head was held high and her shoulders were back. Her hands went into the air and she turned her wrists like delicate parasols. She was definitely dancing from the stomach up.

The sight of such a woman doing such a dance in the midst of this time of celebration stirred something deep inside Christy's gut. Abuela Teresa's fluid, quick-paced dance ended with a spin. She held her head at a tilt and the instant the music ended, she stamped her foot and lifted her right arm into the air with her hand and fingers held in a graceful pose. Her whole body seemed to be one elegant exclamation mark of joy.

The guests clapped and cheered. Bryan rose from his seat, applauding her and looking around at everyone, wildly surprised, as if he had no idea his mother-in-law had such fire and agility hidden inside her.

Carolyn calmly rose from her chair and stepped into the cleared space to join her mother. Christy thought she was going to give Abuela Teresa a hug. Instead, Carolyn exchanged only a dignified glance with her mother before standing beside her with her hands on her hips as well.

Bryan caught on that his bride was now in ready-to-dance position. He stopped clapping and lowered himself into his chair. He gave Carolyn an inquisitive look as she fixed her determined gaze on him and the music began once again.

This time the steps were shared with double the flair as Carolyn and her mother stomped their feet, lifted their arms, and the dance began. Carolyn was the stunning ivory moon orbiting her silver-blue mother earth, reflecting light into the galaxy of observers. It was the most inspiring expression of mother/daughter shared likeness Christy had ever seen. She wished she'd gone to grab her camera. But she didn't want to miss any of the dance. Fortunately, several other relatives were recording the whole thing.

The short number came to a fiery crescendo. Todd started

applauding even before his dad. Christy didn't know if Todd was cheering for the musician or for his new stepmother and grandmother.

Bryan was on his feet again, cheering, applauding, and gazing on his new wife with bemused amazement.

Christy joined them in clapping. Carolyn turned to her and stretched out her hand, inviting Christy to come stand beside her. Christy's eyes grew wide and she shook her head vigorously. "I can't do that!"

Carolyn motioned more insistently for Christy to come to her. She didn't know if it would be more embarrassing to resist vehemently or to quietly acquiesce and be humiliated in front of all the guests if the music began again and she knew none of the steps.

Abuela Teresa offered the same nonverbal invitation to her sisters and one by one they came to her side. The women stood close, their arms around each other's waists, forming a long line.

Rosa came over to Christy and took her by the hand, pulling her into the lineup. "You have to do this. You're one of us now. You're a Woman of the Canaries."

"But I don't know what I'm doing."

"Just follow me," Rosa said. "Always start with the right foot. It's easy. You'll see. Just remember. Always start with the right foot."

Christy stretched her arm around Carolyn's waist, linking her arm with Abuela Teresa. Carolyn looped her arm around Christy's waist and Rosa did the same. The guitar player tapped on his guitar with rapid, staccato knuckle raps. Carolyn and Rosa both extended their right feet. Christy did the same. The flamenco music began once again. This time it was a lighthearted tune. The women all crossed their right foot over the left and Christy followed along, keeping her chin down and watching Carolyn and Rosa for cues.

Right foot, stomp the left foot, five steps to the right, leading with the left foot, another stomp and then the same progression repeated to the other side. Rosa was right. It was easy.

What made the dance beautiful, Christy thought when she watched it back on the video Uncle Bob had taken with his phone, was that the women moved as one. The looping of their arms around each other's waists brought them hip to hip and shoulder to shoulder. When one moved, the others joined in. They looked straight ahead until they got to the second stomp. That's when they snapped their heads in the direction they were to go next. Once their faces turned, their feet followed.

Christy had caught on to the head snap, thanks to Rosa, and within twenty seconds, she was in sync with the Women of the Canaries. She was dancing!

That wasn't the only dancing Christy did on that enchanted night of celebration. As soon as the dance floor was opened to everyone and the guitar music had been replaced by a great mix of popular dance music, Uncle Bob came over to Christy and asked for the first dance.

Christy gave Todd a playful look over her shoulder as she accepted Uncle Bob's invitation. It was as if she was saying, "See? If you won't dance with me, I'll go dance with my uncle." The best part of that first dance, in Christy's opinion, was that she and Uncle Bob laughed more than they danced. It was sheer delight.

The next song had just begun when Todd cut in and with a grin gave Christy a spin. He seemed to be trying his best to make his movements look like they were deliberate and meant to resemble some sort of dance move. However, the entire time Christy kept laughing because no matter what he tried, he still looked like a goofy-footing surfer, balancing on a surfboard and leaning from one side to the other. His arms hung to his side as if he were riding a rolling wave all the way to shore.

Christy could not remember ever having so much fun at a wedding reception. She danced with the little girls in their frilly dresses, holding hands in a circle and taking turns spinning and grinning. She danced with her father-in-law and she danced with her mother-in-law. She even danced with Aunt Frieda, who kept giving Christy uninvited little pats on her backside to make sure the duct tape was doing its job.

Christy laughed from the depths of her belly and kissed her husband soundly after he attempted to give her an impressive dip at the end of the last slow dance.

It was a perfect night in every way.

The stars were high in the unclouded sky when the aunts started the cleanup. Aunt Frieda rallied all the guest to do something before they left, and the teardown happened faster than anything Christy had ever seen at work or at dozens of youth events at church. The patio was cleared and soon, so were all the guests. Christy, Todd, and Bob were among the last to leave after loading several bags of trash and bins of dirty dishes into the back of Rosa's van.

Christy took one last look around the kitchen before going out to the car with a bin of stacked plates in her arms. She glanced out the window and there, on the cleared patio, Bryan and Carolyn held each other, enjoying a lingering slow dance under the stars. It was so romantic. Christy listened to hear the music they were swaying to, but there was no music.

She smiled. That was a Woman of the Canaries out there with her true love.

I know where the music is coming from.

By midafternoon the next day, blissful images of the wedding were fading and Christy felt fidgety in the small apartment. It had rained for over ten hours off and on and it seemed that Todd had played his new flamenco guitar for the same amount of hours. After being cooped up in the apartment, the vibrancy of his music was starting to get to her.

The original plan had been to do some sightseeing during the two days after the wedding before they flew to Kenya. But as their final full day dragged on, sightseeing was the last thing they wanted to do. The rain had already ruined their plans for a beach day and dampened their enthusiasm for a sloshy trek to any of the restaurants or sights the relatives had suggested to them.

Christy spent most of the morning helping Uncle Bob with a project he initiated as a small thank-you for Abuela Teresa. He and Christy had camped out at the dining room table where they downloaded onto Bob's new tablet all the photos and videos he'd taken with his phone. He pulled the images from Christy's camera and did the tedious work of an amateur photographer as he edited, organized, and labeled each picture.

Uncle Bob had inconspicuously started taking photos from the time they arrived that first night at the family dinner in the restaurant by the sea. He had captured a wide variety of images and expressions. Some of the photos Christy had taken of Carolyn as she got ready for the wedding were stunning. The image of Carolyn and her mother holding hands in the backseat of the car on the way to the wedding was, as Uncle Bob said, "award winning."

"I found a place where I can get these photos printed in an album," Bob announced after getting off the phone with Rosa. "It's just up the street in the shopping center. Anyone want to walk up there with me?"

"I will." Todd returned his guitar to its case.

Christy opted to stay at the apartment. She wasn't feeling great and walking uphill in the rain didn't appeal to her at all. The possibility of a nap before a long day of travel was, however, very appealing.

"It's wise of you to sleep now," Abuela Teresa said. "Once you get to Nairobi, it sounds like you will be even busier than you were for this wedding."

"That's true." Christy hoped Katie's wedding dress had arrived. She hadn't been able to get on the phone the last time Uncle Bob called Aunt Marti. According to him, everything was going great. Marti was well rested, the day nurse was a gem, and Christy's mom was already sitting up and able to walk out to the balcony and stretch out on the plush lounge chair. Marti assured Uncle Bob that she had taken care of Katie's dress and Christy shouldn't worry about it.

But she was worried.

Abuela Teresa had slipped out of the living room. Before Christy could head to the guest room for a nap, Abuela Teresa returned and handed Christy a small piece of folded-up cloth.

"This is a gift for your friend."

"For Katie?"

"Yes. The bride. She needs something old, something new, something borrowed, and something blue."

Christy wasn't sure Katie would feel the need to comply with the old adage.

"This can be her something old. It's one of my mother's lace handkerchiefs."

Christy unfolded the dainty fabric and took note of the frayed but lovely lace around the edges. "Did you say this was your mother's?"

"Yes."

"It's beautiful. Are you sure you shouldn't save it for one of your sisters, or daughters or even for Tikki?"

Abuela Teresa put her hands on her hips the way she had right before her blazing dance at the reception. In a firm tone she said, "Christina, when a woman who loves you gives you a gift, you take it, you say 'thank you—*muchas gracias*,' and you kiss her on the cheek."

Abuela Teresa turned her cheek to Christy and waited with a regal posture.

Christy grinned. "Thank you, Abuela Teresa. Muchas gracias." She placed the kiss on her cheek like the first raindrop of spring.

"De nada, mi niña."

"I promise I will deliver this to Katie with much love from you and the other Women of the Canaries."

"No!" Abuela Teresa looked aghast at Christy's comment.

"You will do no such thing. I am giving her this gift. Not them. They can give you their own gifts for Katie if they want. You tell her this gift is from me. *Solamente de mi.*"

Christy laughed.

Abuela Teresa leaned over and gave her a motherly hug. She smelled like lavender.

"Thank you for everything," Christy said. "I loved being here and becoming part of your family. I learned so much from your hospitality."

"You are welcome here any time."

Christy had a sad feeling that it might be a long time before she and Todd would be able to make this long journey again. That evening they'd made plans to break into Bryan and Carolyn's honeymoon week of being alone in their new home. It was the last chance they'd have to be together for a meal and that made Christy sad, too.

She made her way to the bedroom and stretched out on the comfortable bed. The problem with not having a stable home situation right now made the Canary Islands feel like maybe she did belong here. She wished she could be around Carolyn and Abuela Teresa and all the other Women of the Canaries on a regular basis.

At the same time, she couldn't wait to get to Africa and see Katie. It had been way too long since they'd been together, and both of them had saved up lots to talk about once they were face-to-face again.

One thing Christy had determined from this time with these unforgettable women was that her friends and her family mattered to her more than she had ever realized. She didn't want to start comparing and wishing that her mother and her aunt could be as warm and encompassing as the Women of the Canaries. Instead, Christy wanted to accept the women in her family just the way they were. She could be the one to initiate more kindness. She could dispense blessings and pour out the gift of unconditional love and acceptance.

As for strengthening her friendships, Christy thought

about how nurturing it had been to reconnect with Tracy. They had met four times for coffee over the last two months.

Why couldn't it be more than that? Why couldn't we meet once a week? We can meet at Julie Ann's. We'll start our own traditions and become the Women of Newport Beach.

That's when a sobering thought came to her.

How many weeks will we be able to meet? Even though Doug and Tracy are permanently moving to Newport Beach, Todd and I don't know how long we'll be able to stay in the area.

Before Christy could give in to the invisible depression troll that threatened to send her rolling down an emotional hill, she whispered the small words that had become a familiar theme the last few weeks. "Trust God."

She pulled her travel-size Bible from her bag and went on the hunt for some verses she remembered looking up and underlining while she was going to school in Switzerland. That was a long season of waiting and trusting that her relationship with Todd would continue to grow even though they were so far apart from each other for so long.

Turning to Proverbs 3, Christy found the underlined verses 5 and 6. Even though these words of truth had meant something to her in her college years, they now seemed to mean even more in this brand-new season of life.

"Trust in the Lord with all your heart and do not lean on your own understanding. In all your ways acknowledge Him, and He will make your paths straight."

The memory of how she had danced with the Women of the Canaries came back to Christy. They invited her to join them even though she didn't know the steps. She had to be daring and go to them, hold on to them, get in line with them, and then watch how they moved.

"Right foot forward," Rosa had said. *"Always start with your right."*

It seemed to Christy that if she was going to learn the dance of faith in this precarious season of life, she had to do the same thing. These verses told her to trust in the Lord with all her heart.

"From the stomach up," Christy whispered.

Trusting God happens from the stomach up. Not in my head. Not with my logic.

She knew she had to step away from the insecurities and fears of her own limited understanding. She needed to take that first step of willingness and link arms with the One who knew all the right steps because He had danced these steps of faith for many generations with women who fully trusted Him.

Christy smiled. *And now He's inviting me to learn to dance with Him.*

Home of Our Hearts

twelve

*C*hristy leaned over the airplane toilet in the cramped space and emptied her stomach for the second time since they'd boarded this flight. These were not the dance steps of faith she had anticipated when she prayed so earnestly not more than twenty-four hours ago.

She had a bottle of water with her and sipped from it cautiously. Beads of perspiration formed on her forehead and top lip. She wet a paper towel, held it on the back of her neck, and let the cool water from the sink run on her wrists.

I hate being sick.

She didn't think it was anything she'd eaten at dinner last night at Bryan and Carolyn's. Uncle Bob and Todd had eaten the same grilled fish, salted potatoes, and roasted carrots and neither of them was ill.

What did I eat at the airport in Las Palmas this morning?

The nausea passed and Christy finished cleaning up herself and the restroom area. She walked clumsily back to her seat. Todd had moved over so she could have the aisle seat. He looked concerned when she sat down. "You okay?"

Christy nodded. "Yeah. I'm still a little nauseous but I'm okay." She leaned back and turned the overhead vent so she could feel the air flowing on her face. Closing her eyes, Christy hoped she wouldn't have to return to that stifling bathroom.

Todd reached over and covered her hand with his. She drew in a deep breath and slept as deeply as anyone could sleep on a bumpy descent into an airport situated at almost six thousand feet above sea level. Katie had warned her that a lot of groups that fly in from the US and Europe to help dig wells for clean water end up not drinking enough themselves. The altitude and dehydration caused more problems than threats from wild beasts or malaria-infested mosquitos.

"I'll carry your bag," Todd said before they even stood to get out of their seats. "Take it slow, okay?"

Christy nodded. She reached for her water bottle and finished it.

Uncle Bob stepped into the aisle next to Christy's seat. He placed his hand on her shoulder. "Don't get up too fast."

"You guys, I'm okay. Really." Christy rose with only a tinge of dizziness.

"Take this with you, just in case." Todd pulled the folded-up airsick bag from the seat pocket. He stuffed it into Christy's shoulder bag.

She tried to pretend he hadn't just done that. It was embarrassing enough to be sick on a plane behind the closed door of the restroom. She didn't want her husband or uncle to start announcing it. Looking straight ahead, Christy fell into step with the shuffling line of passengers as they exited the plane.

The late-afternoon air felt humid and the airport layout felt confusing to Christy. She let Bob lead the way through Customs. Todd held her hand as they navigated on to baggage claim through the crush of travelers. Christy looked around. The people all around her were a kaleidoscope of shapes, sizes, and colors. She wasn't sure if it was a result of her queasiness or if it was an elemental part of Africa, but the variety of humanity seemed to be a broader spectrum than what she'd seen in Madrid or Las Palmas. Those airports felt like other European airports she had been to. This place felt altogether different.

Christy suddenly felt very white and very American and very far away from anything familiar.

They threaded their way to their designated luggage carousel and kept looking around for any sighting of Eli or Katie. The two of them would be the familiar piece that Christy hoped would help stabilize all the swirling of her senses. The languages spoken by several people around them sounded completely foreign.

Even the light filtering through the open doors that led to the baggage claim felt different. It was evening time. Twilight. But the light wasn't diffused and muted the way it had come through the window at Abuela Teresa's apartment at this time of day. Here the light was dense and persistent as if it were holding out the last note of a song with all the fortitude it could muster.

"Is that your guitar case, Todd?" Bob pointed to a cart being wheeled toward them carrying a mound of oddly shaped luggage haphazardly stacked up.

"Yeah, that's mine. Glad you spotted it."

Todd stepped away to claim his guitar and Bob said, "I'm glad we found the sturdy case for him yesterday. His new prize would have been demolished by now if it were still in the cloth case."

Both Bob and Todd had been pleased with the treasures they found when they'd ventured out in the rain the previous afternoon. Todd came back with the guitar case and Bob had a half-dozen photo albums that had been made from Bob and Christy's snapshots. Bryan and Carolyn loved the album Bob presented to them at their home that night. It made the perfect farewell gift. Unfortunately, it hadn't eased the pain of saying good-bye.

Is my stomach upset as a result of all the emotions I swallowed last night? Abuela Teresa said that's where they go: into my gut. Those were some enormous emotions. I could hardly stand seeing Todd and his dad weep the way they did when they stood there, holding each other when they said good-bye.

Christy tried not to think about the bittersweet parting. Bryan and Carolyn had promised they'd return to Newport Beach in the next few years. But Todd and Christy hadn't been able to verbalize any sort of promise as to when they would return.

All Todd said, after he and his dad pulled away from their emotional embrace was, "I hold you in my heart, Dad. Forever."

Christy had cried and swallowed her feelings and cried some more. Uncle Bob was right there with them, swallowing his tears more than releasing them. Todd had drawn inward and silent. All he wanted to do was sleep. Christy hated feeling so disconnected from her husband, not to mention feeling so nauseous. She had hoped Katie would be there to meet them and that the journey to Brockhurst would be swift.

Todd returned from the luggage cart with his guitar and pointed out a ding on the bottom. "It's not bad. I checked the guitar. It's fine."

She stood back from the airport carousel as the luggage from their flight began to roll toward them. Todd pulled first Bob's suitcase and then his. They continued to wait for Christy's suitcase and she silently prayed that it would show up.

She could feel the perspiration streaming down her back. *Stomach, stay calm.* Now that she was here on Katie's side of the world, she refused to be sick. She didn't want to miss any of her time with her best friend. They had exactly eleven days before Katie would become Mrs. Lorenzo. Eleven days to squeeze in all they'd lost from not having the luxury of their lives overlapping.

Christy's bag came tumbling along and she whispered a relieved, "thank you, Lord." It was bad enough that she didn't have Katie's wedding dress with her. Arriving in Kenya without any luggage would have been even more frustrating.

"Do you think we should wait here?" Todd asked. Katie and Eli were nowhere to be seen.

"Let's go outside and see if they're waiting at the curb." Uncle Bob suggested, sounding weary and looking ragged around the edges. He hadn't gotten much sleep the past few nights on the couch at Abuela Teresa's with her trilling bird as a companion through each night. He said earlier on their flight that his stomach was upset as well, but he hadn't gotten sick the way Christy had. He was blaming his discomfort on the malaria pills they'd started taking. Were they having an overpowering effect on her?

They made their way through the roped-off airport renovation area and stepped out into the cooler air. The swarm of bustling travelers outside was as congested as it had been inside. Christy started to feel woozy again. *Think of something, anything, other than needing to find a bathroom.*

Her tactic worked. But only for about two minutes.

"Todd, I'm gonna be . . . " Those were her last words before reaching into her purse and pulling out the airsick bag.

She didn't have much of anything left in her stomach, and it wasn't as if she was violently ill. But still, who wanted to be sick in public? Christy tried to discreetly fold up the top of the bag and looked around for a trash can.

At the far end of the entrance Christy noticed two men dressed in military uniforms. Both of them carried AK-47s strapped over their shoulders and kept in place by their large, protective hands. Her stomach tightened again. She'd never been in a place where armed guards stood in the midst of the crowds, keeping a watchful eye on all the comings and goings. She wasn't sure if their presence made her feel safer or more vulnerable.

Bob's words about Marti's fears of going into a volatile part of the world returned to Christy, and she knew once again that this was unlike any place she had ever been.

How can Katie feel so at home here?

Christy heard her name and felt a rush of relief at the familiar sound of Katie's voice.

"Christy! Todd! Uncle Bob! Hey! *Jambo! Karibu sana!* Welcome to Kenya! You're here!" With the same exuberance that red-haired Katie Weldon had expended as the Kelly High School mascot, she bounded over a suitcase and swerved past a construction renovation sign. Her arms were around Christy and she was hugging her, rocking her, squeezing her, and laughing her great, contagious Katie laugh.

Through it all, Christy was holding out the airsick bag, trying to make sure Katie didn't accidently smash it open in the middle of her truly joyous greeting. Katie let go of Christy and gave Todd and then Bob an equally enthusiastic hugging/shakedown before turning her attention back to Christy. Her green eyes were lit up and hair was pulled back in a short ponytail. Her sun-kissed face was beaming.

Without pausing for a breath, Katie gushed out all her excited thoughts. "I can't believe you're here! Eli went inside to look for you guys. Oh, it's good to see you, my dearest, most favorite Peculiar Treasure! Is this the biggest God-thing of all time, or what? Sorry we were late. The roads are worse than usual. They're doing repairs on the main highway that goes to the airport. It's awful. You look tired. Are you okay? Here let me take that. Are you guys hungry? Thirsty? If you want, we could go into town to eat. There's a place that serves local meat. It's touristy but we like it. They serve zebra and crocodile. Oh, and ostrich meatballs. Those are Eli's favorite lately."

Christy held up her hand like a stop sign in an effort to keep her friend from saying any more or else she'd need to reuse her airsick bag.

Katie's eyes widened. "Are you okay? You look like you're gonna . . . " Her gaze went to the bag Christy was trying to hold to her side, out of sight.

Christy thought that her flushed face and the airsick bag were pretty significant clues. Surely Katie would take a hint and stop talking about eating ostrich.

Instead of calming down, Katie threw her arms around Christy again and squealed in her ear. Christy tried to pull back, confused by Katie's second round of hugs and squeals.

"Why didn't you tell me? You're pregnant, aren't you? Christy! I'm so excited for you. When did you find out? This is so cool."

"Katie, I'm not pregnant. And what I'm feeling right now is not cool. I was sick on the plane. It was something I ate, I think."

"Or the malaria pills," Bob suggested.

"Are you sure?" Katie asked.

"Yes, I'm sure. I'm not pregnant."

"Bummer. Sorry you got sick on the plane. I hope you're okay now. We've got some water in the car, if that will help. I'm so excited that you're here."

A timer seemed to go off in Christy's cloudy brain. *Wait. What day is this?* She thought a moment and felt her heart-beat quicken. Christy cast a quick look at Todd. It was possible that she could be pregnant. Not probable, but certainly possible. Todd was focused on the luggage and didn't catch her glance.

"Oh hey, there's Eli!" Katie stretched her arm over her head and waved.

Eli headed toward them as Christy conveniently deposited her bag into a large trash can against the wall. She looked up. Eli's brown hair was the shortest she had ever seen it. His trademark goatee had grown back, and for some reason he seemed taller or more filled out. It was as if he fit into this setting more naturally than the rest of them, which made sense since he was a missionary kid and had grown up in this part of the world. The larger-than-life version of Eli strode toward them with the confidence of someone who had the liquid drumbeat of Africa pulsing through his veins.

Eli greeted Todd with a manly sort of handshake that moved into a shoulder-to-shoulder bump and a hearty pat on the back. He gave Christy a warm hug and greeted Uncle Bob with equal enthusiasm even though they had only been around each other a few times before.

"*Karibu sana.* Welcome!"

Christy recognized the greeting since Katie had used it during their video calls in the past. The "Welcome to Kenya" in Swahili sounded more convincing coming from Eli than it ever had coming from Katie through a laptop speaker.

"Here, let me help with your luggage. Todd, you brought your guitar?"

"It's a new one. I just got it in Las Palmas. A guy at my dad's wedding gave it to me."

"I didn't know he gave it to you," Bob said. "That was mighty generous."

"I know. He said we were related now and that the cousins in their family were closer than brothers. Something like that. My Spanish is better when it comes to food, like tacos, burritos, and enchiladas. That, I understand. The reason why he gifted me with this flamenco guitar was beyond my vocabulary skills."

Eli and Todd started talking guitars and music as Uncle Bob took the role of shepherd and made sure Katie and Christy made it across the trafficked area and into the jumble of cars that were parked every which way.

"We have a driver," Katie said. "It's easier than trying to get ourselves into town. Especially with all the detours and the construction right now. Eli does much better driving around here than I do, but his dad insisted that we hire a *matatu* so we'd have enough room for everyone and your luggage, too. By the way, I'm impressed with how compact your baggage is."

Christy wanted to blurt out that it was because Marti wasn't with them with her big luggage. She wanted to confess right then and there that she'd forgotten Katie's wedding dress. But this didn't seem like the right moment to break that news to her. She wished she'd been given more specifics on how Marti had arranged to ship it here. It would feel better if she had the detailed update before telling Katie about her epic fail.

Eli led them to the matatu, which turned out to be a small, white minibus where a young man was seated behind the wheel, his eyes fixed on his cell phone.

Christy got in first and sat by the open window, grateful for the small breeze coming her way. Her head felt as if she'd taken allergy medication. All her thoughts were fuzzy and sounds seemed especially loud. The sun had set and streetlights were coming on as the driver jockeyed for position in the chaotic mesh of cars all trying to leave the airport. She'd never heard so many cars honking at the same time.

"I didn't even ask," Katie said. "How was the flight?"

"Forgettable," Bob said. "My favorite kind."

Christy appreciated that he didn't give Katie a report of her treks to the back of the plane during the flight or any other indicators of how rough the last few hours had been for her. She had a feeling she was becoming more like her mother in that regard. If she was ill, she preferred to be left alone to work it out rather than cause any drama and be the center of attention.

"What about food?" Katie asked. "Did you guys get much to eat on the plane? Are you hungry at all? We have some snacks and water with us here in a bag."

"I'll take some water," Christy said.

"Who else?" Katie turned into their friendly hostess and passed around their drive-time nibbles.

Christy was grateful that it was simple food: carrot sticks, some sort of flat bread torn into small pieces, bananas, and a Cadbury milk chocolate bar. Christy opted for just the bread but Bob and Todd ate everything else.

They bumped along on pitted roads. Christy couldn't help but notice how the driver boldly inched closer to other cars and trucks on both sides of them. He got much closer to the vehicle in front of them than a driver would ever get in the US.

Her stomach clenched and she tried to do the calculations once again and factor in the time difference. It was beginning to seem more possible that she could actually be pregnant.

I am late. By two days. I think. What if I am pregnant?

The thought overwhelmed her. Christy knew she shouldn't assume anything quite yet. She convinced herself that her body was out of sync due to all the travel and time change. Katie had been talking about wedding plans and Christy had been only half listening.

"I'm sorry," Christy said. "I missed that last part you were just saying about the reception at the conference center. Tell me again."

Katie had calmed down considerably since her rambunctious greeting at the airport. It seemed that quiet, steady Eli had that effect on her.

"You know what?" Katie said. "We can talk about all this later. We've got plenty of time. It's rough trying to acclimate especially on this long ride to Brockhurst."

The van hit a pothole just then, jarring all of them.

Katie laughed. "You can see why we call it getting an African massage whenever we have to go into town."

Todd reached over and touched Christy's arm with a steady hand. "You okay?"

"Yes. I'm fine."

"You're doing much better than I did on my first jaunt from the airport," Katie said. "Poor Eli! I think he was ready to turn around and put me on the next plane out of here."

"Not a chance," Eli said.

"We hit a pothole that time and blew out a tire. I thought I'd been shot." Katie laughed again. "I had blood on my back but it was only from a safety pin that snapped open."

Christy wanted to ask why Katie had a safety pin poking into her back but thought best to leave it alone. The thought of safety pins reminded her of the duct tape that had held her together at Carolyn and Bryan's wedding. And that reminded her of Katie's dress. She had avoided making this confession via a phone call or e-mail. The time had come to tell her friend face-to-face that she had blown it big time, but hopefully, if Aunt Marti came through as she promised she would, all would be well.

"Katie, I need to tell you something."

Her friend turned toward her on the narrow bench seat where she and Eli were cozied up in front of Christy and Todd.

"Katie, I forgot your wedding dress. I am so, so sorry. But don't worry because I asked—"

"I already know."

"You know?"

"Uh-huh." She sounded so unflapped about it.

"How did you know?"

"Your aunt told me."

"She did? When?"

"When she called me."

"Aunt Marti called you? Why?"

"To tell me that you'd forgotten my wedding dress." Katie started laughing as if she found the back-and-forth banter to be comical. "Didn't she tell you that she called me?"

"No. She didn't."

Christy turned to look at Uncle Bob. His expression in the passing flash of oncoming headlights made it clear he was as surprised as Christy was.

"Seriously, Christy. Don't worry about the dress. Marti told me about your mom and how crazy everything was right before you left."

Christy felt relieved in the wash of her friend's gracious response, but she still felt confused as to why Katie wasn't be at least a little frustrated. It was her wedding dress they were talking about. She ventured a guess as to why the problem seemed resolved to Katie.

"Did it arrive already?"

Now Katie looked confused. "No. Not until next Monday,

of course."

Christy wasn't sure why Katie said, "of course," unless it was because she expected Christy to know the scheduled arrival time.

The main thing was that Katie wasn't upset or anxious about it, and that relieved Christy's tormented psyche immensely. She thought about how her father-in-law had settled comfortably into the pace of island time when their refrigerator delivery had been delayed. Maybe that was what had happened to Katie. Her time in Kenya mellowed her so much that nothing truly bothered her.

"What is that African saying about don't worry?" Uncle Bob asked.

"*Hakuna matata,*" Eli said the phrase with a lot more authenticity than the way it sounded on *The Lion King.*

"Hakuna matata," Bob repeated. "Your dress is on its way. We can all stop worrying now."

Christy leaned back and tried to relax. Aunt Marti had taken care of everything as she said she would. It made sense that she would bypass Christy and go directly to Katie with the shipping information. The dress wasn't here yet, but it was on its way. Christy was ready to drop the subject but Katie had one more thing to say.

"I'm glad she's coming. I mean, really. How could our wedding be complete without her?"

"Wait. What are we talking about now?" Christy felt bubbleheaded again and thought she'd missed something.

"Your aunt."

"Aunt Marti?"

"Yes."

"What about my aunt?"

"She's bringing the dress with her on Monday."

The air in the van suddenly felt very thin.

Uncle Bob leaned closer to Katie. "Are you saying that my wife is coming here?"

"Yes. On Monday. And she's bringing my wedding dress

with her." Katie's bright eyes were like two headlights as she flashed them on Christy and Todd and then back on Uncle Bob. "Didn't you guys know she was coming?"

"No!" The three of them answered in unison.

"Oh! Well, then . . . surprise!"

Home of Our Hearts

thirteen

$\mathcal{K}$atie had another surprise for Christy the next morning. The two of them were at the coffee bar located inside the main lodge at Brockhurst Conference Center. This was where Katie volunteered as a barista whenever groups were using the conference center. The "Lion's Den" lodge was empty this morning, and Katie had eagerly coaxed Christy to join her here after breakfast so she could demonstrate her skills.

"Go ahead." Katie slid a steaming beverage in front of Christy. "Try it."

This wasn't the first time Katie had presented Christy with one of her tea-based concoctions. The homegrown herbal blend Katie created when they were college roommates had produced a rash on the underside of Christy's forearms and on her neck, so she had reason to be skeptical.

"Go ahead," Katie urged eagerly.

Christy blew across the top of the foamy drink and hoped this new African tea creation of Katie's wouldn't have the same adverse effect as the herbal attempt. Her stomach had calmed down enough for her to eat some hot cereal that morning, and she didn't want to upset the delicate balance.

With a brave bending of her elbow, Christy drew the mug to her lips and took a sip. She felt the soothing touch of the steaming-hot beverage as it slinked down her throat. "Oh, this is nice."

"Told ya."

Christy drew in a deeper breath of the spicy chai tea. The robust flavor came from the added dark chocolate and steamed milk.

"The first time Eli made one of these for me, I thought it tasted like a really good spice cake with great chocolate frosting. Only in liquid form." Katie went back to work preparing the same specialty beverage for herself.

"What's it called again?"

"It's a Malindi Chai Mocha. They're addicting, by the way. So when you have to join a support group one of these days and confess to the others that you have a problem with over consumption of Malindi Chai Mochas, I'm sure my name will come up."

Christy grinned and took another sip. She gazed out the large windows of the upper part of the lodge. When Katie had used the terms *compound* and *headquarters* to describe this place and said that the center was gated with guards, Christy pictured sparse grounds with cement-block dormitories. Christy had seen a few pictures but always thought Katie was capturing only the most appealing corners of the conference center.

Not so. The entire grounds reminded Christy of a well-kept resort with an impressive main lodge surrounded by a number of outlying buildings and clusters of simple, charming stone cottages.

Last night it had been too dark to see much when they arrived. But this morning when Christy and Todd took the path from their cottage to the dining hall for breakfast, she was awed by the rolling green lawns with trimly cut grass that spread out like a thick, inviting carpet. The air was chilly and a fine mist hung over the tops of the tallest trees. They were greeted by birds that had a song she'd never heard before.

Todd had stopped on the way to the dining hall in order to have a look at one of the hand-carved wooden benches strategically placed under a large, sheltering tree along the way to the main lodge. Christy had stood beside him and noticed the tidy flower beds that brimmed with deep magenta-colored flowers. Their circles of fellowship were punctuated by occasional bursts of a delicate, frilly white flower. She felt as if she and Todd were strolling through an English garden located on some parallel planet.

Enjoying another sip of her chai, Christy commented on the view and her first impressions of this surprising place. "I feel like I'm in England, not in Africa. The grounds here are stunning."

"The British influence is pretty obvious, isn't it? I don't know if I ever told you but this conference center was founded by a mission organization from Scotland about fifty years ago."

"I almost expect to see bunny rabbits hopping across the lawn. Like the bunnies that scampered everywhere when we were at Carnforth Hall."

"You won't find bunnies from northern England here," Katie said. "Monkeys, yes. Lots of them. That's why all the windows in the cottages have bars on them."

At the moment it was difficult for Christy to believe this place wasn't as storybook perfect as the setting appeared. However, beyond the tin-roofed cottages Christy could see the looming jungle trees and vines that hinted at the untamed side of the Kenyan highlands. She remembered stories Katie had told her last November about the monkeys that scampered across the roof of her cottage in order to get to the ripe fruit on the loquat tree.

"Do you want to go sit by the fireplace?" Katie asked after she'd finished making her drink and cleaning up at the coffee bar.

"Sure." Christy followed Katie through the vacant lodge to the couch in front of a large stone fireplace. "It feels funny to have this whole place to ourselves."

"Enjoy the peace and quiet while you can. There's a big group coming in tomorrow and they'll be here until Tuesday."

"Will you be on duty as the barista while they're here?"

"Only part of the time. Eli and I managed to clear our calendars pretty much while you guys are here."

The large stone fireplace didn't have a fire going, but the sofa in front of it was still a nice and comfy place to sit. The speckled upholstery carried the permanent scent of wood smoke, and Christy could imagine how inviting this corner of the lodge would be with a roaring fire. "This is your spot, isn't it?"

The past and the present were colliding and Christy found herself touching the couch first before sitting down, because even though she'd never been here before, this spot felt familiar at the same time. It must be because she'd done several video calls with Katie and Eli when they were seated here on this same couch.

"Yeah, this is our favorite hangout spot. We do a lot of cuddling right here." Katie grinned.

"I can see why you love it here."

Katie put her coffee on the end table and confidently rested her feet on the thick wooden coffee table in front of the couch. "The pictures I've sent you didn't tell the whole story, do they?"

"No. They didn't. And it's not just the beautiful grounds. When I met Eli's parents at breakfast, I could tell how much they love you. That's why I said I can see why you love it here. This is your spot in a lot of ways."

"Yeah, I guess it is. I like having a 'spot.'" Katie leaned her head back and folded her hands over her stomach in a posture of complete relaxation. "What's that saying about 'home is where your heart is'? Well, my heart is here and that's because Eli is here. This is home for both of us."

Christy thought about the similar comments Carolyn had made about how Las Palmas was the home of her heart. Both of these two strategic women in her life knew where their place was on this tumbling planet.

A sorrowful sort of jealousy rose in Christy's spirit.

They're home. Carolyn and Katie both know where they belong. I wish I had the same sense of security. I also wish Todd would open up to me about what he's feeling. He liked to process things quietly and privately, but she hated feeling cut off from him this way.

Katie turned her head toward Christy. Her green eyes seemed to glow with a hidden secret. In what could almost be considered a whisper for Katie's usual exuberant standards, she confided in Christy. "I love him. I really do."

Christy pulled all her thoughts back to Katie and Eli and returned a smile as she whispered, "I know you do."

That one, sweet, long-awaited interchange of Katie's glowing heart reminded Christy that she was here to celebrate her best friend's marriage. She and Todd would eventually have a chance to talk through everything they had experienced in Las Palmas. She liked to be left alone when she was sick; he liked to be left alone when he was processing. She wanted to respect that quality in him. For now, it was more important that they be attuned to Katie and Eli and their time of celebration.

"I mean, I didn't even know I was capable of loving someone this much," Katie said. "I thought I loved Rick. And maybe I did love him in a beginner sort of way, like riding a kiddie bike with training wheels. But when the training wheels came off I couldn't balance. The relationship didn't go anywhere. You know all this. You were there. It was just a series of crashes and scraped-up emotions. With Eli though it's the Tour de France on the best racing bike ever made."

Christy smiled at her friend's quirky analogy.

Katie sat up. "No, actually, with Eli it's like a bicycle built for two. A mountain bike, not a racing bike. A mountain bike built to take all the bumps in the road."

Christy tried to remember an African saying Eli had told Katie over a year ago. It became the poignant phrase that motivated Katie to leave everything behind and go to Kenya with him. "What was that saying about going far together?"

"If you want to go fast, go alone. If you want to go far, go together." Katie reached for her mug and wrapped her hands around it. "That's us. We're going far together on an African mountain bike built for two."

She glanced at Christy and added, "Now come on. How romantic is that? An African mountain bike built for two. I've never seen such a thing, but if somebody would write a love song with that imagery, don't you think it would be a big hit?"

"Oh, absolutely."

Katie shifted her position so she could face Christy directly. Her countenance seemed to be sprinkled with happiness glitter. "Enough about me and my perfect life and love story worthy of a top-ten hit song. Let's talk about you."

Christy smiled a protective smile.

"Are you and Todd doing okay? Because you both seemed like you were on automatic pilot this morning at breakfast. Not that I blame you. It took me at least two weeks to get acclimated here. I just wanted to make sure everything was okay."

"It is," Christy said with wobbly confidence.

"Good. Because we are so excited that you guys are here and we have so much we want to talk about with you. I can't believe Eli and I are getting married. I mean, when I think of all the years I watched you and Todd work through your enviable relationship and thought that God had put me on the 'maybe list' . . . "

"The maybe list?"

"Yeah, like maybe He had somebody He wanted me to go through life with and maybe He didn't. It was God's little secret and one I always felt He enjoyed keeping to Himself.

Like a little joke. Only the joke is on me now because I am happier and more at home than I have ever been in my life. Ever."

Christy was still thinking about Katie's comment on Christy and Todd having an "enviable" relationship. From her viewpoint, the many years and the agonizing ups and downs had not been envy-worthy. The way things were between them right now was especially not envy-worthy.

"It makes me wish I would have trusted God more during all those years when I felt stuck in the maybe-zone. He knows what's best for us, Christy. He really does. He accomplishes His purposes for us in His time and in His way. I believe that now more than ever."

Christy felt her heart calming by just being in the glow of Katie's happiness. She was so glad for her friend. Katie's parents, who had never been the nurturing sort, were barely involved in her life and definitely weren't coming to her wedding. That was part of the reason why Katie had originally welcomed the idea of Bob and Marti coming. They were the closest thing Katie had to an "aunt" and "uncle" who were interested in her life.

"So, back to the topic of you," Katie said. "What is your take on this whole thing with Marti? I didn't understand why you guys were so upset in the van last night when I said that she called me and she's coming on Monday."

"I wouldn't say any of us were upset."

"Your uncle sure looked like he was."

"I think he was frustrated that Marti didn't talk it over with him first. It's been hard to communicate because our phones haven't worked as well as we thought they would over here. Plus the time difference has made it difficult to call at a time when my aunt is able to talk."

"But he got ahold of her late last night, right? Isn't that what he said at breakfast?"

"Yes. I wasn't there when he called her, but he said that my mom is doing well, so that's great news."

"But it's not great news that Marti is headed this way?"

Christy considered her answer carefully. "I think it's probably going to be good that she's here. It was good that she wasn't in the Canaries because I don't think I would have had the chance to get to know Carolyn and her relatives the way I did if Marti had been there."

Christy told Katie about the Women of the Canaries, their loyalty and enthusiastic involvement in each other's lives. She told her about Abuela Teresa and how she challenged Christy to "make peace with her curves and honor her bones." She even got up and demonstrated how she had danced with the Women of the Canaries "from the stomach up."

"And Todd danced with me, Katie. I'm sure we looked hilarious but it was so fun. I loved it!"

Katie grinned. "Good. Because I have a pretty good idea we'll end up with some spontaneous dancing at our reception. We're inviting a bunch of Kenyans and they have to sing and dance at everything. It's awesome. You're going to love it."

"I'm sure I will. Todd will love the music. And I'm guessing Uncle Bob will fit right in like he did in the Canaries."

Katie's expression turned more serious. "What about Marti? Do you think she is going to ruin the fun? Because when I said months ago that I liked the idea of her coming, it was because she's always been there, you know? It wouldn't feel right if she wasn't here."

"I don't think she'll ruin anything." Christy hoped she sounded more convincing than she felt. "We won't let her. I know she wanted to be here for you because she loves you, Katie. In her own way, I know she does because of all the ways she helped me with details for your big day. She really wants to be here."

"That means a lot to me."

"I know."

"Do you remember Eli's Uncle Jonathan? Or I guess I should say Professor Ambrose since that's how you remember him from Rancho."

"He married your former resident director, right?"

"Yeah. Julia. Eli and I were both in their wedding last year."

"I remember."

"They were going to try to come but when we decided to move up the date they couldn't adjust their schedules."

"Do you wish you would have kept the April dates so they could have come?"

"No. It wasn't a sure thing that they could come in April either. For us, or I should say for Eli's parents, who live here and know the seasons better than we do, it was more important to schedule the safari before the rainy season was at its peak."

Katie spouted a dozen details about the safari plans: the flight to the Masai Mara National Reserve, the early morning game drive, and the special location they'd selected for their sunset ceremony.

"By sundown next Friday, I will be a married woman."

"Yes, you will." Christy remembered the honeymoon plans from earlier conversations. Katie and Eli would stay at the safari lodgings Friday and Saturday night while the group from the wedding would return to the conference center on Saturday morning. There would be a reception for them in the dining room when Eli and Katie came back Sunday evening.

"As for the rest of the plans while you're here," Katie said, "if you want, we can start making a list now. Or we could wait until the guys get back from their tour of the grounds with Eli's dad, if you think Todd wants to be in on the planning."

"Either way. We want to help any way we can. Put us to work. We're ready."

"Work? What about the touristy stuff? Don't you want to see the Rift Valley from the overlook? Or go feed a giraffe out of the palm of your hand at the giraffe reserve?"

"I'll ask Todd if he has anything on his wish list. I have a feeling he'll say that the safari is plenty as far as sightseeing goes for us." Christy remembered Katie's cute photos she posted after her first visit to the giraffe reserve. "Todd might want to see the giraffes."

"What about your wish list? Do you want to go on a tour of the house where they filmed Out of Africa, or what about Lake Naivasha? That's a really pretty destination. Oh! And if your stomach can handle it we could go into Nairobi and eat at the Carnivore Restaurant."

"Is that where they serve ostrich?" Christy made a squeamish face. Her stomach still didn't like the sound of that.

"Okay, so no ostrich yet. But we definitely have to walk in the tea fields. That's my favorite place to see. And it's super close."

Christy reached over and squeezed Katie's hand. "We don't need to go sightseeing to any of those destinations while we're here, Katie."

"Are you sure? There's lots to see."

"I know. But Todd and I came to see you. You're the destination."

Katie grew quiet. "I've never been anybody's destination before."

"Well, you are now. You and Eli. And what you and I are doing here: being together, talking, just being 'us'—this is what I had at the top of my wish list."

"I have missed being 'us.'"

"Me, too."

"Although," Katie's pout spread upward in a winsome expression, "I am kinda looking forward to Eli and I becoming 'us.' I mean, you were a great college roomie and all, but you've been replaced."

Christy grinned and remembered the gifts she had for Katie. "By the way, is there a chance that someone here is going to have a shower for you? Or have you already had one?"

"No. They don't do stuff like that here. At least not the same way we used to do it back at Rancho Corona."

"I brought some gifts. I wasn't sure when would be the

best time to give them to you."

"Gifts? You can give me gifts anytime. We don't need to plan a party for that."

Christy decided then that she would come up with her own special little time with just Katie so she could give her the nightgown, robe, and the lace handkerchief from Abuela Teresa. She liked the idea of it being a time for just the two of them.

"But honestly, Eli and I don't need anything. We both are low maintenance, as you know. We're just looking forward to setting up our own little nest and being actively married. If you know what I mean."

"I wish I had my camera right now because you are glowing, my friend. Absolutely glowing."

Katie tilted her head and got a mischievous gleam in her eye. "Speaking of glowing, tell me for real. Are you sure you're not pregnant?"

Christy hesitated. "I'm pretty sure I'm not."

"But you could be."

"Well, maybe. I'm not sure. I really don't think I am. But I am, as you put it, 'actively married,' so, you know, there is always some chance of getting pregnant."

"Why don't you take a pregnancy test? That way at least you'll know."

"Where would we get one? At a store?"

"There aren't any stores, like you think of a store, within walking distance from here. Well, at least what you and I would consider within walking distance. But there is a doctor over at the Rift Valley Mission Center who comes here fairly often. I can call him and ask him to bring a pregnancy test with him."

Christy bit her lower lip. She knew she was biting her lower lip and she didn't care. This was a big deal. She'd only taken a home-pregnancy test once before. It was a few weeks after they'd gotten married and her cycle was off schedule. The test was negative, but the whole process had made the fact that she was actively married feel quite real.

It was no small thing for Christy to contemplate the possibility of a child being formed inside her. In a way, she'd rather not know and just keep going until it was clear that her life was carrying another life and therefore everything was about to be radically altered.

Katie lowered her chin. "Hello, Cleopatra. Come on back. You just took a long trip down de Nile, didn't you?"

Christy liked the idea of staying in denial a little longer. "I think I can wait at least a few days to see if my confused body is able to reset to this altitude and time zone."

"I'm going ask Dr. Powell to bring one next time he comes. That way at least you'd have one."

"Okay."

"You're sure you're okay with that?"

Christy nodded.

"Because the thing is, it's not always easy to get medicine and supplies whenever you want them here. It's always better to be prepared."

Christy nodded again. Deep inside though, a resounding question bounced off her spirit. *Be prepared for what? We don't even know where we're going to live. God's mysterious ways and perfect timing could not include a baby for us right now. It just couldn't.*

fourteen

*T*hat night Christy had a crazy dream.

She dreamed that she and Todd had a baby girl. She was born with a big flower-power daisy decal on her bald little head. She kept crying and Christy was trying to get her to go to sleep. The problem was there was no place to put her down to nap, because when Christy looked around in her dream, they were living inside of Gussie the new Bussie!

They were parked at San Clemente State Beach and Todd had a fishing pole strung out into the ocean, trying to catch dinner for them. Christy was wearing a long, tie-dyed, hippy-girl dress that was clinging to her legs. She had on big hoop earrings her daughter kept reaching for and tried to pull from her pierced ears.

In her dream, Christy called out to Todd, and when he turned around, he let go of the fishing pole, even though the tension on the line suggested he'd just caught a big one.

She must have cried out in her sleep because she awoke when Todd roused her. "Hey. Christy. Christy."

She opened her eyes and knew she was in bed somewhere

with her husband in a darkened room. They weren't living gypsy style at the beach in Gussie. They didn't have a baby.

Todd smoothed back her hair and tried to untangle her from the flowing white sheet that was wrapped around her leg. "You all right?"

"It was just a dream," Christy said, trying to get her racing heart to calm down. "A stupid dream." Stupid or not, she knew that her subconscious had combined all her worst fears and put them into a not-so-entertaining midnight performance for her poor jet-lagged brain.

"Were there monkeys in your dream?"

"What?"

"Monkeys." Todd stretched out his legs and readjusted the blankets. "After all the warnings Eli gave us about the monkeys, I think I was dreaming that one had gotten into our bed. Now that I see the sheets, I think it was just you thrashing around. You're my little monkey."

Christy wasn't sure why she let the next sentence pop out of her mouth just then, but it was out. "I was dreaming that we had a little monkey."

"Really." Todd took her comment with good humor. "Boy or girl?"

"Girl. But not a monkey, monkey. She was a baby, baby."

Todd propped himself up on his elbow and leaned close to Christy. "You dreamed we had a baby girl?"

"We were living in Gussie, at the beach, and you were fishing and our daughter had a big flower-power daisy on her bald head. She wouldn't stop crying and there was no place to put her down for a nap."

Todd rolled over and busted up. He laughed the best sort of deep belly laugh. Usually Christy loved it when he laughed like that because it was as if he was releasing a bit of the little kid in him that hadn't experienced much of a childhood.

This time, though, there were far too many elements of her dream that were linked to reality, and that made it a nightmare of Hitchcock proportions to her.

"Todd, it wasn't funny. It was awful."

"Are you kidding? A flower-power decal on her head?" He laughed again. "That's hilarious."

"I'm serious. The dream seemed so real." She reached to turn on the lamp on the end table. It didn't turn on. She tried again. Still no light. Along with the monkey warnings, Eli had made sure they had several taper candles and matches in their room in case the electricity went out.

Todd reached over to the end table on his side of the bed and lit a match from the small box with a picture of a zebra on the cover. The faint scent of sulfur lingered in the air between them while the illumination from the candle gave their room a romantic glow.

He was still slightly grinning as he said, "Look. No monkeys in the bed. No decals on anyone's forehead. Nothin' to be frightened about."

"Unless I really am pregnant."

Now she had his full, sober attention. "Are you?"

"I don't think I am, but how would I know? I mean, I'm a few days late but with all the travel and time changes, that doesn't necessarily mean anything."

"And you've been late before, right?"

"Yes. And those times it seemed to be related to stress, so that's why I'm thinking it's just all the travel."

"Can you find out for sure?" Now Todd was the one with the edge of tension in his voice.

She told him about the pregnancy test Katie was going to ask for from the local surgeon. They lowered their voices and speculated on the details. If she was expecting, the baby could arrive before the end of December. That thought freaked her out.

"I don't feel like I'm ready," she whispered.

He drew her close and held her, using his presence and steady breathing to comfort her. "Our times are in His hands, Kilikina. They always have been; they always will be."

"I know."

"We have to trust God."

"I know." She drew in a deep breath and exhaled slowly. "Todd?"

"Yeah?"

"How are you doing with your dad and everything?"

He didn't move. He didn't answer. Christy immediately regretted bringing up such a big topic in the middle of the night because clearly he wasn't ready to talk about it. She tried to back out as graciously as possible.

"I just want you to know that I really feel for you. We can talk about it whenever you want to talk about it. Or not."

"Okay. Later."

"Later," Christy repeated. It was so hard to step away from that conversation right now. Christy felt that as long as she had put all her middle-of-the-night fears and thoughts out there, Todd should do the same. But he didn't go for adding drama on top of drama. For now, she'd be the one who was processing all her emotions out loud. As Todd said, he'd tell her what he was feeling "later."

"Rest," Todd said softly.

"I love you," she whispered.

"I know. And I love you. Now trust God and be at peace." Todd shifted his position and blew out the candle.

The smoke tickled Christy's nose and made her think of campfires by the beach and all the times during her high school summers that she had gathered with their Forever Friends at sunset. It was her favorite happy place, and at the moment she had only sweet memories of that time in her life. Todd and Doug would play worship songs on their guitars, and she would sing the lyrics that came from Bible verses, like the one in Proverbs 3 she'd underlined in her travel Bible.

"Trust in the Lord with all your heart and do not lean on your own understanding. In all your ways acknowledge Him, and He will direct your paths."

In her mind's eye Christy could see the marshmallows roasting on the ends of long sticks. She could feel the warmth of Todd's navy-blue hooded sweatshirt he let her wear when the sun had gone down and the breeze made the hair on her arms stand up. She imagined she could see the faces of Doug, Tracy, Heather, Katie, and Antonio. She could hear their banter and see Todd's broad smile as he fixed his gaze on her from across the fire pit.

Home.

The singular word filled her mind, unbidden. She couldn't deny it. Newport Beach was the place where she gave her heart to the Lord. It was where she met Todd and where she had returned more times than she could count. And every time she returned there, she felt happy. Deep, soul happy as if she was reunited with an old friend.

With that one beautiful word, *home*, came a sense of peace that felt as thick and comforting as the warm blankets that covered her as Todd held her in a tender embrace. She didn't feel that way about any other place on the earth. Only Newport Beach.

God, You know all things. Why would I feel that Newport Beach is the home of my heart if it's not going to be possible for us to live there? I want to trust You with all my heart. I really do.

She could tell by Todd's breathing that he had fallen back to sleep. Being sheltered by him, in the covering of his strong arms, made Christy think about Katie's comment earlier that day when the two of them were by the fireplace. Katie had said that Brockhurst was her home because Eli was here. Her home was where her heart was.

Is it more accurate to view my home as being wherever Todd is? He was such an integral part of my love for Newport Beach from the beginning. Is that why my heart feels at home there? Do I have it turned inside out? Am I really most at home whenever and wherever I am with him?

Christy let her unresolved questions float off like the high, puffy, butter-edged clouds she had noticed on their walk to the dining hall earlier that evening. She noticed them because they were so unhurried. She could rest now and sleep without knowing the answers to the questions her nightmare had infused into her psyche. She didn't need to know where her home was going to be in December.

For now, her home was right here, under Todd's sheltering embrace.

Over the next few days Christy learned several things about waiting. The main realization was that waiting didn't get any easier the older you got. She thought her difficult years of waiting were behind her now that she and Todd were married. All through their dating years it had been a series of starts and stops, a progression of patience-testing weeks and months. Why did she think life would be smooth sailing once she and Todd walked down the aisle together?

She also learned that waiting could be an action verb.

She'd tried her best to stop waiting for her cycle to "kick into normal." She'd been convinced that it would, as soon as she got enough sleep to conquer her jet lag. But sleep or no sleep didn't seem to make a difference. She tried to stop waiting for Dr. Powell to make his visit to Brockhurst with the pregnancy test. And she tried to stop waiting to know the answer to the question "Am I pregnant or not?" before she entered into the everyday rhythm of the conference center.

If actively waiting was supposed to be a way of testing to see if she was trusting God, Christy was sure she was failing the test.

The large group Katie had mentioned arrived on Thursday afternoon. Christy volunteered to help check in the conferees. It was a group of worship leaders who had come from all over Kenya for their yearly conference. Christy loved watching how the men and women greeted each other with unhindered joy. Some of the women wore brightly colored kaftans with equally vibrant headdresses. Some of the men came in looking as if they'd just played a round of golf, while others arrived in full dress pants and jackets, their dark faces glistening with perspiration as a result of wearing so many layers on the journey up to the refreshing eight-thousand-foot altitude of Brockhurst.

As Christy kept busy helping at registration, Uncle Bob spent time with Eli's dad, Jim. It was fun to see him so engaged and fitting right in with the other men at the mission conference center. He prayed with them and accepted their invitation to join in their weekly staff meeting on Friday morning. Christy never would have guessed her uncle would dive in this way. How would things change when Marti arrived? Would he be free to keep up the pace he'd set with the leadership at Brockhurst?

Christy noticed a different side of Todd, as well. He liked to work. Or more accurately, he liked to serve. He joined Eli and volunteered to help carry luggage to the cabins for the conferees. He and Eli were both working up an appetite as they tromped up and down the hill to deliver the bags to the various outlying cottages.

At one point Christy wanted to laugh because it felt like they were a bunch of little kids playing "hotel." She stood behind the counter with the list of conferees. When the guests entered, they greeted her and each other enthusiastically and told Christy their names. Most of them needed to spell their names for her, but she caught on soon enough. She checked them off the list and handed them their assigned room key.

Katie stood beside her and handed out maps of the grounds, circled their rooms and offered each guest a bottle of water. This sort of helping out was Christy's favorite because it tapped into her gift of hospitality. She loved making people feel welcome and at home. She even perfected the phrase Eli had greeted them with at the airport and said a warm, "karibu sana."

"Do you know what that greeting means?" Katie asked when she and Christy hit a lull in their check-in line.

"Uh-oh. Am I saying something I shouldn't? I heard Eli say it at the airport when we arrived and I've heard other people say it here. I thought it meant 'hello' or 'welcome.'"

"It does. I mean, that's how's it's used. But I love the phrase because in Swahili it literally means, 'draw close.' Isn't that good?"

Christy repeated the phrase. "Karibu sana. 'Draw close.' I love that!"

"I thought you would."

The door opened and the next round of weary but smiling conferees entered.

"Karibu sana!" Christy called out.

"*Asante,*" the group replied with equal enthusiasm.

For the rest of the day Christy made good use of her two Swahili phrases. It amazed her to watch the way Eli interacted with the conferees. He carried on a few complete conversations in Swahili, and he expressed a visible sense of deep respect for all the men who were older than him.

"This is going to sound crazy," Christy told Katie when they sat down to dinner in the crowded dining hall that evening, "but Eli seems like a different person here."

"Different?"

"Like he's taller or older or something."

Katie nodded. "I know exactly what you mean. He flourishes here. In California he was so completely out of the culture of his homeland. He's told me that he felt most of the time that at Rancho he was on the edge just looking in and trying to figure out how to fit in. There's so much he didn't understand about the way we do things and how people treated each other. When he first got there he acted like he does here, warm and outgoing. He hugged all the guys he met and respectfully lowered his eyes and didn't touch any of the girls. You know how odd that made him seem."

"It makes so much sense now."

"I know. This is where he can be his truest self. You should see him in the villages, especially with the children. He's definitely his best version of himself there."

Christy thought about how quick she'd been to judge Eli when she first met him. He seemed odd at times, the way he hung back, always observing but slow to get the jokes and cautious before he entered in. When he did have something to say, it was rich with meaning and intentional. She couldn't imagine how difficult it must have been for him to watch all the surface relationships so many people had on campus during college.

"I can see why Eli was so attracted to you, Katie."

"Are you going to say that odd people attract other odd people?"

"No. You're real, Katie. You always have been. You are who you are all the time. I can see how much that stood out to Eli when you guys were at Rancho Corona. You weren't like any of the other girls who had learned how to put on the fake smile or say things they didn't really mean. You were just you."

"And I can be me here, too. I know I tried to explain this before on one of our calls but in some ways I feel more freedom to be my rambunctious self here than I ever did back in California. It's not at all how I expected things to be here."

Christy nodded her agreement with Katie's statement and swallowed her bite of chicken. "This is so good. I can't figure out what the flavor is. There's lemon and pepper on it, but something else, too. It's so moist."

"We have a great chef here, as you probably noticed."

"I didn't notice the first few days because all I was eating was that hot cereal that looks like cream of rice but tastes like unsalted, soggy popcorn."

"*Ugali,*" Katie said.

Todd and Eli arrived just then, sliding their trays on the table and sitting across from Katie and Christy with the look of two starving laborers. Both of them had politely waited to be the last to go through the buffet line, but clearly the kitchen had not run out of food. Their plates were loaded.

"Who's eating ugali?" Eli asked. "I didn't see any in the line."

"I was telling Christy that's what she's been eating for

breakfast. She thought it was cream of rice."

"Do you like it?" Eli asked Christy.

She tilted her head from side to side. "It's not bad with honey and bananas."

Todd bowed his head and prayed silently before diving in. Christy loved that discipline of her husband's. She often forgot to pause and be thankful before she ate. Todd always seemed to be grateful and never took the gift of having food for granted.

"Dr. Powell is here," Eli said, collecting a stack of baby carrots on his fork. His gaze was fixed on Katie as if waiting for her to react to his announcement.

"Oh, good. I need to see him." Katie gave Christy a glance. She hoped Katie remembered how discreet Christy had asked her to be about the pregnancy test.

Eli raised his chin and kept looking at Katie as if waiting for further explanation. When she didn't offer any more information, Eli said, "Dr. Powell pulled me aside and gave me a fatherly sort of talking to."

"He did?" Katie took a bite of her dinner roll and seemed nonchalant about Eli's statement.

"Yes, he did." Eli put his fork down. "Katie, I think you have some explaining to do."

Todd grinned. "You know what you guys look like right now? Like one of those old reruns of Lucy and Ricky Ricardo."

Katie made her best *I Love Lucy* face as if she were looking into the camera. Her lower lip went slack and twisted. Her eyes grew round and unblinking. She added a rather unattractive throaty sound as if she knew she was in trouble now.

Eli put up both hands as if trying to hold back a tide of unwanted impersonations of television stars he had never heard of since most of his childhood was spent without a television in remote parts of Africa. "I have no idea what you guys are talking about, but Katie, what did you talk to Dr. Powell about?"

Her expression morphed to a serious one. She glanced at Christy and then at Todd as if looking for an okay to let Eli in on what was going on.

"She talked to the doctor about me." Christy kept her voice low. "There's a chance I might be pregnant so she asked him to bring a pregnancy test."

Eli's eyes widened and he started laughing. Loudly.

Christy pulled back. This was not funny to her. She had already gone through so many emotions already as she processed all the possibilities. Why was Eli laughing?

"It's for you, then," Eli said as he caught his breath. "The pregnancy test is for you."

Christy nodded, wishing he would lower his voice. Todd's eyes gave away the fact that he wanted to laugh, too, but was doing his best to hold back.

"How can you guys sit there and laugh?" Her face burned. "This isn't a joke. It's a big deal."

"Kilikina." Todd stopped her by reaching across the table and resting his hand on her arm.

Eli reached across and put his hand on Christy's other arm. "You don't understand. Dr. Powell thought the pregnancy test was for Katie."

"For me?" Katie perked up.

"Yes, that's why he pulled me aside and wanted to have a fatherly talk about repentance and patience and how I needed to be a man of honor."

Christy relaxed. The guys withdrew their rough hands. Katie burst into the same wild and wonderful laughter Eli had given way to. Todd grinned at Christy and gave her a funny little wink. Eli dug into his fork full of carrots as if nothing out of the ordinary had just transpired.

Katie grabbed Christy's arm. "Come on. Let's go."

"Go where?"

"To find Dr. Powell."

"Don't you want to wait until we're finished eating?"

"No, come on. We have to find out if you're preggers and

we have to find out now."

Christy wasn't sure why she let Katie yank her out of her seat and take her cruising through the dining room. They found Dr. Powell seated at a round table in the side annex. He just happened to be sitting by Eli's parents and Uncle Bob as well as several of the administration leaders from Brockhurst.

In an overly "Katie" way, she stepped up to the table and said, "Dr. Powell, this is my *married* friend, Christy. She's *married* to Todd. He's right over there. Remember how I asked you to bring something for my *married* friend the next time you came?"

Dr. Powell's face looked like a sudden sunrise had come upon it. "Oh, I see. If you'll pardon me," Dr. Powell said to the others seated around the table. He stood and reached for his backpack. "Why don't we go into the lounge, Christy?"

Katie followed them and the whole transaction felt awkward and embarrassing. Christy didn't know why these sorts of moments were so much more humiliating to her than they ever seemed to be to her redheaded friend.

The good thing was that she had a pregnancy test in hand and in a few moments she could find out what was happening in her body. At least she thought that was a good thing.

"Come on." Katie took Christy by the arm and directed her downstairs to one of the less-used restrooms.

"I can do this later." Christy was thinking about the yummy chicken going cold on her dinner plate.

"Or you could do it now." Katie didn't slow her pace or give any indication she was going to let up until Christy took the test. "Then you'll know. We'll all know. You need to know. Don't you think you need to know? I think you need to know. Come on."

Christy knew all too well that when Hurricane Katie picked up speed, there was no stopping her. Christy bit her lower lip and took the next step into her future with her best friend pulling her forward.

Home of Our Hearts

fifteen

"*T*his door doesn't close." Christy was sequestered in one of the downstairs bathroom stalls at the main lodge and had the pregnancy kit in her hand.

"Don't worry about it. No one else is in here. All you have to do is pee on the stick, right?"

"Yes. But I'd prefer to do that in private."

"Okay, okay. I forget how American you still are. Here. I'll hold the door shut for you."

Christy opened the box and pulled out the wand. She'd taken one before and this one looked similar to the one she'd gotten from the grocery store at home. She turned the box over to check the directions in order to make sure she did it right.

"Did you do it yet?"

"No. I'm reading the instructions." Christy paused. "Actually, I take that back. I'm not reading the instructions because they're in French."

"Aren't all pregnancy tests about the same?"

"I don't know. This looks similar."

"Just pee on the stick and see what happens."

Christy got herself situated. Her bladder seemed to have suddenly gone on strike.

"Think about waterfalls," Katie said. "That always makes me feel like I have to pee."

Christy tried to ignore her overly helpful friend. She didn't even like hearing Katie say the word pee. It made her think of the way her dad had avoided saying the names of female body parts when they were at the hospital awaiting her mother's diagnosis. She was more of a blend of her mom and dad than she'd ever realized before. Modesty, privacy, discretion. Those didn't seem to be Katie's go-to life themes, especially now that she lived here.

"Okay. I'm done," Christy said.

"What does it say?"

"You have to wait a minute."

"Can I open the door now?"

"Hold on. Okay. Go ahead. You can let go of the door now." Christy stepped out with the wand in one hand and went over to the sink to wash up.

"Can I hold it?"

Christy laughed for the first time since this tumble of events had started. "You want to hold the stick?"

"Yes! I do. Christy, this is an epic moment. You, me, here in a stuffy bathroom, discovering the course of your life." Her eyes widened. "Hey! Todd should be here. Do you want me to go get him and bring him in here for the big reveal?"

"No. Trust me. He'll be fine if he skips this part of it." Christy looked at the stick.

"What does it say?"

"I'm not sure."

Katie leaned in. "What are we looking for? I don't see anything."

"It's supposed to show two lines if I'm pregnant and one line if I'm not."

They stood with their heads together, watching. Christy turned the wand toward the light over the sink and then away from the light. "It doesn't seem to be doing anything."

"Did you do it right? Maybe you need to pee on it again."

Christy was confident she'd done it right. She didn't want to go back into the stall for another try while Katie chattered on about waterfalls and rushing rivers.

"Maybe it's a defective kit. Did it have an expiration date?"

"I don't know. It was all in French."

"Then how do you know for sure that it's not one line for positive and two lines for negative? Oh, wait. Look! There's a line." Katie started to squeal. "That means something!"

Christy didn't see a line. She held it closer to the light.

"Isn't that a line? Yes. That's definitely a line. Or wait. It's two skinny lines, isn't it? Two lines right next to each other. Do you see them, Chris? Those are two skinny lines and two lines is positive, right?"

"I think it's supposed to be two separate lines. This looks like it's filling in and turning into only one thick line. What do you think?" Christy relinquished the wand to Katie and stepped back into the stall to get the box she'd left on top of the tank. She thought maybe the folded-up paper inside would have pictures that would remedy her problem with the language barrier.

Katie followed her into the stall, as uninhibited as if she were a Woman of the Canaries. "I think you could be right. It looks like one thick line now and not two separate skinny lines."

Christy turned in the tight space and bumped Katie's shoulder. Katie let out an unexpected squawk and Christy heard the *plop* before she saw that the wand had fallen into the toilet.

"I dropped your baby!" Katie immediately plunged her hand into the toilet without hesitating.

"Katie, no! Don't. Just leave it!"

Too late. Katie had retrieved the wand and dashed to the sink where she was running the stick and her hand under the flowing water. The sink produced cool water. No hot water. Christy coaxed her friend to pump gobs of liquid soap on her hands. With the water running at full throttle and all the soap being exchanged between the two of them, tiny bubbles began to rise and float over their heads.

"I am so, so, so, sorry, Christy."

"It's okay. Don't worry about it, Katie. Really."

"But I ruined it. Look. It still has only one line. It might have developed into two lines if I hadn't dropped it. I'm so sorry."

A cluster of tiny soap bubbles had attached to Katie's hair and reminded Christy of the crown of baby's breath Katie had worn as a bridesmaid in Todd and Christy's wedding.

She smiled at her endearing friend. A calmness seemed to come over her. "You know what? It's okay. It really is. I'll just have to find out for sure the old-fashioned way."

"What do you mean? You're going to just wait to see what your body does?"

Christy nodded. She could hear Abuela Teresa's firm yet softly spoken words. *"You must make peace with your curves and honor your bones. You must always live from the stomach up."*

"I'm okay with waiting. I really am."

"Well, I'm not okay with it." Katie dried her hands and wadded up the paper towel, then tossed it toward the trash bin but missed. "I want to know now."

Katie bent over and picked up the paper towel, then placed it into the rubbish. When she did, a huge cockroach scampered over the side of the bin and scurried out under the door before Christy had a chance to react.

"Was that what I thought it was?"

"Yeah. They grow big here in the tropics."

It seemed funny to Christy that Katie was so acclimated to the bugs that it didn't creep her out even a little. With a final shiver at the sight of the now-departed cockroach, Christy placed the wand inside a paper towel and folded it up. She reverently placed it gingerly on top of the other tossed-out paper towels in the rubbish bin, so as not to disturb any more creepy dwellers. As fine as she was about not knowing for sure if she was pregnant, it still felt as if she were laying to rest the wisp of a small dream.

In her gut, she knew the test was negative. She wasn't carrying a new little life inside of her. That intuition led her to feel a whisper of sadness and a low hum of loss as she and Katie exited the restroom. What a different reaction they both would have had if the test had been 100 percent positive. Instead of exciting news, they stepped into the lower lobby area with somber faces.

Todd was standing there, only ten feet away from the women's restroom. He was leaning against one of the thick wooden support posts, looking casual with his arms folded in an "x" shape. It was the same posture he took on when he stood on the shore and watched the waves, reading the wind and waiting for a good set before paddling out and giving it his all.

Christy could tell when she saw his face that he had been there the whole time and he had heard everything. She and Katie hadn't exactly tried to keep their voices down, since they were in the lower level of the lodge and they didn't think anyone else was around.

Todd looked slightly amused and at the same time, a little sad and sympathetic toward his wife. He opened his arms and Christy went to him, welcoming his arms around her, feeling the warmth of his body as he held her close and kissed the top of her head.

"Well, I see my work here is done. Take it away, Todd." Katie headed up the stairs. "I'll see you guys later."

"Yeah. Later," Todd said.

Christy and Todd held each other and swayed slightly in a lullaby sort of way.

"You okay?"

Christy nodded. She pulled back and let him see her Mona Lisa smile and clear eyes to prove that she really was okay. "You know, you've been asking me that a lot on this trip."

"I suppose I have. Always for good reason."

"I know. I think my body is jumbled from all the travel. I'm not pregnant. I'm sure of it."

"Because of the test?"

"No. Just in my gut I know I'm not."

Todd lifted her chin with his finger. "You know it would be fine if you were."

"I know."

"God would provide for us like He always does."

"I know."

They kissed, sealing their trust in each other, in the future, and in God's plan for them. When they pulled back, Todd said, "I only have one question. What was Katie talking about when she said they grow exceptionally large in the tropics?"

Christy told Todd about the cockroach, giving an involuntary shiver as she recalled the creepy creature.

"Did he look like this guy?" Todd lifted his foot so Christy could see a smushed cockroach on the bottom of his boot.

"You got him."

"He didn't go down without a fight."

Christy slid her arm around her husband's waist and felt his strong arm cover her shoulders. "My hero."

"My bride."

As they rolled through the weekend, Christy thought several times about how comforting that moment of sheltering security had felt. She and Todd ended up going in different directions to assist with the conference and rarely saw each other during the day. For both of them it was easy to find their place and fit into the rhythm of life at Brockhurst.

On Sunday morning, after Christy had finished her bowl of ugali, honey, and bananas, she decided to spend a few moments on one of the benches under a sheltering tree. It had rained during the night, and as the sun broke through the fleeing clouds, it looked as if the grass had sprouted tiny diamond bonnets. Christy was bundled up in her warmest sweater, jeans, and boots. She wiped the raindrops from the bench and zipped up her jacket against the sudden breeze.

Taking in the lush beauty of her surroundings, Christy automatically started praying for her mom as she had been for the past few weeks. She prayed for Todd and their future. An unexpected thought settled on her.

What if we lived here?

She was used to Todd tossing out lots of possibilities of living and serving in various remote parts of the world. This was the first time her thoughts had initiated such an option. Was it the beauty of this place, or maybe the delight of being back in everyday life with Katie that made her feel like she'd want to live here? Or was this a God-thing, as Katie would say? Was the Lord preparing her heart to move here? The fact that their future was so wide open was certainly a factor in why she was open to the possibility.

A bold little bird with bright-red tail feathers perched on the opposite end of the bench and tilted its head as if looking at Christy. She watched it calmly without moving. With one quick hop it came closer to Christy.

Karibu sana, little one. Draw close.

The bird took one more hop and was only inches away from her. Then with a final lurch, it nabbed a big spider making its way down the side of her jeans.

She sprang from the bench and shook all over, making sure the spider hadn't invited its extended family to crawl over her. She gave her arms and legs another vigorous shake and then shook her head back and forth just in case any critters had decided to catch a ride on her long hair today.

Okay, so maybe this isn't paradise.

Two conferees who had been in a deep conversation coming down the trail had stopped. Christy looked over and noticed they were watching her. One of the men started spontaneously doing what looked like a tribal dance move with his hands over his head and shaking his torso back and forth. Both men were smiling broadly, their white teeth lighting up their expressions.

"Spider," Christy called out, as if that would explain the version of her own tribal dance they had just witnessed.

The men laughed and gave her a friendly wave.

Still feeling embarrassed, Christy started down the lower path and headed for their stone cottage. She knew this fairly idyllic place wasn't a true representation of Kenya. This was a Scottish highland-inspired enclave tucked away at eight thousand feet. It was silly to say that she could move to Africa. This was a bubble. A lovely bubble, but not a clear representation of the people, the culture, or the Kenyan climate.

She reminded herself about the cockroach from the other night and remembered Todd's sheltering arms. She thought about the way she'd decided after her nightmare that like Katie, her home would always be wherever her husband was. The question now was, whether or not Todd was starting to attach himself to this place. Did he feel like he belonged here? He hadn't said anything if he did. But maybe he was gravitating toward living and serving here but was hesitant to tell Christy because of the way she'd responded in the past to his dreamy-eyed looks when he mentioned living in a hut in Papua New Guinea.

Christy picked up her pace. Her stomach was giving her fits and she couldn't get back to the cottage fast enough. After unlocking the door, she dashed in and went to the bathroom.

There was a reason for her clenched muscles. Her body was doing what it had done every month since she was eleven years old. It was just slow in getting in sync this month.

Okay. So, I'm not pregnant. Good to know. I'm okay with that.

What she wasn't okay with were the cramps. Christy went on the hunt for some ibuprofen in her cosmetic bag by the sink. She saw that Todd's phone was plugged in and the screen was lit up but the phone was on silence. A call was coming in. It was her mom's cell phone.

Christy quickly grabbed the phone. "Mom?"

"It's your father, Christy."

"Hi, Dad. How are you? How's Mom? Is everything okay?"

"Your mother is home now. She's right here. She wants to talk to you."

"Hi, honey. How's Africa?"

"Hi, Mom." Christy felt all her tensed, adrenaline-sparked muscles release as she leaned against the cool stucco wall. She could tell that her mom was back to her old self, or at least on her way back to being her sturdy, steady self. "Africa is great. How are you?"

"I'm much, much better. Your father brought me home today and I'm so happy to be back in my own bed. He and David cleaned up the whole house and had a big bouquet of flowers for me in our room. Pink carnations, just like the ones he gave me when we got engaged."

"Dad gave you pink carnations?"

"Yes. A great big bouquet. We didn't have money for an engagement ring. I've told you that before. We spent what we had on wedding bands. But he bought pink carnations for me on our engagement day."

Christy tried to remember any other time that her father had given her mother flowers. She couldn't think of one. Was it possible that her mom was so touched by the flowers in her room now because he'd only given her flowers that one other time?

"I didn't know that, Mom. I didn't know that yours and dad's flower was pink carnations."

Her mom chuckled. "I wouldn't say it was our flower."

"Of course it is. They mean a lot to you. Todd's and my flower is white carnations."

"Is that why you always wanted to keep those dried-up, musty carnation petals in that old Folgers coffee can?"

Christy smiled. It was a secret she'd never shared with her

mother. "Yes. Those were from the bouquet Todd gave me at the end of my summer at Bob and Marti's. He gave them to me in the middle of an intersection and kissed me while all the cars around us were honking."

"I had no idea he kissed you that first summer. You were only fourteen, Christy."

"Fifteen. I had my fifteenth birthday while I was there, remember?"

"That's right. Even so. Fifteen is still awfully young." She sounded as if she was glad that she hadn't known that piece of information until now.

"I know. I was young. Lots younger in experience than all the people I hung out with that summer. And you know what, Mom? I've been wanting to thank you. I mean, really thank you from the bottom of my heart."

"For what?"

"For being brave and for agreeing to let me spend that summer with Bob and Marti. My whole life changed that summer. I wouldn't be who I am now if you and Dad had been frightened of what might happen and refused to let me go." Silent tears were coursing down Christy's cheeks. "I love you, Mom. I'm so grateful you and Dad were brave."

It was quiet for a moment. Christy could hear her mom sniffing and she guessed her mom might be teary as well. "I'll tell you the truth, Christy. It was one of the most difficult things I've ever done, letting you go to California that summer."

"I can imagine."

"Marti was persistent, as you might imagine. I kept saying no, we needed you to stay home because we were going through the awful bankruptcy that caused us to leave the farm that fall. It was more difficult for me to let you go than to take all the steps we had to go through to settle the bankruptcy."

"I had no idea it was that hard." Christy had never thought much of all she had been spared by not being home during those difficult months. She'd never thought of how that season had been for her mother.

"Your father told me I needed to pray for you every day you were gone."

Christy started crying in earnest. Her emotions were all over the place just like her unreliable hormone system.

"And I did," her mom said firmly. "I prayed for you every day."

"Thank you so much, Mom. You have no idea how much that means to me. I love you." The sentiment flowed from a place deep inside her heart. She wanted to get to know her mother as a woman, the way she'd shared such sweet times with the Women of the Canaries. She wanted to understand what her mother's life had been like and if she had any dreams or wishes. She wanted to hear more stories of pink carnations and what her mother felt like when she found out she was pregnant with Christy.

Those conversations were for another time. What was at the forefront of Christy's thoughts at the moment was that her mother hadn't said why they'd called. Her dad wouldn't have placed the call unless there was something important to be said.

"Aside from being back home and in your own bed, how are you healing up? Have you been back to see the doctor?"

"Yes, and everything is as it should be. The lab reports came back negative so there's no concern that the growths were malignant."

It took a moment for the words to settle on Christy since her mother delivered them with no emotion. She wanted to make sure she'd understood correctly. "Are you saying every-thing is fine?"

"Yes. The polyp was benign," her mother repeated. "There were no cancerous cells."

Christy sighed with relief. "I'm so glad, Mom. This is the best news."

"Yes, it is. That's why your father said we should call. He wanted you and Todd to know. We left a message on Bob's phone, but could you tell him as well?"

"Of course."

Christy's mom paused and then added, "I'm going to pray for my sister every day she's there, just like I prayed for you that summer. I've prayed for her for a long time, but because of all the painful things she went through earlier in her life, she just won't let God get close to her."

Draw close. Karibu sana.

"I understand. I'll be praying, too. When we get back, I'll come down and see you right away."

"I'll look forward to that. Good-bye, honey. I love you."

"I love you, too, Mom."

Christy held the silent phone and stood unmoving for a few sweet lingering moments with her back pressed against the cool wall. "I have an amazing mom." She realized she'd said the words out loud.

Returning Todd's phone to where it was plugged in, she let it recharge and thought about the best way she could recharge as well. The Sunday morning worship service was starting soon. Maybe it had already started. Todd and Eli had been invited to play their guitars with the rest of the expansive worship team. Everyone on staff at Brockhurst said it was the one Sunday morning service they looked forward to every year when this group showed up. The musicians came with African drums and handcrafted instruments as well as keyboards and guitars. There would be dancing and singing that raised the roof, according to Eli's announcement at breakfast.

Christy flopped on the bed. The way she felt right now was not conducive to singing and dancing in the aisles. She gave herself permission to take a nap and couldn't stop thinking about her mom.

I have missed so much by not welcoming my own mother into my life. Why didn't I start to draw closer to her sooner?

Her thoughts filled with images of Abuela Teresa and Carolyn. They had orbited each other so gracefully. Carolyn was a golden moon held on course by the silver earth of her mother's abiding love. It was clear to her that no matter where a daughter went and no matter how close she thought she was to her mother, the two would always be linked by invisible currents of complicated love that would always ebb and flow.

Christy resolutely confessed to herself something she'd never realized until this moment.

My mother will always be my original home. She will always be in my heart.

Home of Our Hearts

sixteen

*C*hristy stayed sequestered in her cozy little guest cottage and took a deep, restorative nap after the encouraging call from her mom. The rain woke her sometime later and prompted her to draw back the curtains and take in the drenched landscape. Wrapping the extra blanket around her shoulders, Christy pulled the corner chair up to the window and watched the rain. She could hear the army of determined droplets as they continued to march across the roof and parachute over the edge, making a soft landing in the flower beds.

Several of the conferees gathered under large, blue umbrellas and nimbly made their way back to their cottages. One of them was sharing an umbrella with Katie. Christy loved watching her gregarious friend smiling and chatting as she approached Christy's cottage. Christy waved but Katie didn't seem to notice her at the window.

Christy opened the cottage door and welcomed in the cold, moist air as well as her smiling pal.

"Hey! There you are. I didn't see you at the worship service." Katie took off her jacket and quickly unlaced her boots, leaving them behind the door. "Are you okay?"

"Yes. I'm fine. But . . . " Christy paused before making her announcement. "I'm definitely not pregnant."

Katie made a pouty face.

"I know. I'm relieved, though. And I got to talk to my mom."

"How's she doing?"

"Great. Her lab results came back all clear and she sounded good. I think it was possibly the best conversation I've ever had with her. I feel so relieved."

"I can see how you would. That's great, Christy." Katie jumped right into talking about how amazing the worship service had been and how Todd and Eli were both in their element that morning as they stood on stage with the rest of the large worship team. "It was epic. I wish you'd been there."

For a moment, Christy felt slighted. She wanted to talk about her mom and their encouraging conversation. She wanted to tell Katie how eager she was to get back to California so she could see her mom and keep this new friendship side of their relationship growing. Then Christy remembered how distant and uncaring Katie's mother was and realized it might be too painful for Katie to hear Christy give a glowing report about her mom right now. She changed the subject and told Katie this was the ideal time for her to pull out the gifts she'd brought with her.

"Presents?" Katie's green eyes lit up like Christmas lights. "Yes, please!"

Katie made herself comfortable on Christy's bed. She crossed her legs the way she used to do when they were college roomies and she was settling in for a heart-to-heart conversation.

"This is so exciting, Christy. You have no idea."

"I remember what it was like when I was at school in Basel. Whenever I got something from home. It is a big deal." Christy flashed back on all the times her aunt had sent her care packages with makeup and magazines, chocolate chip cookies and warm clothes such as sweaters and scarves. Her mother had written newsy letters once every two weeks on the same stationery that had butterflies fluttering down the side. She wished now that she hadn't thrown all those letters away.

"I hope you brought me something from Bargain Barn," Katie said. "I miss that place."

"No Bargain Barn items for you on your wedding night, my friend."

"Did you say wedding night?"

"Yes, I did. This is real stuff. Not preworn. Nothing but the best for you on this occasion."

Christy pulled from her suitcase three very smushed gift bags with crumpled tissue paper and flattened ribbons. She held them up and playfully tried to blow into the bags to fluff them back up. "They've suffered a bit of jet drag, I'm afraid."

"They look like they came from Bargain Barn and that's almost as good!"

Christy laughed. "You're right. They do. They look awful. It's what's inside that counts though, right?"

Christy peeked before handing her the gift bag that contained the expensive, smooth undergarments that would accent her figure under the wedding dress.

Katie unabashedly peeled off her several layers of rainwear. Christy looked away, as she'd done at the spa in Maspalomas, while Katie tried on the elegant new undies.

"This is so nice. I don't think I've ever had anything this nice in my life, Chris. Thank you so much."

"You're welcome. It looks like the fit is good."

"The fit is perfect. Eli is going to be amazed."

Christy wanted to tell her friend that when it came to pretty under dainties on the honeymoon, they didn't tend to stay on very long. But it would be more fun to let Katie discover that for herself. "Now the next gift."

Katie pulled the elegant nightie from the flattened bag and held it up with a look of amazement. "This is for me?"

"Yes. Of course it's for you. You're the bride, remember?"

"Oh yeah. I am, aren't I?"

"Yes, you are." Christy waited for a vote of approval. "Do you like it? I wanted to get you something for your honeymoon that would make you feel feminine."

"This is gorgeous. No, it's beyond gorgeous. It's . . . wow. I love the way this material feels. What is it?"

"Silk."

Katie's eyes widened. "Silk?"

"Yes, and by the way, you'll need to wash it by hand. Don't throw it in with the rest of your jeans and sweatshirts."

"It's so beautiful, Christy. I don't know what to say."

Christy was feeling pretty pleased with her gifts for Katie. She really liked giving gifts that others liked and had always felt bad when she'd given something that appeared cheap or poorly made. She'd done that a number of times over the years. But not this time.

Katie had slipped the ivory silk nightie over her smooth, fancy undies and practiced an exaggerated catwalk across the floor. She turned and gave Christy a pouty model look. With a funny accent she said, "This is the real Katie Weldon, dahling. Deal with it."

Christy laughed. "You're not supposed to wear that until you become the real Katie Lorenzo, darling. It's for your honeymoon. And so is this."

Christy handed her the third dismal-looking gift bag and Katie pulled out the matching robe. She held it up and burst into tears.

"I've never been showered with so many beautiful things before. I'm overwhelmed here." The true "real Katie Weldon" cried happy tears and thanked Christy multiple times as she tried on the robe, turned around in front of the little mirror over the sink, and tried to get a view of the additional detail on the back of the gown.

"This is unbelievable. Thank you, Chris. Thank you so much."

Christy received Katie's cheery and teary hug.

"I have one more gift." Christy returned to her suitcase and remembered the handkerchief from Abuela Teresa. "Actually, I have two more gifts."

Katie was back on the bed, wearing all her new lovelies and smoothing her hand over the kimono-style sleeves. "I'm never taking this off. This feels like butter. No, it feels like the underbelly of a baby bird."

"When did you ever feel the underbelly of a baby bird?"

"Well, never. But if I had, this is what I think it would feel like. It's the most elegant, beautiful, comfortable thing I've ever owned. Ever."

Christy smiled and handed her another smashed gift bag. "This one is from Tracy. There's a card inside."

Katie pulled out the gift first. It was a bottle of body wash and a bottle of lotion both in a tropical fragrance that made the whole room smell fresh and delicious as soon as Katie tried some. "I smell like a ripe papaya."

"I think it smells good," Christy said.

"That's what I was getting at. Eli's favorite fruit is papaya. He's going to love this. How did Tracy know? This was so kind of her."

Christy told Katie how they'd gone shopping together and it had been Tracy's idea to send body wash and lotion since that was one of her favorite shower gifts when she and Doug got married. "We sampled at least a dozen lotions, and this one just seemed like something you would like."

"You got that right. Again. I love it. Tell Tracy thank you for me."

"I will. Don't forget the card. She put it inside the bag."

Katie had already tossed the bag on the pile with the other rumpled gift bags. She fished inside and pulled out the card. As soon as she removed it from the envelope, she burst out laughing.

Christy hadn't seen the card so she didn't know what image was on the front of it. She tried to see what had sent Katie into such a fit of laughter.

"A mountain bike built for two! Look at this! Is this a God-thing or what?"

The front of the card did, indeed, have a cute little drawing of a bride and groom in traditional American bridal apparel riding off into a sunset on a bicycle built for two. Trailing behind them was a string with several bright balloons. Inside the card said, "Two are better than one for they have a good reward for their labor. Ecclesiastics 4:9."

Christy was amazed, too. "That is a God-thing. What a cute card."

"She wrote a note here on the inside." Katie skimmed the personal note and said, "I love this verse Tracy wrote in the card. Listen to this, 'And in Him you, too, are being built together to become a dwelling in which God lives by His Spirit.' Ephesians 2:22."

Katie looked up at Christy. She looked like Queen Esther on a bed of colorful African fabric pillows. Her wind-blown hair, still damp from the rain, had formed tiny curly-cues around her face. Ever since she put on the silk gown and robe, she had settled herself on the bed in a graceful, elegant position that seemed befitting of royalty.

If it weren't for the fact that Katie was wearing a nightie, Christy would have grabbed her camera and captured the moment. Katie looked in every way like a beautiful, untainted dwelling place of the Holy Spirit.

Just then, they heard voices outside the door and the sound of Todd's key in the lock. Christy ran to the door and held it shut, calling through the opening, "Hold on just a minute. Don't come in yet."

"Okay. Are you all right?"

"Yes. I'm good. Katie's here. She was trying on some stuff."

"Good, because Eli's with me and we were wondering where you two were hiding."

"Eee!" Katie scooped up her clothes and scrambled for the small bathroom area so she could close the door and change. "Don't let him see me. This would spoil the surprise even more than if he saw me in my wedding dress."

"Give us two minutes," Christy said.

"How about twenty seconds. It's raining out here, you know."

Christy waited until the bathroom door was soundly shut before she unlocked the door to their guest cottage. Todd and Eli hurried inside with a blast of cold air on their heels. They were soaked and stood by the door dripping. Todd carried a covered plastic bin in his arms.

"I brought lunch. I didn't know if you'd gotten anything to eat. I didn't see you at the worship service."

"I'm really sorry I missed it."

"Is Katie in the bathroom?" Eli asked.

"I'm changing," Katie called out.

"Well, don't change too much. I like you just the way you are." Eli grinned at his own sweet line and waited for Katie to reply.

"You're going to like me even better on Friday, Mr. Lorenzo. You just wait and see."

Eli's grin was manly and bashful at the same time. "That's all I've been doing, Katie Girl. Waiting to see."

Christy and Todd exchanged surprised expressions at the flirty interchange they'd never heard before from these two lovebirds.

"Should we leave you two alone?" Todd asked.

"No!" the two of them answered in tandem from their opposite sides of the cottage.

"We can't be trusted," Katie said.

Christy and Todd looked at Eli. He gave an innocent shrug. "She's probably right. We've come this far. Better not to leave us alone until Friday night. After that, everybody better leave us alone."

Christy wanted to laugh out loud at this previously unseen version of quick-witted, affectionate Eli. She swallowed her laughter and it looked like Todd was doing the same.

Katie emerged from the bathroom wearing her jeans, sweater, scarf, and thick socks. Her hair was pulled back in a ponytail. All the Queen Esther aura and majesty was gone except for the trace of eagerness and pure joy that still shone on her face. She had a bath towel in her hands that was wrapped up in a big ball. Christy deduced that she'd rewrapped her gifts in the towel in order to keep them hidden from Eli.

"Are those towels for us?" Todd put the lunch bin on floor and moved toward Katie.

"No! Sorry. Special cargo coming through." Katie carefully placed her towel wad on the bed.

Eli and Todd stepped past her and pulled towels out of the bathroom to dry their hair and faces. They pulled off their shirts and hung them over the rod in the shower. Katie and Christy watched their shirtless men with equal appreciation.

"Hey, no peeking," Eli said. "Goes for both the bride and the groom."

The girls turned around and shared a grin as Todd rummaged in his bag for two shirts. "I need to do some laundry pretty soon."

"Hang it outside," Katie said. "Free wash and dry here. All you have to do is wait for the sun to come back out."

Todd ignored the suggestion and came over to the bed to give Christy a kiss. "Do you want a sandwich? I brought some food back for you."

"Sure. Thanks." She hugged him and whispered the reason why she'd missed the worship service.

Todd gave her an adoring look and kissed her again, a kiss of deeper understanding than what it might appear to Katie and Eli who were now standing close with their arms around each other.

"Do you think they want to be alone?" Katie asked Eli. She said it loud enough that it was obvious she wanted Christy and Todd to hear.

"I don't know. What's this thing they keep doing with their faces so close together like that."

"I know. What is that?" Katie said playfully. "It looks like their lips keep running into each other."

"It does." Eli had turned to Katie and with his arm around her shoulder, pulling her close. "It seems like they're doing something like this." He kissed her. And from the look on Katie's face when they pulled apart, Eli had kissed her good.

Todd stepped in between them, pushing them apart. "Okay. Hold it right there. I believe you. You two can't be trusted. Just a few more days. That's all you have to wait."

Katie gave Eli one of her playful pouts. "Busted by the purity police."

They all started laughing. Christy opened the top of the plastic bin and poured the rain water that had collected on it into the small trash bin. Inside was enough food for a family of eight who had skipped lunch and breakfast. "How hungry did you think I might be?"

"I missed lunch, too. So did Eli. His mom put that together for us."

"Perfect. An inside picnic. It looks yummy."

Katie discreetly slid her gifts back into the gift bags and stuffed the tissue paper in the top. Christy quickly made the bed and spread the extra blanket out over the top. They put the bin of food in the center of the bed, and the four of them took to the four corners and had a rollicking indoor picnic as the African rains tap-danced on the tin roof.

What Christy loved most about that fun and sweetly close time with Eli and Katie was that the two of them opened up in a serious way about their relationship. They asked Christy and Todd for advice. They shared a few fears and questioned a few hows about their honeymoon expectations. Both of them said they had hoped to have a chance to talk with Christy and Todd like this, as a couple, because they hadn't been able to discuss these intimate topics yet with anyone else.

Christy loved being drenched in the sweet fellowship that poured down inside their cottage that afternoon. She thought about how often in California they would just sit and watch TV when they were at Bob and Marti's. When was the last time she and Todd had been intentional about inviting people over for conversation like this? It didn't have to be fancy. This kind of closeness as two couples happened because they had been able to come to Kenya. Christy was so grateful. She was grateful to her aunt and uncle for helping with the airfare and grateful to her mom once again for letting Christy go during a difficult season in her own life.

That night, when they were alone and getting ready to hop into the warm bed, Todd started telling Christy about the worship service. The electricity had gone out again and they had once again lit the taper candle on the bedside table. Christy loved the romantic glow it gave to the room.

"We played for over an hour. People were singing like I've never heard people sing before. It was from the heart. So loud and joyful." He laughed at the memory of it. "Some people were dancing. Such freedom and a childlike sort of adoration for God. I loved it, Chris. I'll never forget it."

"I wish I'd gone."

"I do, too." Todd was quiet a moment, and Christy started to feel bad that she hadn't made more of an effort to go to the worship service.

"Hey, you did what you needed to do to take care of yourself. I support your decision. Besides, it sounded like you were here at just the right time to get the call from your dad."

Christy nodded. "That was a God-thing, wasn't it?"

"God's perfect timing. He's always right on time."

They cuddled up under the covers and Todd added, "Unlike Marti's flight."

Christy popped her head up. "What did you just say?"

"Didn't I tell you?"

"Tell me what?" It drove Christy crazy whenever Todd forgot to tell her significant details.

"Bob said that Marti's flights were rerouted or rebooked or something. She didn't mind because she was able to get on those nicer planes with the beds. She'll arrive on Tuesday instead of tomorrow."

"Well, that's good to know." Christy resisted hitting her forgetful husband with her pillow in the dark because she didn't feel like starting something she couldn't finish.

Home of Our Hearts

seventeen

Christy slipped her hand into Todd's and the two of them fell into step behind Katie and Eli on their way to the tea fields for a picnic breakfast. It was barely dawn on Monday morning and Eli had set up this small adventure because he wanted to show them where he had proposed to Katie.

Eli's and Katie's well-worn boots looked like they were familiar with the wide path of rich, red earth that was a thoroughfare for people from the nearby village. They passed several people already that morning on their way to the fields for their workday. Their greetings were friendly and their clothes were colorful. The children that tromped by going in the opposite direction were all dressed in blue plaid school uniforms.

Christy tried to imagine what it would be like to grow up here and walk many miles to get to school each day. She was glad that she and Todd had worn their boots this morning, too. The shady parts of the trail were still muddy from the heavy rains and the terrain was uneven.

Katie clutched Eli's arm. "Doesn't a donut sound good

right now? When was the last time we had one? Remember the ones we got when we went to Strawberry Peak Lookout?"

"What kind were they again?"

"Old-fashioned buttermilk. So dangerously good. Remember how the bakery guy brought them in while they were still hot?"

Eli gave Katie an affectionate look. "That was almost a year ago."

"I know. So much has changed in a year. We've changed. For the better, I think."

Eli nodded his agreement. Once again he looked taller to Christy. He looked like he belonged here and so did Katie.

Their journey continued, Hobbit style Christy decided, as they ventured out of the Shire and into a world she had never imagined. After the last half a mile of thick, junglelike foliage and a winding, hilly path, the four friends rounded a curve in the road and all of them stopped.

Spread out before them, as far as their vision could stretch, were rows upon rows of perfectly lined-up bushes that ran up and down the rolling, verdant hillsides. In the marigold light rising over the tallest hill behind them, the green leaves covering the tea plants appeared to be the great, uneven scales of an enormous dragon that was sleeping on its belly, warming itself in the fresh morning sun.

"Oh." It was the only word that managed to escape from Christy's enraptured spirit. "Oh."

"I know," Katie said, her voice hushed and her head resting on Eli's shoulder. "It's magnificent, isn't it? I never get tired of this place, this view. It stirs something inside me every time we come here."

"That's probably because we almost always bring food with us," Eli said. "That's why your stomach gets stirred up."

Katie swatted Eli's arm playfully. "No, what stirs in my stomach is something else much more romantic than food. It's like the view sees me at the same moment I see it. It always calls out a welcome. But since I don't speak tea field I don't know how to answer back. Except to tell God that I think He made a beautiful world and I love this part of it."

"That was surprisingly poetic," Eli said.

"It was, wasn't it?" Katie looked as if she'd surprised herself with her romantic thought. "See what you've done to me, Lorenzo? You've turned me into a mush-heart."

"A mush-heart?"

"Yeah, I didn't used to be this poetic, did I, Christy?"

She was taking her time letting her eyes memorize the panorama. It took her a moment to pull out a response to Katie's question. "Well, there was that one time in England when you and Sierra got pretty mushy about your dreams for the future."

"Oh, Sierra! I miss Sierra," Katie said. "How is she? Do you know? Have you talked to her lately? Is she still in Brazil?"

"Yes, she's still in Brazil. I owe her a nice, long e-mail."

"So do I," Katie said.

Eli pointed to an open, grassy knoll to their left. "You guys want to head up the hill and finish your reminiscing up there?"

"Somebody's ready for breakfast." Katie grinned at Eli.

"I'm not gonna deny it."

Christy wanted to linger and take pictures since the lighting was so mellow. Sometimes when she rushed to frame and freeze a moment like this, she regretted it later. She would look back and feel that in her eagerness to take a picture, she had missed the chance to draw in the 3-D reality of the moment. She wanted to do that now, standing completely still, feeling the chill of the morning air on her face and breathing in the rich scent of the brick-red earth that still carried a heady fragrance after the immersion of the African rains.

"Is it okay if we stay here a few more minutes and take some pictures?" Christy asked.

"Sure."

"Do you think anyone would mind if we walked through the fields?" Todd asked.

"Not at all. You can even help the workers, if you want." Eli pointed to a half-dozen laborers in the distance who had cloth satchels strapped across the front of them. "Just make sure you only pluck the top two leaves and the bud. That's the only part of the plant they use to make tea."

"No wonder it has to all be done by hand," Todd said.

Christy headed for the closest rows of evenly trimmed tea bushes. She never expected them to look the way they did, like a thick hedge that was so long, it stretched up and down the hills for miles.

Todd walked ahead of her, extending his arms slightly to his sides as he strode between the rows. His flat palms skimmed the tops of the tea plants as he walked. Christy started snapping pictures. Her surfer boy had found a new place to reach out and balance himself inside of God's nature. He looked like he was surfing through the tea fields as he walked. An ocean of green lay before him.

Turning and grinning at Christy, he said, "Let's get one of these."

"One of what?" She snapped a shot of his unshaven face with the fresh sunlight illuminating his silver-blue eyes. She loved his little-boy expression.

"One of these. A tea field. This is unbelievable. Have you ever seen anything like this?"

"No. It's the perfect time of day to come here, too. The light is amazing."

"What do you think, Kilikina? We could move here and buy a red-dirt hill and plant tea. I'll help lead worship somewhere on Sundays, and you can take all the photos you want every day."

Christy lowered her camera so they could see eye to eye. "How serious are you right now?"

"Serious enough. Why?" Todd looked intrigued. "Would you ever consider moving here?"

"Maybe."

"Maybe?"

Christy gazed out over the landscape and spoke the truth that had risen to the surface. "The thought of us living here doesn't freak me out." She turned and smiled at Todd. "Crazy, huh?"

Todd strode toward her, his gaze fixed on her expression. He took her hand and scanned her face as if searching for something.

His intensity made her nervous. "Todd, I'm not saying that . . . "

He put his finger to her lips. "Don't say anything. Let's just leave the possibility here like a seed in the ground. We don't have to know yet if it will grow or not."

Christy nodded, feeling a rush of peace. She was grateful that Todd hadn't pressed her to commit to the fanciful inklings of this place one way or the other. It was enough to speak honestly and be content to wait patiently.

"Here," Todd said. "Let me have the camera for a minute. The sunlight is right behind you and it's lighting your hair on fire. You are such a beautiful woman, Kilikina."

Todd snapped a few pictures and Christy tried to act natural. She looked out over the hills. Next, she looked right at Todd and gave him a loving grin. Then for fun, she lifted her right arm in the air and tried to strike the pose of a Flamenco dancer, flipping her chin up and looking as exotic and fiery as she could.

Todd grinned. "Work it, baby. That's right. The camera loves ya."

Christy laughed. *I feel so over-the-moon happy right now. So blessed. Filled to overflowing.*

She suddenly started crying.

"Hey." Todd stepped closer and wiped her tears with his thumb. "What is it? Why are you crying?"

Christy drew in a ruffled breath of the cool Kenyan highland air. "I just got so filled up with happiness that it had to leak out somewhere."

Todd tilted his head back and laughed. "You never stop

surprising me, Kilikina. You really love it here, don't you?"

"I love being here with you. I love that we can be here for Eli and Katie. I love our life. I love God. I even love the romantic notion that since we don't know what's next, we have to live inside the mystery." She paused. "Well, actually, no. I take that back. I don't love that we're about to be homeless again in a few months, and I don't love having to wait to find out what's going to happen. But I love being on the journey with you, Todd. I really do."

The hopeful expression on his face made Christy want to kiss him something fierce. The rising sun had slipped over the top of the hill and shone in Todd eyes.

That face, those eyes.

"You need to be kissed," Christy said. "Right now." She took Todd's scruffy face in her hands and gave him what might possibly be the most romantically passionate kiss she had even given him.

She drew back and he opened his eyes only halfway, like a man still caught in a dream. Christy lowered her chin, surprised at her own fervor. Todd pulled her back and whispered, "Oh, yeah? Well, I'm not the only one who needs to be kissed right now." He responded with an equally passionate kiss.

They lingered in a close embrace, standing in the wide-open space of the dirt road that circled the base of the hill where Eli and Katie had gone to set up the picnic. Christy knew that Todd was thinking the same thing she was thinking but neither of them spoke their secret wishes out loud. Sometimes during their marriage, at moments like this, she felt like they had to practice as much patience as they had over the years they were dating. It was a good thing they'd had so many years of exercising restraint.

Todd reached for her hand and laced his fingers between hers. "Come on," he whispered in a husky voice. He held on tightly and led the charge up the hill. "We better go chaperone Katie and Eli. Young lovers shouldn't be left alone in this place."

Christy smiled and had a feeling she'd be smiling all morning.

They found Katie and Eli calmly sipping tea when they got to the grassy knoll. Before they even sat on the blanket, Todd said, "Christy wants to move here."

"Really?" Katie's eyes lit up. "Seriously? You're not messin' with us, are you?"

"No. Well, yes, but no." She glanced at Todd. "I just like it here. A lot."

"We do, too," Eli said.

"What's not to like?" Katie asked. "I mean, where else in the world can you find a breakfast view like this and be able to sit here with your favorite people in the entire galaxy and sip tea? Seriously. Who wants Newport Beach when you can have this?" Katie lifted her mug into the air. "You can have your tea field and drink it, too."

They all laughed.

"Here, hold your mug," Katie said. "I'll pour you some tea."

"You guys know we can always use help with the clean water ministry," Eli said. "There would be plenty for both of you to do. Not to mention that Katie and I would love having you here."

"We're going to start to pray about it," Todd said. "Deliberately pray."

"Good. 'Inquire of the Lord,'" Eli said, keeping on the serious track with Todd. "That's what my mom calls it. She prays about everything. I'm convinced she prayed Katie over here."

"And I'm so glad she did." Katie pointed to the stack of dried toast. "It's not old-fashioned buttermilk donuts but it's pretty good with this homemade marmalade."

Eli reached for a knife. "When my mom prays she always says, 'Your kingdom come and Your will be done.' If God wants you here and if you're asking Him what He wants,

He'll bring you here. I believe that. What I've seen too often is when people show up here because they think Africa needs them. They want to help God out somehow. It's much better to humbly ask God what He wants. He doesn't need our help. He wants our hearts."

"Agreed." Todd lifted his cup and gave it a sniff. He wasn't much of a tea drinker but he was always interested in trying new things. "We'll pray."

"I'm suddenly feeling very unspiritual." Katie bit into a piece of toast covered with orange marmalade. "I didn't exactly fast and pray before coming here. I came for love."

Eli grinned. "But here's the thing, Katie. You prayed a lot during your last semester at Rancho about what to do next. I know you did. I prayed a lot, too. So did my mom. It was more like you prayed in steps. Each time you were brave enough to take the next step, those steps kept you moving forward until you ended up at the airport, ready to go."

"That's true. During my last semester all I did was pray about what God wanted me to do next. I guess I did inquire of the Lord. It wasn't as impulsive as a leap. It was a series of small steps, like you said."

"I think that's the way God usually leads us: step by step." Todd pointed at Katie. "Think about where you were two years ago when you started praying about what to do after college. Can you imagine what you would have said if you prayed only one time and God told you, 'Okay. Here's my answer. Move to Africa and marry Eli'?"

Katie laughed. "I would have said, 'That's never going to happen.'"

"Exactly. We say that we wish God would answer our prayers immediately, but I think that if He did, we'd run the other way. We need the gift of time. We need the grace of small steps."

"I like that. I definitely needed the grace of small steps to end up here." Katie grinned at Eli. "And I'm so glad this is where God brought me."

Eli reached for Katie's hand and planted a kiss on it. "Me, too."

"Well, if we ever do end up here," Christy said, "I want you guys to remind us of this first small step this morning. It feels like a big step for me. I just want to be open and willing to go wherever God wants us to go."

Todd gave her a great smile over the rim of his mug of hot tea. She smiled back.

Eli stretched out on his back as the sun was climbing in the sky and warming the earth. He bent his elbows and put his hands behind his head. "There's a place in the book of Acts. I think it's around chapter 17 when Paul was in Athens. He's talking about how God made the world. All of it. He made every nation from one man and they spread out over the earth. Then he says that God determines the exact times and places where they should live."

Christy tilted her head back and took in the view of the expansive blue sky Eli was staring into as he spoke.

"I believe that," Eli said. "I believe God is intricately involved with where we should live and who we should be in community with. I also believe He appoints how long we should live there."

Christy was convinced that God had appointed for her to live in Newport Beach during the summer she turned fifteen. He had given her then the people who now were at the forefront of her life. She believed more than ever that He would show them His appointed time and place for wherever they would live next.

The four friends continued discussing the challenging topic of understanding God's will for their lives as they gazed out at the tea fields and enjoyed the toast, marmalade, cheese, and tea. What she liked most about their easy conversation was that she felt as if they were all equals, eager to know God and understand His desires for them. None of them shared as if they had God all figured out and were now telling the others what He wanted them to do.

The sun was high above when they finally packed up the remains of the picnic and headed back. Eli and Todd led the way on the dirt path, carrying all the stuff. Katie and Christy followed close behind.

"So, your aunt arrives tomorrow," Katie said. "Are you ready for her?"

"I think so. Are you?"

"Of course. I'm the one who wanted her to come. I'm glad she's coming."

"I'm glad she's bringing your dress. I still feel awful that I forgot it."

"Hey, I dropped your baby, you forgot my dress. It's all good. It'll all work out with Marti, too. You'll see."

"I hope so." Christy realized she was more nervous about Marti's arrival than she'd let on. An infusion of drama into their happy circle was inevitable. "To be honest, sometimes I just want to shake her."

"No, you can't do that. You don't shake babies."

They walked a few more feet before Christy asked, "What did you just say?"

"Eli's dad told me one time when we had some unbelievably inept volunteers here, that they were babies when it came to knowing God and trusting Him. Then he told me you don't shake babies. It messes them up."

Christy walked beside Katie in silence before saying, "You're right. I need to learn how to be more patient with my aunt."

"Now that's funny because I'm the one who is usually saying that same thing to you, that I need to be more patient. Because love is patient, right? It's the foundation for any lasting relationship." Katie raised her voice so the guys could hear. "At least that's what Eli and I learned in our premarital counseling sessions. Isn't that right, snookums? Love is patient."

"Yes, dear," Eli said over his shoulder in a comical voice. "Whatever you say, dear."

Katie grinned. "Whatever I say, huh? Well, I'd say we're

ready to make it real. I've got a wedding dress arriving special delivery tomorrow, you've got the rings. What do you think?"

"I think I'd like to take you as my wife."

"Oh you do, do you? Well, that's a good thing because I was thinking that I wanted to make my home with you for the rest of my days."

"And nights?" Eli asked quickly.

"Oh yes. The rest of my days and especially the rest of my nights."

Eli kept looking straight ahead as he walked. Katie's face was radiant as she waited for his comeback. Christy hadn't seen this side of Eli before. She loved that he was such a perfect match for Katie and her quirky wit.

"Then what do you say about putting on that white dress, Katie Girl, and I'll show up with the preacher?"

"I can do that."

"I'm thinking Friday, around sunset maybe?"

"Really? This Friday?"

"Sure. Why not?" Eli said. "Let's meet at the Masai Mara. What do you think? Is it a date?"

"Well, I don't know . . . " Katie's coy voice was cracking Christy up.

"You don't know?" Eli stopped and turned to face Katie and take in the full view of her impish expression.

"You left out one important detail."

"What's that?" Eli asked.

"If I do show up and make good on my promise to marry you, are you gonna kiss me?" She had her hand on her hip and was staring him down. "I mean, like really kiss me good?"

Eli's expression appeared unflinching, but the light in his eyes made it clear that he was loving this. He gave Katie a casual shrug and turned back around, heading down the trail next to Todd.

"Only one way to find out," Eli called out over his shoulder. "Show up on Friday. And bring your lips."

eighteen

$\mathcal{C}$hristy missed her aunt's grand arrival at the conference center on Tuesday. Secretly, she was disappointed that she didn't get to be one of the first to greet Marti with "karibu sana." After praying for her so much the last few days, she was more hopeful than ever that Marti would draw close to God here in Africa. Christy felt His presence, His very breath so close here. She wanted that for her aunt, too.

As soon as Marti was settled in their guest cottage, she sent Uncle Bob to round up Christy, Katie, and Eli's mom, Cheryl, so they could see how Katie's dress fit. Christy left the dining room where she'd been helping set the tables for dinner. She stopped at her cottage first and picked up the handkerchief from Abuela Teresa and joined the other two women.

They arrived at the same moment and knocked on the door of the guest cottage. Marti appeared in the doorway, wearing a long, colorful, African-looking kaftan. The look surprised Christy since she hadn't seen this outfit before. It seemed as if Marti had watched a documentary on Africa and then went shopping with the intent purpose of matching her wardrobe to what the women in the film were wearing.

"*Jambo!*" She greeted each of them with a Newport Beach hostess sort of air kiss off the right cheek. She expressed her congratulations to Katie and to Cheryl and gave Christy a side squeeze as she asked, "Were you surprised?"

"Yes. We were all really surprised that you were able to come."

"And really glad," Katie added. "Thank you for making such a heroic effort to be here and to bring my dress."

"Of course. It was much more grueling than I expected. Such long flights. But I can tell you all about that later. Let's see this dress on you, Katie. It's waiting for you right over there."

Katie headed for the bathroom and then stopped. "Would you guys mind if we went over to my cottage? Christy helped me move everything in yesterday and get it all set up for when Eli and I move in after our honeymoon. I kinda had this vision of trying my dress on over there."

"What a romantic thought." Marti touched her heart with her perfectly manicured hand. "Point the way, Katie. And Christy? Will you do the honors of carrying the gown? I have several other items I'd like to bring along. Here, Cheryl. Would you mind carrying this bag for me? Where are those helpful porters when you need them?"

Christy was surprised at how perky her aunt was. She wondered if the advantage Marti had was that she'd made the trip in the first-class cabins on all her flights. Or maybe she'd just taken a dose of her serenity pills. Whatever the reason for her fresh and friendly approach, Christy hoped it would last.

The movable bride's party followed each other single file up the hilly path, through the beautiful gardens to Eli and Katie's new stone cottage-home-to-be. Christy couldn't help but feel that everything was practically perfect at this moment for her Forever Friend. Todd was right. God worked out getting the dress here. She wished now that she had trusted God and her aunt a little more wholeheartedly.

Arriving at the door of Katie's cottage, Christy noticed a bright yellow-and-brown bird that flitted out from under the overhang. She turned her neck to see under the eaves. It was as she suspected. The bird had been building a nest. The sight of the protruding twigs and trailing bits of string and vines touched Christy deeply. She thought of how only a year ago, her best friend was about to graduate from college with no idea of what the future held. She planned to move in with Todd and Christy temporarily and everything she owned fit into her car. What a difference a year had made.

If God can give Katie a garden cottage and give that little bird a place to nest, He can provide a home for Todd and me. I just know He will. I'm open to wherever He leads us. Here or Newport or someplace we haven't even thought of yet.

She entered the cottage smiling. It felt so good to be thinking things through with faith and not with fear.

Katie's new nest was a cozy five hundred square feet and had all the basic essentials of the cottages where the guests stayed. However, their cottage had enough room to add a love seat in the corner and an efficiency kitchen that included a tiny refrigerator, a cooking plate, and two cupboards for cups and plates and pans.

She and Katie had set up a bookshelf yesterday with some specific books that were important to Eli. He had grown up doing a lot of reading and living in places where books were often hard to come by. Even though he could upload any title he ever wanted now, he still valued the feel and the experience of turning the paper pages of his favorite books.

Marti, however, was stunned at the sparse accommodations. She said she understood why the room she and Bob shared was so compact. They were merely guests. Shouldn't the people who lived here and served for such a noble cause be given more than just a cracker box for their living quarters?

Neither Katie nor Cheryl had a reply. They both seemed completely content with the arrangements. Getting the party started, Katie hung the garment bag on the upper door frame of the bathroom and unzipped it slowly.

"Remember that it still needs to be steamed," Marti said from her place on the love seat. "Don't look at the wrinkles."

Katie flashed a gleeful grin at Christy, and the two of them pulled the crumpled gown from the garment bag. Katie stepped back and had her first look at her wedding dress.

"I love it."

"You haven't even tried it on," Marti said. "Let us see how it fits. I know Christy is confident she can make the necessary alterations, but I'm concerned that if there are too many adjustments, she won't be able to get it done in time."

Katie collected her new undies from her dresser drawer and chose the privacy of the bathroom instead of stripping down in front of her future mother-in-law and Aunt Marti. Christy thought that was a good choice. A few minutes later, Katie took two steps out. "Can you zip me?"

"It doesn't zip. It's all buttons. Tiny pearl buttons. Be patient." Christy went to work getting each pearl into the right loop. "There. Turn around."

"Let's see the full view."

Christy followed Katie as she stepped into the center of the room. Her arms were out to the side and she spun around, grinning all the way. Marti took a moment to tilt her head and look at Katie as if she were observing an unfinished work of art. Christy knew that look all too well.

"It's lovely." Cheryl pressed her hands to her cheeks. "Oh, Katie. You look beautiful."

"It needs to be taken in on the sides," Marti said. "I'm sure you want it to be as close fitting as possible to show off that slim torso of yours. And of course the length is probably all wrong. Too long, don't you think, Christy?"

"It depends on what shoes she's going to wear." Christy stepped in front of Katie and decided to follow the example

Cheryl had set. With a warm smile she said, "You look gorgeous, Katie. The dress really suits you. I can see why you liked this one so much."

Christy wasn't wowed with the dress, but she was wowed with the way her tomboy friend looked so gorgeous in the dress. Katie glowed.

Marti seemed to still be looking for the TV version of a "yes moment," but none of them had gotten teary eyed when they saw her in the dress.

"I think the fit is perfect." Katie swayed from side to side. "What do you think, Christy?"

She began to pinch the fabric on either side, pulling it in a quarter of an inch.

"That would be too tight. I want to be able to breathe. I don't know how it looks to you guys, but I like how it feels. I don't want it to be taken in. And I think the length is going to be just right, Marti, because my boots have thick soles so I'll probably be half an inch taller when I put them on."

Marti stopped her. "Did you just say 'boots'?"

Katie nodded.

Marti looked to Christy as if expecting this to be one of Katie's jokes. Christy returned a supportive shrug. If Katie wanted to get married in boots, then she should.

"Eli and I are both wearing boots. It's our thing."

"Your 'thing'?" Marti's expression seemed to twitch slightly. Christy wondered if her serenity pills were wearing off and she was about to go into one of her critical, take-charge moods. "How about if we simply consider your other options, Katie? Where are your shoes? Do you have a nice, simple slip on? Something in silver, perhaps?"

Katie started laughing. "This isn't exactly a place of silver slippers. I only have three pairs of shoes." Katie pointed to her all-purpose athletic-style tennis shoes by the door next to her boots. "And I have a heavy-duty pair of sandals. I love my boots. I'm gonna wear my boots."

Marti looked as if her brain was trying to process the

thought of a woman only owning three pairs of shoes. "You know what? We have one more day before we leave for the safari and your wedding. What if we head to Nairobi and go shopping first thing in the morning? I'll have Robert call the driver who brought me here from the airport and make the arrangements."

"If you want to go shopping tomorrow, great. Have fun. Cheryl and I have been through every store in Nairobi and there's no way I'm going to do that again. Ever. I'm wearing my boots. End of story."

Marti fussed some more but Katie held her ground and Marti backed down. It surprised Christy to see how quickly her aunt gave in.

I'll have to remember Katie's skills in sticking to her own opinion the next time my aunt tries to bulldoze me into something. If Katie can stand on her own two boots, so can I.

"Okay. Fine. Now, what about the rest of your ensemble?" Marti's arms were folded and her tone was crisp. "Do you have a veil?"

"No."

"No veil?" Marti looked surprisingly cheerful all of a sudden. "You do realize that this dress needs some serious accessorizing. And I do mean something other than boots."

"Eli wanted me to wear a wreath of flowers like I wore at Christy's wedding. I'm just wearing the wreath. It's right here." She went to the dresser and rolled back the tissue that covered a head wreath fashioned from dried flowers that were white and pale blue with tiny greenery tucked in. It looked handcrafted and was simple but lovely. Katie plopped it on her head.

"Katie, dear, I want you to consider, just for a moment, what it might look like if you had a nice sheer veil, cascading over your shoulders." Marti bustled over to the garment bag and fished into the zipped-up pouch on the back side. "You see, I took a risk and brought a veil for you. Just in case you might like it. If you don't, that's fine. But how will we know for certain unless you at least try it on?"

Marti pulled out a sheer white veil and gave it a good shake. "You'd want to wear your hair down of course. Go ahead. Take out the clip. There. Now give your hair a light shake. Yes. Just like that."

Katie removed the wreath of flowers and gave her red hair another swish as if it were an Oriental fan. She bent her knees to lower herself so Marti could place the veil over the top of her head.

The three women now stood in a half circle around Katie viewing her reflection in the bathroom mirror.

"Yes, just like that," Marti said. "Then the wreath would go on top. Let's try it."

"May I?" Cheryl asked.

Katie handed her the wreath and Cheryl majestically lifted the bridal crown and placed it on her head, sliding it slightly to keep it in place. "Oh, Katie, you look so beautiful."

Katie took in her reflection in the mirror and her eyes shone with the ancient fire of young love. "I'm going to be a bride," she said in a low voice.

"A stunning, bride," Marti said. "I knew from the moment Christy showed me your dress that you needed something simple and elegant to complete it."

"Thank you, Aunt Marti." Katie turned and gave her a robust hug.

"Did you call me *Aunt* Marti?"

Katie glanced at Christy. "Did I?"

Christy nodded.

"Sorry. I meant to just say Marti."

"No, please. Call me Aunt Marti. I like being your adopted aunt. And I won't deny that I am thrilled you like the veil."

Christy kept thinking of the tender moment when Abuela Teresa presented Carolyn with the special heirloom wedding veil. That was the sort of moment she wanted Katie to have and here she was, feeling honored and beautiful and very much like a bride.

And it was my aunt who managed to make that happen.
Amazing.

"I just knew you'd look lovely in a veil." Marti stood back, admiring her handiwork. "I don't know if it's part of what the bride wears at weddings here, but it's the perfect accent to your gown."

"Veils are actually a big part of African wedding traditions. Not sheer veils like this. Here, they cover the bride from head to toe in local colorful fabric. When I say head to toe, I mean she is completely covered."

"I went to a wedding like that a few months ago," Katie said. "Eli had to explain to me what was going on because they lined up the bride with other women about the same size who are also covered head to toe. Then the groom has to walk down the line and pick the one that is his wife-to-be."

"What if he picks the wrong one?" Christy asked.

"He better not!" Katie said.

Christy said, "It reminds me of Jacob in the book of Genesis and how he wanted to marry Rachel but he didn't know until the next morning that he'd married Leah. I always wondered why Jacob didn't know which bride he ended up with."

"They could have been covered from head to toe like Waturi was at the Kikuyu wedding Katie's talking about," Cheryl said.

"Or the groom could have been drunk," Marti suggested.

Christy started laughing and Katie joined her. It wasn't that Marti's theory wasn't plausible. What made Christy laugh was the way her aunt was fitting in and turning this into the sort of bridal party Christy had hoped Katie would have.

"When we lived in Zimbabwe," Cheryl said, "there was a local wedding tradition that the bride would be covered with a long veil and the groom's family would pay to look at her under the veil."

"Why?" Katie asked.

"It all goes back to the bride-price. For centuries it's been expected that the groom would come up with a price equal to the value of the woman he wanted to marry. We had a friend who paid nineteen goats to get his wife."

"They still do that?" Christy asked.

"It sounds barbaric in this modern age," Marti said. "Can you imagine having your value as a woman reduced to a certain number of goats?"

"They still do it in some places," Cheryl said. "It's how some tribes here have operated for centuries. They select honored representatives from each family and they meet to discuss the value of the bride and settle on a price. I think that's what started the tradition of looking under the veil at the bride. The groom's family members wanted to have a look before the wedding to make sure the representatives did a good job and found a bride who was worthy of the groom."

Christy stepped closer to Katie. "As a representative of this bride's extended family, I am here today to say that she is definitely worthy of her groom."

"Well then," Cheryl said. "I hope you have nineteen goats to back up that declaration."

"No, but I do have something for Katie. I forgot to give it to you the other day in my room." Christy went to her shoulder bag and pulled out a folded-up piece of tissue paper, the only wrapping she could find for the special handkerchief Abuela Teresa had sent for Katie.

"This is a gift for you from my new grandmother-in-law. It belonged to her grandmother who was from Spain. It's quite old, so that's why it's a little tattered. It's for you to use in case you tear up at the ceremony."

"It's so delicate. Wow. It's beautiful, Chris." Katie studied the lace edges and then handed it back to Christy. "I can't keep this. It's too valuable. It's from your new family. You should keep it. I'm worried that I might damage it."

Christy pressed the handkerchief back into Katie's hand. She remembered the words that Abuela Teresa had spoken to her when she also tried to refuse the valuable gift. "Katie, when a woman who loves you gives you a gift, you take it, you say 'thank you"—*asante*—and you kiss her on the cheek." Christy turned her cheek to Katie the way Abuela had offered her cheek to Christy.

Katie looked at the handkerchief and folded it back into the perfect square it had been pressed into. In the most humbled tone Christy had ever heard tumble from Katie's lips came the words, "Asante."

Since Katie seemed too far out of her comfort zone to offer a kiss, Christy leaned in and kissed the still-veiled bride-to-be on her freckled cheek.

Cheryl and Marti, who had been observing the tender interchange of friendship, looked as if both of them might need their own handkerchief right then.

"Oh, and one more thing," Christy said. "Abuela Teresa said that the handkerchief is supposed to be your something old. You know that rhyme about something old, something new, something borrowed, and something blue? And the veil is the something new."

"The something blue is the flowers in your wreath," Cheryl suggested.

"I'd like to add my contribution," Marti said. "It matches your halo. It's also blue."

Marti removed a dainty necklace from her neck and held it out to Katie. Christy had seen this necklace a number of times. It seemed to be one that Marti wore often on average days. It had three small stones in a cluster. The center stone was a bright-blue sapphire, flanked by two small diamonds on either side.

She held it out to Katie. "This was the first piece of jewelry Robert gave me. It's always been very special."

Katie blinked in surprise. It took her a moment to reach out and take the necklace from Marti. With glistening eyes, Katie seemed to be remembering Christy's admonition of how a woman receives a special gift from another woman. "Thank you so, so much, Marti. Asante." Katie bravely leaned over and gave Marti a little kiss on the cheek. "I've never been given such a beautiful gift."

Marti pulled back, caught off guard by Katie's response. "Did you think I was giving this to you? I thought you were looking for something borrowed."

Katie did a commendable quick rescue. "Oh, yeah, exactly. That's what I mean. Something borrowed. This is perfect. Thank you."

A tense moment passed between the four women before Katie said, "I guess I better get out of this wedding dress so we can start to get the wrinkles out of it."

Katie removed the floral wreath first and handed it to Cheryl for safekeeping. She gave the veil to Marti and turned around so Christy could start unbuttoning all the tiny pearl buttons on the back of the dress.

"You know," Marti said. "I almost think the back of your dress is more visually stunning than the front. What about if you wear the veil over your face so it hangs to your shoulders in both the front and back? That way it won't hide the lovely buttons and you can have the veil drawn back and over your head when the moment comes for Eli to kiss his bride."

Katie had begun shaking her swishy red hair before Marti had even finished her idea. "Nope. Not gonna happen. I'm going to say 'I do' with an unveiled face. The beautiful buttons will just have to take a backseat this time."

"It's your choice, of course," Marti said.

"Of course," Katie playfully echoed.

Marti had returned to the love seat where she'd left the gift bags she'd brought from her room. She cast a wayward glance at Katie's boots lined up by the front door, still caked in mud from the weekend rains. The other three women were all watching Marti carefully.

Katie said, "I will clean them, of course."

"Of course," Marti said, mimicking Katie. "Something old, something new, something borrowed, and something ridiculous."

"That's what we're going for," Katie declared. "Every couple should include something ridiculous."

"Like butterflies released at the end of the ceremony?" Christy reminded Katie of her determined idea that Christy should have butterflies at her wedding.

"Hey, it worked with the two doves I released at Julia's wedding. Are you saying that was ridiculous?"

"Yes," practical Cheryl answered for all of them.

"I have no idea what you're talking about," Marti said. "All I know is that if you want ridiculous, Katie, then go ahead and have ridiculous. It's your wedding. Your day. And that's why I'm here. To share your special day with you. Now what do you say to getting out of your dress and opening some of these little shower gifts I brought for you?"

Katie made eye contact with her across the room. "More gifts? Marti. You're spoiling me. I'm so glad you came."

"Well, that was the reason I came, wasn't it?" Marti shifted on the love seat. "I certainly didn't come all this way to see the elephants."

nineteen

Christy buckled her seat belt and reached across the narrow aisle to grab Todd's arm. She had every intention of holding on for dear life for takeoff because this was the smallest plane she'd ever been on.

The cabin was open to the cockpit. Bob, who was seated closest to the front, was carrying on a conversation with the pilot as he checked his instruments and got the engine revving. Marti sat behind him, her big floppy hat and large sunglasses guarding her private thoughts as much as hiding her eyes. She was sedately applying hand sanitizer from the travel-sized bottle in her bag. Marti had been using hand sanitizer regularly and it was starting to bug Christy. It seemed like Marti was silently giving the message that everything around her was dirty.

Eli's parents appeared completely relaxed as if this were the same as taking a bus to school every day. If Marti's compulsive de-germing bothered them, they didn't show it. Christy turned and looked at Eli, who was across from Katie, grinning like it was Christmas morning.

The full plane edged down the airstrip at a different airport than Nairobi international airport where they'd arrived over a week ago. The roar of the engine was too loud to carry on a conversation. Christy just kept holding on to Todd across the aisle and vacillated between squeezing her eyes shut and turning to peek out the window.

As effortlessly as a sailboat skimming along on a day of gentle breezes, the plane lifted off the tarmac and rose into the cloud-filled sky.

She released her death grip on Todd's arm and shot him a "sorry" sort of grimace. She was afraid she'd left nail marks in his skin. Turning to gaze out the window, Christy drew in the bird's-eye view of the sprawling, diversified city of Nairobi. The roads were clogged with cars and busses and the familiar white shuttle vans. The roofs of large houses were easily visible as well as the top of a large shopping mall, business offices, and lots of mature green trees along the streets.

Katie tapped Christy on the shoulder and pointed out the window at the sprawling area that was void of anything green or growing. It looked like a huge field of brown cardboard and corrugated tin roofs.

"Kibera," Katie shouted. "That's the slums."

Christy had heard of the slums of Nairobi and all the many ways that Eli's dad and his team had worked to get clean water to the people living there. She had no idea it was so vast.

The plane continued to climb and the clouds blocked the view until they flew into an open patch where it looked like acres of green farmland below. Christy noticed areas where houses were clustered together in the middle of the rolling acreage.

The terrain took a sudden, dramatic drop and it appeared as if the world had cracked open. An enormous rift ran as far north and south as she could see. The Rift Valley. *I hope Marti is seeing this. She was the one who did all the research about this place.*

The landscape began to change to a less lush sort of green, and great stretches were flat and yellow like an abandoned desert. The sound of the propellers made it too difficult to try to call out to any of the others on the flight and ask questions. Christy settled into her seat and let the steady hum of the engines lull her as she took in the beauty and dramatic majesty of the views below.

As the plane came in lower, it was easy to make out the occasional baobab tree that stood like a singular umbrella on the parched-looking terrain. Leaning closer to the small window, she saw movement on the plain below. It looked like a herd of zebras. The plane continued to descend and Christy focused more clearly. It was zebras! A dozen or more were charging to a grove of scrawny-looking acacia trees near a narrow river. The urgency of their movement and the way they disappeared into the grove was thrilling. She looked around to see if any of the others were glued to their windows the way she was. Uncle Bob turned toward Christy and gave her a thumbs-up. He seemed to be enjoying this as much as she was.

When the group exited the small plane on the narrow landing strip, it was immediately evident that they were no longer in the highlands. The somber yellow stretch of grazing land was void of wildlife. The terrain was flat except for one hill not far from them that looked like a great mound of mashed potatoes covered with melting butter.

The air was dry. The temperature had increased significantly and all of them, except Eli, were wearing more layers and heavier jackets than needed. A quickened breeze greeted them and threatened to take Marti's hat and toss it to the four winds. The flat landscape made it easy to watch the shuttle as it came their way with a cloud of dust trailing behind. There were no other vehicles for as far as the eye could see.

The hotel was located on the backside of what Christy thought looked like a hill of mashed potatoes. The rooms were built into the hill and were designed, according to Cher-

~ 221 ~

yl, in the same style as the mud huts of the Masai people. Katie was the first to say what Christy was thinking. "This place looks like Bedrock. Like on *The Flintstones*? You know, yabba dabba do!"

As usual, her comparison of real life to old television programs left Eli shrugging. No one was shrugging when they entered the lodge and walked past the pristine swimming pool to their individual rooms. The porters who led the way with their luggage opened each door with a grand gesture of welcome.

All eight of them congregated in the room Christy and Katie would be sharing that night. It had four-poster beds with romantically draped mosquito nets, rugs, and chairs covered in what looked like cheetah skin. Sliding glass doors led out to small balconies.

Christy stepped out on the balcony to take in the wide view. It was one stunningly long stretch of golden fields interrupted here and there by large clumps of dense trees. At the horizon, the vast sky appeared liquid and flowing. Clusters of lazy clouds floated in the ocean of pure blue bliss as if they had nowhere in particular to go visit that day.

The world seemed to be a hushed place.

"What do you think of the Mara?" Eli stepped out on the balcony and leaned on the edge. "It's like nothing else, isn't it?"

"It is. And the sky is . . . "

"Like no other sky," Eli said.

They stood in quiet, mutual admiration for the unwritten poetry that hung in the air around them. This was a place of mystery and ancient beginnings.

"Wait until you see the stars tonight," Eli said. "Whenever I look up at them, I know where I am. I'm home."

Christy loved that thought.

"I wanted to say thanks, Christy." The words tumbled out awkwardly, as if Eli hadn't planned to say them.

"For what?"

"For coming. It means so much to both of us to have you and Todd here."

"We wouldn't have missed it for anything."

"I know," Eli said. "Even for a medical emergency in your own family."

"My mom's doing well, as you know."

"Yes." He looked shy as if he had something to say and couldn't find the words.

Christy waited. Just like the surroundings here, she didn't feel rushed and neither should Eli. A large, brightly colored lizard scurried across the balcony railing. It paused to take in Christy and Eli and then went on its way.

"I want you to know that I'm going to take good care of her."

His words fell like soft rain on Christy's heart. She smiled her softest smile. "I know you are, Eli. I know this is where she belongs. These are her stars, too. This is her home. I miss her like crazy and I'm going to go back to missing her like crazy when we return home next week. But I know you are the one God handcrafted for her and this is the place the two of you are supposed to be."

Eli nodded solemnly. "Thanks for saying that. I think I've been waiting for the blessing."

"Did you think we weren't in favor of you guys getting married?"

"No. Not you and Todd. Or Bob and Marti. It's Katie's parents. Their absence and complete lack of communication has been harder than I thought it would be. I'm so close to my parents. Katie and I have received their blessing. It infuriates me that Katie's parents are so uninterested." He scowled and looked out onto the unspoiled landscape. "I just don't understand how parents can choose to ignore their own child and withhold their blessing."

"I know," Christy said quietly. She was grateful that Eli understood Katie's soul-wound so clearly and felt it as well, as if the two of them were already one heart. She wished she and Todd could do something more to give Katie and Eli that sense of blessing that was so important to him.

Uncle Bob had been standing near when Christy and Eli were talking on the balcony. Christy knew he had overheard their conversation because that evening, after a bountiful buffet dinner, he had arranged for dessert and Katie's favorite chai tea to be served to the group outside around a fire pit on the terraced hotel grounds.

Bundled in sweaters and gathering close around the amber flames, Christy felt the familiar happiness of being around the fire pit, Newport Beach style. Instead of plump marshmallows on the end of sticks roasting over the fire, their dessert was served on trays held by kitchen staff in white coats.

"This is why I was so persistent about staying here," Marti announced. "Five-star service in such a remote place is luxury at its best, don't you think?" Marti was reclined in a lounge chair and enjoying the personal attention of the staff a little too much. She liked sending them off with a wave of her hand and holding her teacup up from her saucer only slightly before one of them was at her side, refilling her cup.

"I'm not complaining," Katie said. "And the crème brûlée is stellar, I'll tell you that. It's so good. Thanks for setting this up, Uncle Bob and Aunt Marti."

Christy liked hearing Katie refer to Bob and Marti as if they were her aunt and uncle. It was evident they liked their new titles as well.

"It's our pleasure," Bob said.

"Yes. Of course it's our pleasure," Aunt Marti added. "I imagine you and Eli will enjoy your tent-camping experience for your honeymoon starting tomorrow night, but I felt it was important that we make our entry into this wild place with a bit more comfort."

Todd reached over and slipped his arm around Christy's shoulders drawing her closer. He whispered in her ear, "Do you think we should say something?"

Last night the two of them had stayed up way too late

talking and praying and discussing their future. Ever since their walk in the tea fields, they had both been praying about moving to Kenya and finding a place to serve at Brockhurst. Christy thought it would be a long process of waiting and listening and praying before they knew what they should do. But for both of them, the answer had come in a few days and it had been crystal clear.

"If you think now is a good time to tell them, sure."

"What are you two whispering about?" Katie asked. "I hope you're not planning any groomsmen shenanigans on the night before our wedding."

"No. Nothing like that." Todd glanced at Christy and she gave him an affirming nod. "We were talking about our future and what we think God has for us next."

"And it's not here, is it?"

Christy was surprised at Katie's immediate reply. "Why do you say that?"

"I've been praying, too, you know. This morning on our way here, I just knew. You're not coming. Not anytime soon, at least."

Christy and Todd exchanged glances in the firelight.

"Well, yeah," Todd said. "That's the conclusion we came to, too. We don't know why, but the impression was strong for both of us. We're not moving here. At least not now."

Marti fidgeted in her chair. "When did all this happen? I had no idea you were even considering such a thing."

"We've been praying about where we're supposed to live and what we're supposed to do next," Christy explained. "I thought the other day that this might be the place. But now I think it was more a matter of my just being willing and open to go anywhere. It was a big step for me in trusting God. I can't believe you came to the same conclusion, Katie."

"That's what happens when your life is knit together with someone you know by heart." Katie smiled at Christy and then turned to Eli. "Guess it's just you and me, Mr. Elisha Lorenzo. For better or worse. After tomorrow there's no turning back. So if you're going to change your mind, this is your final opportunity."

"Not gonna happen. No turning back for me. You're stuck with me, Miss Katie Weldon." Eli reached across the chair and intertwined his fingers with hers.

Christy was surprised at how easy it had been to break the news to Eli and Katie. The possibilities they'd talked about during and after their tea field picnic had gotten all of them dreaming about doing life together. But God had something else for them. A different place to live during this next season.

Christy tilted her head back and drank in the view of the endless shimmering stars in the African night sky. Todd followed her lead and gazed with her.

"These aren't our stars," she whispered.

"No, they're not," Todd whispered back.

All of them were looking up at the stars now. Eli's dad, Jim, recited a line from a poem: "'Silently one by one, in the infinite meadows of heaven, Blossomed the lovely stars, the forget-me-nots of the angels.'"

"Longfellow," Uncle Bob said before any of them could ask where the quote came from.

"That's right. You a fan?" Jim asked.

"On occasion. I'm definitely a fan of your stars here in Africa."

Cheryl said, "You know that we're happy to share our stars with you anytime. All of you would be welcome back here to stay as long as you wish."

"Thanks. We might have to take you up on that," Uncle Bob said.

"We?" Marti asked.

"Sure. We. You and me. I'd come back. But first, I have something I want to do on this, our first visit."

Marti looked completely flustered.

Uncle Bob rose to his feet, which also surprised Marti. "I have a few things I'd like to say to the happy couple, if the rest of you don't mind."

Now Christy was surprised. Her uncle had been such a quiet, behind-the-scenes, go-along-for-the-ride sort of companion on this trip. It felt out of character for him to get all eyes on him for any reason.

Uncle Bob cleared his throat, and in the romantic glow of the flickering campfire he spoke as an ancient elder. "Eli, you are a man of integrity, deep faith, and great humility."

He's blessing him! Uncle Bob is giving Eli the blessing he said he wished he could have gotten from Katie's parents. This is perfect. So perfect.

"I charge you, to love your wife as Christ loved the church and gave Himself up for her. Always consider her needs, always be tender with her, and always lead your family with vision and compassion. With Christ as the head of your home, as He is the head of the church, you will continue to experience His blessing."

Christy had never seen this side of her uncle. She loved the way he was blessing her friends. The moment felt spontaneous, but she was pretty sure he had done some serious planning that afternoon while the rest of them were enjoying the swimming pool and Marti was getting a massage. His voice began to crack as he turned to Katie and pronounced his blessing on her.

"Katie, you are a woman of deep joy and intense loyalty. You are beautiful and caring and filled to overflowing with compassion for others. You will be an excellent wife, and should God choose to bless you with children, you will be an exceptional mother. Give yourself fully to your husband and follow his leading. Trust that Christ is leading you alongside your husband and that His ways for you are good. Set your affections always on the Lord and He will continue to bless you and give you His peace."

The group sat in surprised and silent reverence of this beautiful and unexpected moment under the canopy of stars. The wood snapped in the open pit and a thousand flickers of light danced heavenward in the night sky.

That was so beautiful. It was perfect. Christy watched the bravely burning ashes float upward.

In the pause of the moment, Todd pushed his chair back and rose to his feet. He moved over to where Katie and Eli sat and stood behind them. He gave a nod to both Jim and Bob and both of them got up and stood behind Eli and Katie, with Jim directly behind them. Jim placed his hands on Katie's and Eli's shoulders as Todd and Bob placed their hands on Jim's shoulders. The three men formed an arrow aimed at the soon-to-be-married couple.

With his face to the heavens, Todd's deep voice rumbled out the blessing that had soaked into Christy's heart more than once during their early years. "Eli. Katie. May the Lord bless you and keep you. May the Lord make His face to shine upon you and give you His peace. And may you always love Jesus first, above all else."

"May it be so," Uncle Bob said.

Jim added a tender prayer and the men stepped away from the couple. Christy felt her heart racing. It seemed as if here, by the fire, under the stars, the presence of God's Holy Spirit was encircling them, lifting each of them up the way the sparks rose from the fire.

No one spoke.

It seemed from the expression on Katie's face in the light of the flickering flames that she was overwhelmed. Blessed. Filled up.

Christy could never do anything to change the void in Katie's life that was created by her uncaring parents. But she and her husband and aunt and uncle could give their undaunted support and unswerving love. It was not the same, but it was enough, and Christy could tell that Katie was filled to overflowing with the gift of words.

Eli held Katie's hand as both of them stared into the fire. Katie wiped her tears and leaned her head on Eli's shoulder. He let go of her hand and wrapped his arm around her, drawing her close, taking her to his side and sheltering her. He whispered something to her and she nodded.

Todd reached over and took Christy's hand. Jim and Cheryl did the same.

Bob moved his chair so he could grasp Marti's hand. That's when Christy noticed Marti was sobbing. Her chest was trembling and the tears were coursing down her face. She was a muffled mess. It was a beautiful moment in every way.

When Christy thought of their sacred gathering the next morning, she remembered Todd's voice as he sang, ushering the group from awed silence into heartfelt worship. First it was a song he and Eli knew and Eli joined him, the two men's voices blending like a well-twisted rope: strong and dependable, able to go the distance. The next song was familiar to all of them except Marti. She pulled out her bottle of sanitizer and gave her palms a squirt. The rest of them sang the beautiful song twice, holding out the note at the end as if it were earnest enough to welcome the dawn.

The dawn did come, but not until after they'd all returned to their rooms and slept deeply. It was only minutes after the dawn arrived that all of them were gathered in the hotel lobby meeting their drivers and loading into the two Jeeps that would take them on the early morning game drive.

The solemnity of their time by the campfire seemed to still settle on them as they held on and took the bumpy road out into the vast game reserve. Both Jeeps had a driver, a guide, and a rifle.

She thought all eight of them would be able to ride together in the same vehicle, but they had to divide up into two Jeeps. In the end, she was glad it worked out that way because she and Todd ended up with Katie and Eli. Aside from their breakfast in the tea field, this was the first and last time the four of them would have the fun of being on what could be considered a double date.

The top of the Jeep was open and once they were out on

the dirt trail, all four of them stood up on the seats so their heads and arms popped out of the top of the vehicle and allowed Christy to get her camera balanced and steady as she started taking pictures.

The first wildlife they came upon was a herd of impalas that looked like gentle brown deer or antelopes but with long, curved, black antlers. They also saw warthogs and some scary-looking, scraggly hyenas. Katie was the first to see a herd of zebras ahead.

"No two are alike," the guide said. "Their stripes are their own. No other zebra has the same pattern. It's like a fingerprint."

Christy captured lots of pictures because the zebra weren't at all hesitant to come close to the Jeep. Some even lifted their noses to have a better look at the four half bodies that popped out of the open top.

As the driver continued on, they didn't see any animals for several miles. He drove a little faster and the four of them held on tight as they laughed and the wind slapped them in the face. Katie squealed when she spotted the first giraffe. The driver turned down a narrow dirt trail and came within fifty feet of the stunning creature. It turned its head and twisted its long neck, taking in the sight of the Jeep.

"Look! There's a baby giraffe right behind the mama."

Beside her was a baby giraffe on spindly legs, pressing in close to its mother's side. Christy couldn't take pictures fast enough. Through her lens the giraffe's mottled coat appeared smooth and sleek. The mother giraffe turned toward them and Christy got a picture of her beautiful brown cow-like eyes and long lashes. She snapped a shot of the baby's tail that reminded her of a short rope that had gotten terribly frayed at the end. The baby giraffe flicked it back and forth as if it had just discovered what it could do.

"When a giraffe calf is born it drops six feet to the ground. Within an hour it is standing and walking." The guide pressed the button on his walkie-talkie and reported to the other driver that they were observing a mother giraffe and her calf.

They drove on. The relative flatness of the reserve made it seem as if they could see for days. On the straight horizon they could see several singular baobab trees that looked like tiny umbrellas floating on top of a tropical drink.

"Look over there." Eli pointed to the right and called down to the driver. "Is that a pride?"

The driver turned and began heading that direction at a slow speed so as not to startle any of the animals around them. The guide said, "Best to sit inside now."

They took their seats behind the closed windows, and Christy had to remind herself that this wasn't a ride at Disneyland. They were in the wild. These animals weren't tame. This could become a precarious situation at any moment.

The guide checked in on his walkie-talkie with the guide in the Jeep that Bob and Marti and Jim and Cheryl were in. He let them know they were headed toward a pride of female lions. The other vehicle came up alongside them. As the driver approached the five female lions, Christy thought she had never seen anything so majestic and golden in her life. Roused from their morning sunbath, they came toward the vehicles with long, deliberate movements, a force to be reckoned with.

"They remind me of the Women of the Canaries," Christy said to Todd. He grinned and kept his eyes fixed out the window. For someone who wasn't much of an animal lover, he seemed enthralled with the lionesses.

"There's the boss," the guide said.

In the tall yellow grass where the pride had been spread out, a great male lion rose from its lounging position and shook his golden tangle of a mane.

"Aslan," Todd whispered in Christy's ear.

Her heartbeat quickened. She loved the images of the lion in the Narnia tales. When she first read the stories, she wanted to be like Lucy and bury her face in the fluffy mane of the one who appeared in those imaginary lands with justice and deep love.

Now that she was staring through the window of the Jeep at a real lion, Christy felt a thrill and tremor at the sight of the wild beast. It was crouched in the uneven dry grass about twenty feet away from the vehicles. The female lions came closer, moving as a cohesive group, each of them looking in all directions. They passed in front of the vehicles across the dirt road and kept going, paying little attention to the two Jeeps with their engines running.

"That was amazing," Katie said. "Did you see the scars on the one in front? She is one tough gang leader."

Christy noticed that the guide was watching the lionesses with his hand on the pistol in the holster on his belt.

"Looks like the girls were a decoy," Eli said. "Here comes the king."

The lion, with its head forward, came striding toward them through the grass. The great lion approached the vehicle with even paces. It stopped ten feet from them and raised its head, shaking its tangled mane. The sunlight turned its noble eyes into two shiny nuggets of amber as it seemed to stare past the vehicles, watching the movement of something smaller and tastier that moved in the grasses on the other side of them. The females were circling the desired prey and the boss was looking on. The Jeeps didn't seem to be more than an annoying block in the road.

"Do you think it'll roar at us?" Katie asked.

"He doesn't look bothered enough," the guide said. "Lions rest or sleep twenty hours a day. The females do the hunting. He's taking it easy."

The lion settled into the yellow grass at the side of the road and sat, paws forward, head held high, just like the many statues of great lions Christy had seen when she was in London. The lionesses disappeared from view over a slight knoll. The lion waited for the females to call him for breakfast.

Christy snapped one more shot of the king of the jungle in his regal pose before the Jeeps continued down the road to where another herd of giraffes were heading down the middle of the dirt road. They were fascinating to watch with their long strides in which they swung both legs on the same side of the body forward at the same time.

"Giraffes walk and graze all day. Some male giraffes grow to twenty feet tall. Sixteen to nineteen feet is average."

The sun was in their eyes now as they drove. It was only midmorning but already it seemed that the animals that had come out for their morning kill were finding their patch of shade for the day and wouldn't venture out again until dinnertime. The driver had taken them in a circle, and in the distance they could see the mashed-potato hill where their hotel was located.

"That went fast," Katie said.

"We have to get you back before lunch," the guide said.

"I won't complain about that," Todd said.

The guide radioed the other vehicle to say they were returning to the hotel. As he waited for the reply, the first thing all of them could hear through the walkie-talkie was Marti's voice.

"We can't go back yet. We didn't see any elephants. I didn't come all this way to go on a safari and not see any elephants!"

Christy and Katie burst out laughing.

"Oh, Aunt Marti," Christy said.

Katie leaned closer to the driver. "What do you think? Could you find us some elephants?"

The driver and guide exchanged glances. "We really shouldn't."

"Hey, it's my wedding day today," Katie said.

"Really?"

"Yes," Eli said. "We're getting married at sunset. What do you guys think? Can you give us a special gift on our wedding day and take us to see the elephants?"

They exchanged glances again and the guide said, "Okay, we will. But you must not tell anyone at the hotel that we kept you out longer than scheduled."

The four of them looked at each other excitedly and promised not to say a word. Katie asked if she could borrow the walkie-talkie. Pressing the button she spoke louder than necessary.

"Hey, Aunt Marti, we're goin' on an elephant safari. Tell your driver to try and keep up with us."

With that, their driver took a turn off the wide road and headed off into the Serengeti. The thrill of the hunt was on.

twenty

$\mathcal{T}$he wild lions and giraffes and even the two elusive elephants they found in a remote cluster of trees were all forgotten once the road-weary group was back at the hotel. They brushed off their dusty clothes and helped themselves to the buffet lunch. The conversation quickly turned to wedding details: when to leave, what to take, what happens when.

In a few hours Katie and Eli would be married.

Marti wanted a rundown of the events and Christy was grateful her aunt had asked because it helped Christy figure out what she needed to do to help Katie get ready. The ceremony was to be held at a different location only a few miles away by the river.

"Why don't you go back to the room," Christy suggested as soon as Katie had finished eating. "You can jump in the shower and I'll get everything you need pulled together."

"Sounds good." Katie put both arms over her stomach. "I think I ate too much. It was all so good."

Eli stood and helped pull out her chair.

"My! What a gentleman you are. I think I'll marry you."

Eli gave her a grin. "I'll think I'll let ya marry me." He leaned in for a quick kiss and Katie turned away. She covered her mouth and muffled a low belch.

"Sorry!" She started laughing. "You sure you still want to take me as your one and only?"

"For better or worse," Eli said.

Everyone at the table seemed to enjoy the banter between the easygoing bride and groom. Christy thought of how different this was from any other wedding she'd been to or been involved with over the last few years. The union was truly all about Eli and Katie and finding a way to exchange their sacred vows in a place and in a way that represented their personalities. She shouldn't be so nervous about making sure she remembered the details of what they needed to bring with them to the wedding site. No one else was nervous. Why should she be?

When Christy returned to their room twenty minutes later, she could hear Katie singing in the shower. She smiled. Christy didn't remember singing in the shower on her wedding day. On their honeymoon, yes. On her wedding day, no.

"I'm back," Christy called out.

"Did you bring the stuff from Cheryl's room?"

"Yep. I've got everything. I'll get your dress ready."

"Good. I cleaned my boots so they're ready to go."

Christy removed the dress from the garment bag and plugged in the steamer to do some final touch-ups. While the steamer was warming up, she decided to get out her camera and take some shots of the gown and veil. Christy hung the gown near the window where the tawny light from the afternoon sun gave the room a blissful, dreamy glow. She placed the chair with the leopard print next to the gown and placed Katie's cleaned-up hiking boots in front of the dress.

Chery had kept the bouquet in a small ice chest to keep the flowers fresh. Christy took the bouquet out and placed it on the chair. She played with the arrangement until she was able to get it just right in the light. With a few quick snaps she felt she'd captured a fun part of Katie's wedding that would make a great gift. She'd decided already that she'd do an album for Katie the way she and Bob had put one together for Bryan and Carolyn. This would make a great "before" picture.

The bathroom door opened and the blushing bride emerged with a thick white towel wrapped around her head and the plush hotel robe tied around her waist. She trotted over to where Christy stood before Christy had a chance to dismantle the surprise.

"I love that. Did you get a picture?"

"Yep. I was going to try to surprise you." She had another sudden inspiration. "Here. Hold this."

Christy handed Katie the bouquet and took some fun, zany shots of Katie beside the mosquito-netted bedpost with the towel on her head, covered up in the white robe, and holding the wedding bouquet. Katie struck several of her mock model poses and the two of them laughed until their sides hurt.

The rest of the afternoon rolled along with as much ease as if the two of them were back in their college dorm or hanging out at a high school sleepover. Christy got the dress steamed, took a shower, dried her hair, and put on her make-up while Katie stretched out on the bed and took what she called a "lioness nap."

Christy slipped into her bridesmaid butterfly sleeved dress and decided to follow Katie and Eli's lead and go with her boots instead of the dainty slip-on shoes she'd brought for the wedding. After trucking through the mud and uneven paths since arriving in Africa, Christy felt the boots were a much better choice. She cleaned them in the bathroom, being careful not to get any mud on her dress.

The last thing she did to get ready was put in the pearl earrings Todd had given her.

"Let me see." Katie rolled over in bed and took in Christy's appearance. It was the first time she'd seen Christy in the dress she'd selected. Christy held out her arms so Katie could get the full butterfly effect.

"Perfect."

"I'm glad you think so."

"It's exactly what I wanted. A little bit princess, a little bit superhero, and just the right shade of blue. I love it."

"Good. Now let's get you into your perfect dress."

"Let me go get my hair figured out first. And I thought maybe I'd brush my teeth in case that guy tries to kiss me again."

It took Katie only half an hour to get her easy hair to cooperate and fall into its usual swishy position. Christy helped her with her eye makeup, applying more than Katie would usually ever wear but just enough to accent her natural loveliness. Katie brushed her teeth, rolled on a little extra deodorant, and declared she was ready.

Christy helped her slip the dress over her head and then went to work on all the buttons.

"It's a really good thing you didn't take the dress in after the way I pigged out at lunch. I'd be bursting at the seams."

Christy smiled when she remembered the duct tape solution to her too-tight dress at Carolyn's wedding. For the first time it struck Christy how extraordinary it was to be part of these two completely different weddings during the same month. All her earlier thoughts of the two events had been stuck in planning mode. She focused on the details, not the sacredness. Now that the moment was here to accompany her best friend as she was about to head down the aisle, Christy caught a glimpse of the immense privilege this had been.

She and Katie didn't have an overly sacred moment while Katie dressed. They'd had plenty of sacred moments in the past two weeks, and Christy knew that Katie felt ready and honored and very much loved. That's what mattered the most.

The two friends took turns lacing up each other's boots as they put their feet up on the leopard-print footstool. Then Christy placed the veil on Katie's head in front of the bathroom mirror and fixed the "halo" as Katie had started calling the floral wreath.

"Now where's the necklace?" Christy asked.

"It's wrapped up in a tissue in my cosmetic bag."

Christy froze.

Katie caught her expression in the mirror. "What's wrong?"

Christy didn't say a word. She went over to the trash bin and pulled out several wadded-up pieces of tissue until she found the one that contained Marti's necklace. "I thought it was a used tissue from when I was doing your eye makeup."

"That was close," Katie said. "You know it's only on loan."

"I know." She unclasped the necklace and placed it around Katie's neck.

"That's the trouble with being entrusted with nice, expensive things. You have to worry about them."

Christy made a mental note to be sure to remind Katie to return the necklace to Marti tonight before they went their separate ways. She stood back and admired her friend. With a big smile she said, "Any final words, Miss Weldon, before you become Mrs. Lorenzo?"

Katie's reply was interrupted by a knock on the door. Marti and Cheryl had come to see how the bride was getting along. Marti had on a pair of wide black silk pants, a silk top with several long gold necklaces, and a brightly colored long silk jacket that fluttered on the sides as she entered the room. Cheryl wore a simple light-blue dress that was short and similar to what Christy was wearing, without the butterfly sleeves.

"Well?" Katie emerged from the bathroom. "What do you think?"

Cheryl was the first to speak up. She was also the first to tear up. "Katie, you look stunning."

"The veil makes the outfit," Marti said. "Don't you think?"

"Yes. I love it. Thank you again."

Marti stepped closer and offered her cheek for Katie to kiss, in keeping with the new pattern of how to respond when receiving a gift from a woman who loves you. Katie pressed a rose petal of a kiss on Marti's cheek.

Christy thought Marti should be the one offering kisses to the bride.

Marti turned her head. "You might as well kiss me again because I've talked to Robert and we've decided that you should keep the necklace."

Katie's mouth opened but no words or kisses came out. Christy remembered how Katie had just said that having expensive things was a burden. She hoped Katie would still say thank you and accept the gift.

With a second kiss for Marti, Katie said, "Thank you. This means a lot."

"Always remember that it's from both of us. Bob and I both wanted you to have it."

"I love it. Thank you."

Christy was so grateful Katie responded the way she did. It seemed this was the only way Marti knew how to extend a blessing and Katie seemed to pick up on that.

"We should be on our way," Cheryl said. "I'll get your bouquet. Is your bag all packed?"

"I just need to throw in my cosmetic bag and toothbrush."

"I'll get it." Christy double-checked the bathroom to make sure nothing else had been left. Once Christy was convinced they had everything they needed, she grabbed her sweater and joined the procession of women as they ushered the bride through the lodge and into the same Jeep they'd ridden in on their safari. The guys had gone ahead in another Jeep and would be waiting in their places when the women arrived.

The wedding location was under a distinctive, large tree with a twisted trunk. Katie called it the marriage tree because it was two trees that had been planted close together and trained to twist around each other until they grew into one inseparable trunk. The tree had sprouted double the canopy of any of the singular trees in the same encampment and was planted beside the river. In the river was a hippo pool.

Christy thought Katie had been kidding about the hippo pool, but as soon as they arrived, she could hear the loud grunting sounds of the "water horses" as Cheryl called them. The four women took the long way around to the marriage tree and had to pass through the lodge and by two of the ten outlying tents.

Marti stopped at the second tent. It was very large and was built on a wooden platform. Two comfortable-looking lounge chairs were positioned in front of the open flap door. The inner screen door was zipped up. Inside was a four-poster bed with a mosquito net that looked like the ones at the hotel where they'd stayed. There was a beautiful, plush rug, two nightstands with ornate lanterns, a leisure chair with a footstool, and a dresser with an oval mirror. It looked like something from a romantic film about royalty going on an African safari a hundred years ago.

"Katie, I had no idea these tents were so well appointed," Marti said. "The website doesn't do them justice."

"The one Eli and I are staying in even has a clawfoot bathtub with running water."

"You're kidding." Christy had thought Katie was making these details up when she talked about them earlier, just like she thought the hippos were a joke.

"Ours is one of the more remote tents. The lodge staff will bring us breakfast in the morning. Do you guys want to see the hippo pool before we go to the marriage tree?"

"I do," Christy said.

"Hey, that's my line," Katie said. "I'm the one who came here to say, 'I do.' But not quite yet."

Christy loved seeing Katie so calm and in her usual state of silliness. All of this felt natural in spite of the exotic surroundings.

Katie hiked up her wedding gown and Christy did the same with her long bridesmaid dress as the four women traipsed through the grass to the overlook. Indeed, below in the muddy waters were at least eight hippos. Two of them were submerged so the only thing visible was their eyes and the top of their heads with their funny gray ears. Christy remembered her fifteenth birthday date to Disneyland with Todd. They'd gone on the Jungle Cruise boat ride and when the guide said something about the hippos only being dangerous when they wiggled their ears, a mechanical hippo rose from the water and its ears wiggled. The staged hippo moment had so surprised Christy that she practically jumped into Todd's lap.

She smiled to herself thinking how long ago that was. Never did she ever imagine then that she and Todd would end up married and in Africa, next to a real hippo pool. She missed Todd. It had only been a few hours since she'd seen him at lunch, but she missed him and couldn't wait to see him when, for the second time that month, they took their places and stood beside a bride and a groom they both loved very much.

Christy captured a bunch of quick photos and they tromped back to the path that led to the marriage tree. Marti was the only one wearing nice shoes and Christy could hear her muttering about how they were ruined now. Cheryl checked her watch and looked up at the sky as if gauging the amount of daylight left.

The men stood in a circle under the tree. Lanterns hung from the lower branches. A large rug was spread at the base. There were no chairs. Only four nicely dressed men, all gazing on Katie with great admiration. Especially the man in the white long-sleeved shirt and black pants. Goatee boy looked all grown up. Ready to take Katie to be his wife.

The easygoing mode that had prevailed so far meant that when it came down to this crucial moment, none of them had thought through how the ceremony would begin.

"This is ridiculous," Marti spouted. "Katie needs to walk down the aisle. Since there is no aisle, we shall all envision an aisle. Here. Jim, you're the officiating minister. You stand right there in the center of the rug. Todd, you stand there. No, back one step. There. Eli, you stand here between them."

Marti turned to the women and Bob. "Cheryl, since there are no chairs, you'll just have to stand. I suppose you can stand wherever you wish and I will stand beside you. Christy, you come down the aisle first."

"I could just stand by Jim," Christy suggested. "That way Katie would be the only one who comes down the aisle."

Marti stomped her muddied shoe. "No. You need to come in as the bridesmaid, Christina. There needs to be some traditions of Katie's motherland incorporated in this ceremony and that's the first one. Next, Katie, you will come down the aisle holding your bouquet in front of you. When you get to the front, you will hand your bouquet to Christy."

No one seemed to mind Marti's passionate last-minute organizational efforts.

"Did I leave anything out?"

"Yes," Katie said. "I want to add one more American tradition. I want to be walked down the aisle, even though there is no aisle. Uncle Bob? Would you do the honors?"

"I thought you'd never ask, sunshine."

Marti clapped her hands together. "Marvelous! Now, places everyone."

It would have seemed to Christy that they were going through the motions of putting on a play, except for the fact that Katie was every inch a bride. This wasn't dress up or backyard summer theater. This was Katie's wedding and by the look on her face, it was everything she had ever dreamed it would be.

The group took their places. Christy had no flowers to carry so she casually clasped her hands in front of her and rolled her shoulders back. Her camera was slung over her shoulder on a long strap. As she had done in the Canary Islands, she started with her right foot and with a soft smile resting on her lips and on her heart, she took the twelve steps toward the marriage tree, gazing on her husband's handsome face.

She caught a glimpse of Eli. The moment seemed to have suddenly gotten very real for him, as well. He was staring at Katie with an intense expression. Christy paused and took a picture of Eli, of Jim, and one of the base of the marriage tree. Then she stepped forward, turned, and took her bridesmaid place, feeling the flutter of her sleeves when she did.

Uncle Bob offered his arm to Katie. She tucked her left hand through the opening and held the bouquet with her right hand. Her face was pure sunshine. The light breeze ruffled the edges of her veil. Christy took lots of pictures. When Uncle Bob delivered Katie to her place in front of Jim, he took the camera from Christy and stepped back, next to Marti. Katie handed Christy her bouquet and stood facing Eli. He took her hand in his and they faced his father together, ready to be united as man and wife.

The next fifteen minutes were filled with wonder. Absolute wonder.

The sun was setting and the colors of twilight encompassed the tree with a muted radiance that seemed to reflect off of Katie's white wedding gown. The lit lanterns began to glow in the ebbing light of the passing day. A great flock of white birds flew over their heads and came to roost in the tree for the night.

Jim had some notes on a paper that was folded inside his opened Bible. He talked about the sanctity of marriage and how God instituted the union of man and wife in the very beginning, starting with Adam and Eve. Then he turned to a passage in Ephesians that he said was the life verse he and Cheryl had chosen for Eli. When Jim read the verse, Christy felt the words go deep into her heart as well. It may have been Katie and Eli's verse, but she wanted to share it with them.

"'Christ will make his home in your hearts as you trust in him. Your roots will grow down into God's love and keep you strong.'"

Jim looked at Katie and Eli, giving them a serious admonition. "This is a great promise. This is the good news. That Christ will make His home in your hearts. He wants to be at home in you, in your hearts. Notice the next part says, 'as you trust in Him.' That's your part. Place all your trust in Him. The resulting blessing is that your roots will grow down into God's love and keep you strong."

Jim asked Eli and Katie to face each other. He asked each of them if they choose to enter into the covenant of marriage before God and these witnesses.

Eli looked into Katie's eyes and said, "I do."

Katie replied with a firm, "I do."

Jim asked Todd for the rings, which he pulled from his pocket without a hitch. Eli took Katie's hand and held it up high. Katie had told Christy earlier that this was an African tradition. Hands raised toward heaven indicated they were declaring their bond openly, before the whole tribe and before God. Eli slipped the ring on her finger. Katie did the same, lifting Eli's hand in the air and urging the ring to slide over his knuckle.

A time of prayer followed. Eli prayed first, dedicating their marriage to the Lord, and then Jim prayed, placing his hand on their joined hands, asking for God's blessing on their union. Both Eli and Katie said, "Amen."

Jim smiled at them. "Elisha, my son, you may now kiss your bride."

Eli took his time. He placed his right hand on Katie's cheek and waited for her to draw near to him. The moment Katie leaned toward Eli, he covered the rest of the distance and kissed her with a tender passion that was evident to all of them. Christy could hear her camera clicking and was glad Uncle Bob was capturing this moment before all the natural light was gone.

Katie and Eli drew back. Christy tried to hand Katie her bouquet but she was too caught up in the joy of the moment. She linked her arm through Eli's and he drew her close, covering her hand with his and grinning at her affectionately.

They started down the invisible aisle with their arms linked and their eyes locked on each other.

Todd began spontaneously singing one of the worship songs they had all sung last night. Christy couldn't hold back. She started singing with him. Uncle Bob joined in and the close circle followed the newlyweds across the lawn area, singing loudly.

Eli started swaying to the singing and Katie joined him. They stopped in the middle of the grassy area and held each other in a waltzing position. With lots of laughter and a few twirls, Eli danced with his bride, simultaneously kissing her and singing to her.

Christy handed the bouquet to Marti and took the camera from Uncle Bob so she could capture the moment. She trotted around the front so she could get the lantern-lit tree in the background of the dancing couple. Eli held Katie's middle back and dipped her as the song came to an end. Christy caught a gorgeous shot of the flickering light from the lanterns coming through her veil as it touched the ground.

Eli kissed her soundly on the lips while he had her in the dipped position. It looked awkward rather than romantic so Christy only snapped two quick shots. The two of them laughed and straightened up into a more dignified position with their arms around each other's waists. They whispered and headed for the pathway lit by glowing lanterns. Christy could hear Katie giggle and she felt so happy for her. So happy.

The rest of the wedding party followed the pathway and came to the private wedding dinner that had been set up for them under a cluster of trees not far from the river.

"Oh, my," Marti said. "I didn't expect this. It's so elegant."

A long table was prepared for them with glowing lanterns encircling the area. A staff of four, wearing white pants and chef's jackets, stood ready beside several carts on wheels.

Christy and Todd took the seats directly across from Katie and Eli. She wanted to stare at her radiant friends, but first she needed to stare at the table as Marti was doing. It was covered with fine white linen and folded cloth napkins. Each place was set with gleaming fine china and weighty silverware complete with all the proper additional forks and spoons. They had crystal stemware and china cups and saucers. A row of votive candles ran down the middle of the table and cast an even more romantic glow around them, as if this could possibly be any more romantic that it already was.

Todd lifted his water glass to offer the first toast before anything else was said or done or explained or offered for their wedding feast that evening. His timing was perfect. They needed to toast this extraordinary moment. Everything about Katie's wedding had been perfect. Exactly as Katie had dreamed it would be.

"To the King and His Kingdom," Todd said. "And until the day that we join Him at the wedding feast of the Lamb, may Christ be at home in our hearts as we trust in Him."

The sound of clinking stemware and heartfelt agreements echoed around the table like a burst of embers fluttering into the night sky. Even Aunt Marti made her voice heard as she offered the final whispered, "Amen."

Christy looked up toward the heavens. Overhead, all the stars of the African night had come out in their full brilliance and were gazing down on the happy gathering.

The forget-me-nots of the angels.

This was a night of celebration. This was a night of deep joy.

twenty-one

*C*hristy put two pieces of bread into the toaster and pressed down on the lever. She stood in the kitchen of Todd's dad's house and stared out the window at the early morning fog. She was thinking of Africa. Again. Dreaming and remembering, hoping the vibrancy of her memories never faded. She'd returned there a hundred times in her thoughts ever since they'd gotten home over a week ago.

It was Saturday morning and as soon as Todd came downstairs, they were going to jump into Gussie the Bussie, pick up Doug and Tracy, and go on their long-awaited surfin' safari to San Clemente State Beach.

As familiar as all those plans sounded and as natural as it felt to be going for a drive in Gussie with Doug and Tracy, Christy quietly wished she was going back to Africa this morning. She wanted to see it all one more time. The marriage tree. The giraffes. The bird's nest in the eaves of Katie and Eli's stone cottage. The tea fields.

Oh, the tea fields in their early morning majesty!

She wanted to taste the distinct flavor of ugali with honey

and bananas. She wanted to repeat their visit to Nairobi Java House and have another Malindi Macchiato and Masala fries the way they did on their last day before going to the airport.

In the mist outside her window, Christy could envision the last image she had of Mr. and Mrs. Eli Lorenzo standing at the airport, both crying as they said good-bye.

The toast popped up and Christy jumped.

Todd was beside her and she hadn't heard him come downstairs. He reached for the toast. "You want jam on yours?"

"Hmm?"

"On your toast. Do you want some jam?"

Christy looked at him. "We saw a lion up close."

Todd grinned. "Yes, we did. And you danced with the Women of the Canaries. That was almost as amazing as the lion."

Christy took her piece of toast and bit into it without anything on it. "I think my brain is still jet dragged. My emotions are so confused."

Todd spread peanut butter on his toast and chomped into it just as his phone signaled that a text had come in. He wiped his thumb on his T-shirt and checked the message. "Hey. It's from my dad. Check it out." He turned the screen so Christy could read it.

LOOKS LIKE I HAVE A BUYER FOR THE HOUSE. UNEXPECTED. VERY COOL. BOB WILL FILL YOU IN ON DETAILS.

"Already?" Christy read it a second time and looked up at Todd. Her heart felt as if it had jumped into her throat. She put down her piece of toast and waited for Todd to say something. He just kept eating.

"Are you going to text him back?"

"No."

"Don't you want to know more? Like how much longer we can stay here?"

Todd checked the message again. "He said Bob would fill

us in on all that. We'll call him later."

Later! Grrr!

Christy walked away. She was so frustrated with her husband's easygoing approach to all this. She didn't want to say something she'd regret, but her overloaded emotions felt like they were about to burst through her skin. She went upstairs to their bedroom and made the bed with furious, exaggerated motions. Her tears, like her frenzied feelings, were brimming over her eyelids and sliding down her lower lashes.

Faith, not fear. Trust God. Trust Him, Christy. His ways are mysterious.

She reached for a tissue to wipe her eyes and blow her nose.

I wish we'd decided to go back to Kenya to live there. At least we'd know what we were going to do now.

She didn't mean that. The decision not to move to Kenya had been confirmed several times. It was an answer but not the right answer for them.

Christy tossed the decorative pillows she'd made onto the top of the bed in one crazy heap of fury. Last night when the Friday night gathering had come to their house and everyone was so glad to see them again, Christy thought *this* was the answer. This house, this group of people, this town. This was where God had appointed them to live for the next season of their lives, the way Eli had described during their breakfast in the tea fields.

Did I talk myself into believing that just because I wanted so badly for it to be true? If not this place and these people, then where? And with whom?

"Christy?" Todd called up from the bottom of the stairs. "You ready to go?"

She didn't answer. Her heart was pounding furiously again. She could hear Todd's heavy footsteps taking the stairs two at a time.

"You okay?" He stood in the doorway, looking befuddled as to why she would be upstairs, sitting on the edge of their bed with tears streaming down her face.

"No," she replied in a wavering voice. "I'm not okay. But I want to believe that I will be."

"That's an honest answer." Todd crossed the space between them, sat beside her, and wrapped his arms around her. "And you know what Proverbs has to say about honest answers."

"What? That they should be kept to oneself?"

"No. 'An honest answer is like a kiss on the lips.'" To demonstrate the verse, Todd leaned in and kissed her tenderly on the lips.

His affection didn't cancel what she was feeling but it did help a little. "It just frustrates me that you don't feel the way I do about things. I know you can say that it's my hormones or that you feel the same things but don't show them. But Todd, you hold so much in."

"That's how I process. That's why I want to go surfing. That's where I do my best thinking and praying."

"I know, but sometimes I need you to process out loud with me just a little before you go into your monk mode or off to your surfing cone of silence. I hate having to try to think things through by myself. I process out loud."

"I know."

"It just doesn't seem fair that I leave you alone so you can process stuff, but then I need you to not leave me alone when I need to process stuff."

"Okay. Makes sense. I'm here. I'm listening. What do you want to process?"

"This!" She motioned to the whole house with her arms. "How can you not be flustered that this house, your dad's house, has just sold? Not to mention that we need to find a place to live and we don't have jobs yet."

Todd rubbed the back of his neck. "We both have interviews this coming week and I've got two boards I'm working on in the garage right now, so we're moving forward on the income part. We'll call Bob when we get back from the beach and find out how much longer we can stay here. Then we'll put the word out that we're looking for a place and start looking for apartments online. We'll find something. God will provide. He always does."

It helped Christy to realize that Todd had, in fact, lined up the next steps in his thoughts and was approaching their dilemma with logic and leadership even though he didn't give away any hints that that was what he was doing.

He gave her another kiss, this time on the cheek. "We have to trust God in all this."

"I know," Christy said quietly.

"We should get going. Doug and Tracy are probably waiting for us. When we get back we can talk about everything as much as you want, okay?"

"Okay." Christy got up and pulled her Rancho Corona University hoodie out of the closet. She followed Todd downstairs and the two of them grabbed the stack of beach blankets she'd put by the back door late last night. The leftover snacks from the Friday night gathering were in a bag on top of the blankets along with some drinks.

Christy got in the front passenger seat and tried to stay cheerful as Todd backed down their short driveway. This was their big "Gussie Reunion Day" with Doug and Tracy. All of them had been looking forward to this time together. She didn't want to ruin it by being moody.

·Doug and Tracy came out the front door of her parents' beach house as soon as Gussie pulled up. Tracy's mom stood at the door holding Daniel who was waving good-bye with one hand and holding a toy truck in the other.

Doug slid the side door open and practically leaped inside. "This is awesome!" He reached through the open space between the front two seats and gave Christy one of his famous "Doug hugs." His exuberant spirit immediately made her feel better. Ever since she first met Doug he had been passing out great hugs and making frequent use of the word awesome. In her mind, if anyone else ever said "awesome," they were just quoting Doug.

"Christy, don't you love this? Whooo! What a morning!"

Tracy climbed in, all bundled up and beaming. "You guys, this feels like we're having a major flashback in time, doesn't it? She's a sweetie, Todd. You found a gem when you found Gussie. I've got to take a picture of this. Smile, you guys!"

They rumbled down the freeway chattering, laughing, and teasing each other about memorable moments during their high school years. Christy kept watching Todd as he drove, leaned over the big, round steering wheel and confidently checking the rearview mirrors. She had wondered if he might have had some unspoken fears about driving a VW van again since the demise of Gus was a serious car accident on the freeway that sent him to the hospital. His hands still bore the scars from all the stitches. If he was at all nervous, it didn't show. He couldn't stop smiling as Doug reminded him of one "awesome" memory after another.

"I'm so glad we got to go on the maiden voyage of Gussie with you guys," Tracy said.

"You almost didn't get to," Christy said. "When we drove down to Escondido to see my mom on Wednesday, Todd wanted to take Gussie. I told him you guys would never let him hear the end of it if he hadn't waited until today."

"You got that right," Doug said.

"How is your mom doing?" Tracy asked.

"Really well. She says she's still slower than she was before the surgery, but she's feeling better than she has for a long time." Christy thought about how sweet her conversation had been with her mom during their visit on Wednesday. She was so grateful for the way she and her mom were growing closer.

"That's good to hear. I know it was hard for you guys to leave knowing she was recovering from surgery. We prayed for you a lot."

"We could tell," Todd said. "Thanks. Or as they say in Kenya, asante."

"Tell us more about Africa," Tracy said.

Todd jumped in, talking about the worship and the great time they had dancing to the local Christian group that provided the music at the reception. Over two hundred people came to the reception held at the conference center after Eli and Katie returned from their honeymoon. The kitchen and camp staff put on the entire event. It was, as Todd was describing to Doug and Tracy, "epic" with more food and more laughter and more dancing than Christy could have ever imagined. Katie and Eli loved every minute of it and apparently Todd did, too, since it was one of the first things he wanted to tell Doug and Tracy about.

They had arrived at San Clemente and were pulling the surfboards off the roof when Christy noticed her phone buzzing. A call was coming in from Aunt Marti. Deciding to let it roll to voice mail, Christy went ahead and sent her aunt a text letting her know they were at San Clemente and would be home after noon.

Marti texted back: TEXT ME AS SOON AS YOU GET HOME.

Christy tucked her phone into the front pocket of her hoodie and trotted down the trail to the beach with her arms full of blanket and snacks. Tracy chatted about how things had been for them that week as they were adjusting to their new home. They had moved into a bungalow on Balboa Peninsula that her parents owned and rented out during high season.

"It doesn't feel as small as I thought it would," Tracy said. "We eat most of our meals out on the back patio since it's so private, and that makes it feel as if we have another complete room. We're just glad to be able to live here so close to my parents. What about you guys? Any updates on how long you get to stay where you are now?"

Christy spent the first half hour of their time on the beach updating Tracy on all the details and thoroughly processed her feelings on it all. She told Tracy about the dream she had in Africa and said, "I think I've even made peace with the option of living in Gussie."

Tracy laughed. "Just think of how much time you'd save on cleaning."

Christy laughed. It felt good to laugh with Tracy. It felt good to get all her feelings out with a trusted friend. Maybe the best thing for her marriage was to have regular times to process her up-and-down emotions with her close girl-friends and not try to get Todd to turn into her best friend or expect him to understand the way a girlfriend would. He was her husband. That was different. She needed to respect the differences and so did he.

Tracy and Christy looked out at the waves and spotted their guys, who had both caught the same wave. Christy noticed the beach was filling with more people now that the sun had come out in full springtime beauty. She glanced to her right and saw the lifeguard station that held a powerful memory. That was where she had broken up with Todd so he could pursue his dream of being a missionary to Papua New Guinea.

Unlike all the other memories they'd talked about on the way down here, this memory Christy felt in her gut. She and Todd had stood there, by the lifeguard station, dreaming about the future. She knew she had to let him go. So she took off the gold ID bracelet Todd had given her with the word Forever engraved on it, and she gave it back to him. Todd crumbled in the sand and both of them knew that if they ended up back together again one day, it would be a God-thing.

And here she was, all these years later, living in the midst of the very God-thing neither of them dared to ask for. They were married. They were learning how to trust God together.

With a deep breath, Christy prayed, from the stomach up, and asked God to do another God-thing and find a place for them to live in Newport Beach.

It wasn't long before the guys headed back to their wives with their surfboards under their arms. They shook their shaggy manes at the girls just as they'd done during their high school years. And Christy and Tracy squealed, just as they'd done in high school.

"Doug says I need to grow up," Todd announced.

Doug laughed. "Yep, that's exactly what I told him." He shook his head, indicating that wasn't what he said.

Todd sat beside Christy on the blanket and stretched out, leaning on his elbow. "You know how I've been processing this whole thing with my dad and Carolyn and how they're so far away?"

Doug jumped in. "I told him he could be as bummed as he wanted, but eventually he'd have to realize that he's a married man. His home is with you, Christy."

Todd reached into the snack bag and pulled out the bag of chips. "He was right. Brutal, but right. I have a family to lead."

Christy gave Doug a grateful smile. For weeks she had tried to extract from Todd his true, deeper feelings about his dad's marriage and new life. He'd convinced her in Las Palmas that the matter was resolved. Apparently though, in guy fashion, he'd still been processing all the changes. Doug was able to say things to Todd that Christy wanted to say but had refrained from speaking.

Where would we be without such good friends?

"Why don't you guys start a Canary fund?" Tracy suggested.

"What's a Canary fund?" Doug asked. "You think they need to get a bird?"

"No, it's like my mom's Sister Fund. My mom and her sister are really close, but her sister lives in Minnesota. Both of them save up, and every two years they use the money to get together and spend time with each other. I know how much your dad means to you, Todd. The two of you could both save up for regular reunions. That way it won't feel like you're never going to see each other again."

"I like that idea." Todd turned to Christy and she nodded

her agreement. Inwardly she was thinking that she needed to do the same thing with a Peculiar Treasure Fund so she and Katie could set up reunions, too.

They talked and snacked for a few more minutes, but Todd let them know he was eager to get back because he and Christy needed to talk to Bob about what's happening with the house.

They loaded up their stuff and the guys strapped the boards back to the roof of Gussie. It was only twelve forty-five when they dropped Doug and Tracy off at her mom's. Todd called out, "Later," and Gussie puttered down the street like a happy old dog on a leash, going for a walk in her familiar neighborhood and sniffing all the flowers as she went.

Todd pulled into the driveway. Christy started unloading the van and smiled when she heard Todd whistling as he unfastened his surfboard and took it around to the outdoor shower to wash them off. Over his shoulder he called out, "Next time, Kilikina, we'll get you out there surfing with us."

Christy shook her head and shook the sand out of the beach blankets. She was content to have the kind of beach trips they'd just had. Her spirit was calmer and so was Todd's. This morning was exactly what they needed. She did a quick clean out of the fast-food bags and brushed the sand off the passenger seat.

A car pulled up—it was Bob and Marti's. She remembered that she hadn't texted her aunt back.

"I'm sorry," Christy said as soon as Marti was out of the car.

"Sorry for what?"

"We just got home. I didn't have a chance to text you yet."

Marti waved her hand at Christy the way she had waved it on their last day on the safari as she systematically summoned and dismissed the uniformed attendants who brought her fruity beverages by the pool.

Christy couldn't tell if her aunt was summoning her or dismissing her. One thing was certain: Marti was a woman on a mission. And not the sort of mission work Eli and Katie did in Africa.

"Where's Todd?" Marti asked.

"Around the side of the house washing off the surfboards."

"Robert? Would you like to get him for me?"

"Sure thing." Bob had his messenger bag slung over his shoulder. Christy guessed he'd brought over his laptop so they could finish editing all the photos from Katie's wedding. "Let's go inside."

Marti led the way with a bounce in her step. "Where's your verse, Christy?"

"My verse?"

"Yes, last January when you had the party here and all of us wrote on the floor, you wrote a verse about God being able to do exceedingly abundantly above all we could imagine. Where is your verse?"

"Well, it's in Ephesians. Chapter 3, verse 20."

"No, no. I don't mean where is it in the Bible. Where did you write it on the floor?"

"In the living room. In the corner."

"Where? Take me there."

As Christy led her aunt to the corner where Christy had written on the cement foundation of the house, Bob and Todd entered through the back door.

"This way, boys," Marti called out.

They joined Christy and Marti as they stood on the carpet next to Narangus, the half surfboard/half VW bus bench seat Todd had turned into their most distinct piece of furniture.

"What's going on?" Todd asked.

"Christy wrote a verse here at the house blessing party," Marti said. "Tell him the verse."

Christy repeated Ephesians 3:20–21 even though she knew Todd knew it. "'Now to Him who is able to do exceedingly abundantly above all that we ask or think, according to the power that works in us, to Him be glory . . . forever and ever.'"

"Forever," Marti repeated, looking quite pleased with herself. "That seems to be an important word for the two of you."

Todd caught Christy's attention and with his eyes he asked, What is going on?

Christy shrugged and they all waited for the next line in Marti's theatrical performance.

"I think the two of you should live in this house forever. Or at least until you outgrow it with too many children."

"Well, we'd love that," Todd said. "But I'm sure Bob told you that it sold."

"I know." Marti's voice turned high and squeaky. She had a crazy grin as she opened her arms wide and announced, "I'm the one who bought it!"

Christy stopped breathing for a moment. She and Todd looked at each other.

"And I've decided to rent this lovely home to the two of you."

"But Marti, we can't . . . "

She held up her hand to stop Todd's protest. "Let me finish. I've been saving money for quite some time, waiting for an investment property to come along, and this is the one I decided to buy. I will rent it to you for one hundred dollars a month for the first six months."

"That's ridiculous. Do you know how much my dad charged for rent?" Todd said.

"Yes. And I know what kind of tenants your father ended up with. I want someone who will take good care of the property. I also have a fair idea of what your income is, and I'd say that one hundred dollars will leave you enough revenue to pay the electric bill and buy groceries. But after six months, once you have jobs and more money in the bank, I'll adjust the rent to whatever is reasonable based on your income at that time, not on the value of the house."

"Aunt Marti, this is a . . . " Christy couldn't find the right word.

"A God-thing, like Katie would say?" Marti grinned. "I

know, isn't it? It's exceedingly abundantly above what the two of you would ever ask or think or even imagine. Robert and I want to do this together. I had the funds, he drew up the papers and is ready to complete the transaction with Bryan."

Uncle Bob patted his messenger bag, indicating that he had the papers ready for them to sign.

"Well? Do we have a deal?" Marti asked.

Todd rubbed the back of his neck and looked at Christy. Then he looked at Uncle Bob.

What is he thinking? What is he going to say?

Christy had qualms about the way Marti tended to tie strings to her gifts and wondered if Todd was thinking the same thing. She remembered, however, the way that Marti had given Katie her valuable sapphire-and-diamond neck-lace and insisted that Katie receive it as a no-strings-attached gift. Maybe Marti was changing. Maybe she was drawing near to God so He could make His home in her heart.

Tears gathered in Todd's eyes. "Marti, this place is and always has been home to me."

"I know," she said with stately pluck.

Christy turned from Todd's befuddled, teary expression to look at Uncle Bob. His eyes glistened, too, like African stars filling the night sky.

The forget-me-nots of the angels. Oh, Father God, You didn't forget us, did You?

Bob grinned at Christy. "So? What do you say?"

Her throat tightened. "It feels too good to be true."

With her hands on her hips, Marti said, "Christina. When a woman who loves you gives you a gift, you take it, you say thank you, and you kiss her on the cheek." She tilted her head and lifted her chin, waiting.

In unison, Todd and Christy went to her, both offering a great big kiss followed by a never-before-experienced group hug with Uncle Bob encompassing his arms around all three of them.

They drew back and Todd started laughing his best little-boy laugh. Christy slipped her hand in his and gave him three squeezes. He responded with the same. She looked into his screaming silver-blue eyes and Todd spoke the words that reverberated throughout every memory-filled corner of her heart.

"We're home, Kilikina. We're home."

Here is where it all began

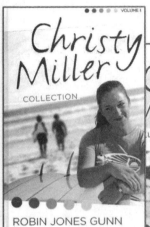

ROBIN JONES GUNN

ROBIN JONES GUNN

ROBIN JONES GUNN

ROBIN JONES GUNN

Christy Miller Collection
Vol 1: Books 1-3
Vol 2: Books 4-6
Vol 3: Books 7-9
Vol 4: Books 10-12

Follow Christy and her Forever Friends on an unforgettable journey through the ups and downs of high school.

The Friendship Continues

Sierra Jensen Collection

Vol 1: Books 1-3
Vol 2: Books 4-6
Vol 3: Books 7-9
Vol 4: Books 10-12

Christy and Sierra meet in England and the adventures pick up speed in the Sierra Jensen Series.

Sierra's Story Continues in:

Love Finds You in
Sunset Beach, Hawaii

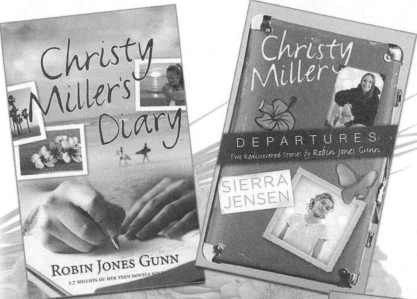

Katie Weldon Series

#1 Peculiar Treasures
#2 On a Whim
#3 Coming Attractions
#4 Finally & Forever

Katie Weldon

Join Christy's best friend, Katie, as she takes the world by storm during her final year of college.

Christy & Todd
The Married Years

When Christy and Todd face life-altering
obstacles will they drift apart? Or will they
grow in their love for each other and the
One who brought them together?

Forever With You   Home of our Hearts

Welcome to Glenbrooke

ROBIN JONES GUNN
secrets

ROBIN JONES GUNN
whispers

ROBIN JONES GUNN
echoes

ROBIN JONES GUNN
sunsets

ROBIN JONES GUNN
clouds

ROBIN JONES GUNN
waterfalls

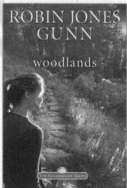

ROBIN JONES GUNN
woodlands

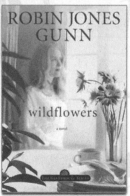

ROBIN JONES GUNN
wildflowers

Join the women of Glenbrooke who gather in a quiet town where souls are refreshed.

#1 Secrets
#2 Whispers
#3 Echoes
#4 Sunsets
#5 Clouds
#6 Waterfalls
#7 Woodlands
#8 Wildflowers

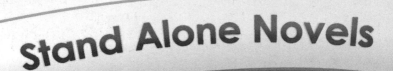

Stand Alone Novels

Under a Maui Moon
Canary Island Song
Cottage by the Sea
Gardenias for Breakfast

A Favorite Choice for Book Clubs.
Discussion questions included in the
back of each book.

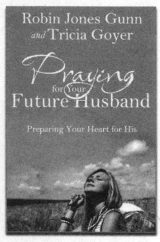
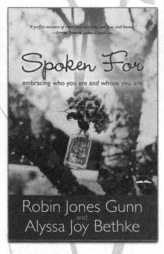

List of Robin's Books

The Christy Miller Series Vol: 1, 2, 3, 4

Christy & Todd Married Years:
  #1 Forever With You
  #2 Home of Our Hearts
  #3 One More Wish

The Sierra Jensen Series Vol: 1, 2, 3, 4

The Katie Weldon Series
  #1 Peculiar Treasures
  #2 On a Whim
  #3 Coming Attractions
  #4 Finally & Forever

More Stories about the Forever Friends
  Christy & Todd: The College Years
  Love Finds You in Sunset Beach, Hawaii
  Christy Miller's Diary
  Departures

Glenbrooke Series
  #1 Secrets
  #2 Whispers
  #3 Echoes
  #4 Sunsets
  #5 Clouds
  #6 Waterfalls
  #7 Woodlands
  #8 Wildflowers

Sisterchicks® Series
  Sisterchicks on the Loose
  Sisterchicks Do the Hula
  Sisterchicks in Sombreros
  Sisterchicks Down Under
  Sisterchicks Say Ooh La La
  Sisterchicks in Gondolas
  Sisterchicks Go Brit
  Sisterchicks in Wooden Shoes

Stand Alone Novels
  Under a Maui Moon
  Canary Island Song
  Cottage by the Sea
  Gardenias for Breakfast

Non Fiction / Women's Studies
  Praying For Your Future Husband
  Victim of Grace
  Spoken For

Visit Robin's online shop at
shop.robingunn.com

ROBINGUNN.COM

one more wish

*C*hristy closed her eyes.

"Go ahead," Todd said. "Make a wish."

Maui. I wish Todd and I could go to Maui.

Returning to Maui had been a secret hope ever since she and Todd had gone there for their honeymoon over four years ago. Now that her aunt and uncle were planning a trip for the fall, Maui had been on her mind for weeks.

Christy opened her eyes, took a quick breath, and victoriously blew out all candles. The circle of friends gathered around the kitchen counter gave a cheer.

"Wait till you taste this carrot cake." Doug began pulling out the tiny candles so his wife could start cutting slices for everyone. "It's gotta be Tracy's best recipe so far. Not that I want her to stop experimenting, since I'm her official taste tester."

Todd slipped his arm around Christy's waist and leaned close to murmur into her long nutmeg-brown hair, "So, what did you wish for?"

"I can't tell you," she said playfully. "If I do, it won't come true."

"I think we can all guess what she wished for." Tracy put down the cake knife and used both hands to shape an invisible bubble in front of her belly.

A baby. Christy's heart did a little flutter. *Oh, yes please. May this be the year!*

"Light the candles again," Christy said. "I need to make one more wish."

"Too late," Doug said. "The cake has already been cut. Guess we have to eat it. You first, Christy. Go for it."

"Interesting," Tracy said. "If you didn't wish for a baby, then what did you wish for? Now I want to know, too."